THE UNDERTOW

Christopher Wakling was born in 1970. He has worked as a teacher and lawyer. *The Undertow* is his third novel, following *On Cape Three Points* and *Beneath the Diamond Sky*. He lives in London.

Also by Christopher Wakling

ON CAPE THREE POINTS

BENEATH THE DIAMOND SKY

CHRISTOPHER WAKLING

THE UNDERTOW

PICADOR

First published 2006 by Picador
an imprint of Pan Macmillan Ltd
Pan Macmillan, 20 New Wharf Road, London N1 9RR
Basingstoke and Oxford
Associated companies throughout the world
www.panmacmillan.com

ISBN-13: 978-0-330-44321-0
ISBN-10: 0-330-44321-6

1 3 5 7 9 8 6 4 2

A CIP catalogue record for this book is available from
the British Library.

Typeset by Intype Libra Ltd
Printed and bound in Great Britain by
Mackays of Chatham plc, Chatham, Kent

For my sister, Katie

Nay, come up hither. From this wave-washed mound
Unto thy furthest flood-brim look with me;
Then reach on with thy thought til it be drown'd.
Miles and miles distant though the grey line be,
And though thy soul sail leagues and leagues beyond,–
Still, leagues beyond leagues, there is more sea.

Dante Gabriel Rossetti, 'The Choice'

There is nothing so hard as not deceiving yourself.

Wittgenstein, *Culture & Value*

PROLOGUE

Blink, and your eyes open to the possibility of a different world. The risk of change, for better or worse, is always there; it hangs in the gap between heartbeats, tracks the second hand round the clock-face, lurks in the pause separating each breath. Life can veer off course in any given moment.

I forgot that. I grew complacent. Defy the gods, and eventually they'll punish you: sooner or later something unexpected will happen to change the familiar contours beneath you and send you spinning off the map.

My story begins with a telephone call. I was sitting in my office, staring through the wall-length window beyond my desk. Outside, February lashed at London's rooftops: dusk, rain and wind. Inside, I had just tucked my right foot behind the stem of my swivel chair, and was tapping silently at the carpet with my toe, rerunning the meeting I'd returned from as I moved the seat from side to side. The phone rang. A number I didn't recognize showed on its screen. I adjusted my headset and pressed receive. 'Wilson Taylor.'

A pause followed. I began to think the caller had hung up.

'Hello?' The speaker was a woman.

'Wilson Taylor. Can I help?'

'That's Mr Will Taylor in London, England, right?' Her

voice was tentative and she had some sort of accent. A new-business enquiry, I assumed.

'Yes. Of Taylor Blake. What can we do for you?'

Another pause. Then, 'Right. Good. I'm glad to have reached you.' The speaker did not sound glad. She hesitated again. A light came on in the office block across the street, on one of the floors beneath mine, and a tiny figure moved from left to right across the room. In the time it took whoever it was to pass into and out of frame this third pause became ominous. I suffered a premonition that the caller was about to tell me something awful. She sounded Australian, which somehow mattered. My toecap dug harder into the carpet behind me and my swivel chair stopped moving.

At the other end of the line the woman drew breath, galvanizing herself. When she spoke again it seemed she was trying to recall a script, having inadequately rehearsed what she had to say.

'I'm Jo Hoffman. Dr Jo Hoffman. I work in the emergency department at a hospital here in Byron Bay. In New South Wales, Australia. Do you know where that is?'

I found myself confusedly answering her question. 'Of course. New South Wales, yes. But no, not Byron Bay.'

She pressed on. 'I believe you have a daughter. Anna Taylor. Who has been . . . is travelling in—'

'I know where my daughter is. Sydney. She called me from there the last time we spoke.'

Another pause, more audible breathing, and then the doctor continued. She sounded young, but her voice was increasingly sure of itself, picking its way sensitively through difficult terrain. Even as the anger and fear engulfed me I experienced an odd nervousness – for the doctor – in the pit of my stomach. It had fallen to this young woman to break news to me, and I could hear an apprehensive sympathy in the pauses between her words. I felt sorry for her. She wasn't to blame for whatever she had to tell me, and in any case I somehow already understood the situation she had to explain, ahead of her exact description. It seemed cruel to make her go through with the details. I heard 'accident, sea,' but stopped listening. The impossibility of what she was saying sat in silent opposition to the inevitability of its being true.

I say 'details', but in fact Dr Hoffman knew very little then about the disaster she was relating. It would be some time before I was able to put together a full account, longer still before I could make any sense of what had happened. But analysing the causes of catastrophes is part, at least, of what I do for a living, so even as she told me the basics, what I saw – or, more exactly, what I *felt* – was the gaps in her explanation, the room for manoeuvre, the holes in which to hope.

Picture a vast scimitar of shoreline. Boulders stand proud to the left, dividing this part of the beach, in front of the little town, from the miles beyond them around the bay. And off to the right, where the blade of sand narrows to a distant tip, a lighthouse juts from a low spur of land, marking Australia's easternmost point: Cape Byron. Ahead, in the foreground, the Pacific is cut by white wave-tops, but beyond the break the aquamarine deepens to a silvery blue, shimmering in the glare.

Though only mid-morning, the sun is brutal. It scores black shadows beneath the trees along the front, draws outlines round the few sunbathers dotted along the beach. An incapacitating heat, with no wind to disperse it, seems to hover above the sand. Through it the sea appears distant, as if behind a translucent screen. Yet the suck and thump of waves is ever present, blotting out all other sounds, so that the holidaymakers crouching beneath their hats, dripping sun-cream, melting in the stillness, seem actors in a dumb show.

Gil and Beth Defoe, an English couple in their late thirties – my age – emerge from between the trees. Gil holds a paper bag containing two bagels away from the heat of his body, as if carrying something distasteful. He's an academic. His wife, Beth, a theatre nurse, pushes up the brim of her hat and rolls a can of cold drink across her forehead. They pause at the back of the beach, afraid of breaking the tree-line, of tackling the heat without shade. In silence they sit down at the base of a pine tree and start to eat, staring at the view.

A sea eagle slices sideways overhead, wheels, and hangs above them. They don't notice. Gil upends his drink, his face turned to the sky but with his eyes screwed shut. He starts a conversation about his geological research. While he's talking Beth spots the nick of a sail, far out to sea. Her gaze slides nearer to shore, rests on a swimmer in the shallows opposite where they are sitting. The swimmer pauses, raises an arm in mock salute, then carries on towards them. Gil lowers his drink and looks out to sea too, distracted by a jogger loping through the heat along the water's edge. He hurts for her. While he watches she comes to a halt, puts her hands on her hips and stares at the horizon.

In the other direction, Waller, one of two lifeguards monitoring the stretch of water between the flags, has already followed the jogger – Vee, an old schoolfriend – out of sight.

THE UNDERTOW

He leans back in his chair, extends the shade of his hat-brim with a broad hand, and takes in the sea eagle. It seems tethered in its stillness, riding an unseen updraught. Invisible, yet Waller understands about currents here, both in the water and in the air. The expanse of land at his back has been heating up since dawn; the thermal is a prelude to a westerly wind which, on its way inland, will blow the surf to a useless chop within the hour.

Waller looks back out to sea. The tide is retreating; soon the sandbar will show pale in the gaps between waves. Since eight o'clock, when he set out his flags, the nearest rip has worked its way northwards, towards him. The lifeguard doesn't tell himself this, because he doesn't have to. He sees the undertow – a flatness in the water, the point where the waves seem most reluctant to break – and knows, as he knows the sun will set at night, that it won't come any nearer before the tide turns. He reclines his chair, thinking of the iced tea he sent his colleague to fetch from the surf club, and puts his big hands behind his head.

I'm setting this scene deliberately because, in the accident's aftermath, it has preyed on my mind. I've craved definition in the picture of this beforehand state. And yet it's impossible for me to know how much of what I've described is true. I wasn't there. The details necessarily came afterwards, in my investigation, in what the witnesses said, in conversations and reported speech. Some of the colour I've probably embellished. Did the lifeguard say he'd put his hands behind his head, for example? Am I sure Gil Defoe carried the sandwich bag away from his body? Or are these specifics that

5

I've added myself? Perhaps it doesn't matter. All that really counts is that until this moment these people, who were later implicated in one way or another, remained oblivious to what was unfolding before them. If they'd noticed what was happening earlier, if their collective gaze had focused on the problem a minute, or even seconds beforehand, the accident might have been prevented. But the swimmer was half-way out of the water before the tourists opposite him on the beach, the jogger running along it, or the lifeguard in charge of the flags understood that he was waving for help.

Waller, the lifeguard, still leaning back in his chair, ran the sun along the curve of his hat-brim, squinting. The surf unfurled, regrouped, peeled forward again. Out of the corner of his eye he saw Vee loping back down the beach. He reached for his binoculars, raised them and looked at her for a full second. Strange. She could never have made it to the lighthouse and back since she passed him last. As her magnified image drew closer his unease grew. He saw that she wasn't jogging: she was in full flight, running fast above the water's edge. Her mouth was open and one of her arms was raised. She was waving and shouting at him.

The lifeguard later said he didn't remember turning the binoculars seawards, but he knows he must have done so. His next memory is of accelerating through the waves on the surf-club jet-ski, which, with his renowned diligence, he'd reversed nearer to the retreating surf a quarter of an hour beforehand. Evidently he hauled it from its stand and down the final yards of wet sand into the water without help; proof, if it were needed, of his adrenal panic in those seconds.

Back down the beach Beth Defoe had also seen the jogger waving at her friend emerging from the water. It wasn't until the runner took off in the other direction, leaving the swimmer, now on his knees in the shallows, to continue with his staccato saluting, that anything seemed wrong to either of the Defoes. Gil stood up to look more closely at what was going on. There was something odd about a grown man on his knees in the spume, waving at nobody, and yet, whoever he was, he appeared happy enough. They were some fifty yards away, through the shimmering heat; perhaps the figure was waving at *them*; maybe he had mistaken them for somebody else. It was almost tempting to wave back.

But before Gil could smile to himself both he and Beth were distracted by the lifeguard's jet-ski, glancing across unbroken wave-backs. Something orange trailed in the ski's wake. A sled, slapping the white-water, into and out of view as the machine crested and dipped behind the swell. The lifeguard was standing up above the saddle. He checked the jet-ski and turned it hard, cutting a fan of water into the air. Then he set off again on a different tangent.

'Looks like fun,' Beth said to Gil.

Gil didn't respond. By now he was certain that something was wrong. He walked a few paces nearer to the sea, squinting at the jet-ski as it tacked wildly through the sheet-metal glare. The lifeguard was looking about. Still standing up out of the saddle, he threw the machine left and right, a hundred yards from shore. The swell rose and fell. From their vantage-point up the incline of sand Gil couldn't see anything where the lifeguard was searching; there was nothing visible in the water at all.

Except the man in the shallows, who was still on his

knees, waving. The jogger had doubled back towards him again, lifting her feet high to clear the surface of the water as she ran out to the man. In the seconds before she reached his side he stopped waving and slumped on to all fours, shaking his head slowly. She bent to pull him upright, a hand under his arm, but he crumpled as she did so, sliding face down into the water. By now Beth had dropped her bagel and stepped past Gil on her way to help.

Gil stayed where he was, watching the lifeguard, who slowed into a sharp turn, dipped in the lull between waves, and seemed to stop. But only for a second. As the next surge lifted the machine Waller was driving it forwards again, aiming at the beach. It looked like he had realized that the swimmer in difficulty was already out of the sea: certainly the jet-ski and sled, a blur now cresting the shore-break, thumping through it to outrun the white-water, had not stopped for long enough to pick up a passenger. Gil breathed out in relief. Beth was half-way to the water's edge, and the jogger had already managed to help the swimmer to his feet. Perhaps he had cramp. Whatever the matter with him, it couldn't be that serious. Gil wiped his brow and retreated a step into the shade, then stopped in surprise as the lifeguard, steering with one hand, accelerated the jet-ski through the remaining yards of shallows, flat-out up on to the wet sand. The machine slewed to a halt, the sled skidding sideways. Gil saw that somebody was on it. The lifeguard's other hand, flung out behind him, was clamped round a young woman's wrist.

Waller later maintained that Anna could not have entered the water between the flags. There was no way, he said, that he would have missed her and her friend swimming south, out of the safe zone in front of him and towards the current that took them out to sea. Of the many assumptions made in the aftermath of the accident, I found this easiest to accept. Even if it had been compulsory to swim in front of the life-guards, which it wasn't, Anna would have considered such a rule unfounded and swum where she wanted. I taught her a healthy scepticism for authority. I don't blame Waller for what happened. If he hadn't sent his junior to buy drinks, if he had happened to train his binoculars down the coastline and out to sea before the jogger ran back to raise the alarm, then perhaps, perhaps. But he didn't, and given the vast expanse of Byron Bay he couldn't be expected to keep watch over more than his patch.

The accident wasn't Waller's fault, I accept that. Neither, of course, do I blame the jogger, or the Defoes. Beth and Gil, from Hull in East Yorkshire, had stepped off a long-haul flight into Brisbane airport just hours before they arrived at the beach, and although their failure to see that the swimmer was waving for help is appalling, it is understandable. They were still in a different world. Luckily the jogger, Vee, wasn't. A local resident – she and her boyfriend run a holistic retreat on the outskirts of town – she was alive to what a raised arm at sea meant and responded as soon as she saw it. She alerted the lifeguard: she gave Anna her chance.

No, when I learned what went on while Anna struggled in the water, I felt no venom for the players on the beach. I can accept that their involvement had to do with fate, not fault. Where I had immediate difficulty, however, was with the other swimmer and the moment of his decision, the moment when he left my daughter face down in the water and struck out for shore.

Gil Defoe was also stunned by this aspect of what had

happened. The horror of the boy's choice hit him as soon as the jet-ski slid to a halt and he saw the lifeguard dragging a girl's body sideways off the sled. It made him stop on his way down to tell Beth that she should leave Vee and the boy and offer her help to the lifeguard instead. Only the white sand above the wave-line, so hot that it burned his feet, prompted Gil forward to steer Beth to where she was needed most.

Anna was still on her side when the Defoes made it to the lifeguard. He was kneeling over her, two broad fingers pressed hard into the side of her neck, which was blue-grey despite her tan. He was muttering, to himself, to Anna, to nobody, 'Come on, now. Not now, no, come on.' After a pause he repeated, 'No, no, no,' scooped Anna up again – small across his chest – and laid her down flat on her back, a few paces up the beach.

Gil trotted after him, pointing at his wife and saying, 'Nurse.'

'Right. Righto.' Waller seemed to take this in. Sweat dripped from his unshaven chin. 'Not breathing, no pulse. Help me.' He wiped sand from Anna's lips – her face was covered with it – and hooked his thumb and forefinger into and out of her mouth. 'You start compressions.' He pointed at Anna's chest, clamped her nose shut between his thumb and forefinger, and bent down over her face. 'I'll sort out the airway.'

I see the three of them, Waller, Beth and Gil, grouped round Anna, outstretched on the foreshore. While the other two began the kiss of life, Gil stood to one side panting heavily, uncertain of what to do. The outline of his foreshortened shadow lay across Anna's legs, connecting him to her struggle. She was wearing underwear and a vest top, which had gone see-through in the water. This detail makes it look as if she hadn't planned on going to the beach, let alone swimming. Yet Anna was keen on her swimsuits and bikinis. Given the slightest chance of a dip, she'd have worn one beneath her clothes, just in case. Nevertheless, she wasn't wearing a costume that day. While Beth, hands together, leaned into the work of pumping on Anna's chest, pressing hard – I saw the bruises later – the vest rose up, over her breasts. After a minute or so of Beth's compressions and Waller's surrogate breathing Anna's mouth and nose flooded with watery vomit.

As Waller spat, wiped his mouth on his arm, and bent over Anna again, the other lifeguard arrived in the beach pick-up. He shook the radio handset at Waller from the cab, then jumped down and strode into the circle carrying a red bag. They dragged Anna's top higher still and began sticking pads to her chest, talking in jargon. Gil Defoe stumbled backwards and sat down, out of the conversation. Looking out to sea he saw other swimmers, unaware of what had happened, carrying on regardless. He felt light-headed. Pulling himself together, he decided to go and see if he could help the boy, who was still with the jogger. As Gil said later to me, 'I thought I wanted to help him, but it was more complicated than that. He was all right. The girl wasn't. Since I couldn't do anything useful for her, I wanted to find out what had happened to put her in that state.'

The jogger had an arm across the boy's back. She looked up at Gil as he approached and shrugged her shoulders. A silent 'What now?' The boy was squatting on his heels, holding his head in his hands and rocking backwards and forwards. His back was beaded with sweat, yet he had goose-bumps and was shivering. His streaky blond hair was pasted to his forehead. Gil bent down next to him, looked into his face, saw an open mouth, eyes wide and blank. Vee was stroking the boy's arm, whispering reassurances, but Gil asked his question.

'Are you and the girl together?'

'Boyfriend.' His voice was hoarse.

'Can you tell us what happened?'

'Kept slipping.'

'What's that?'

'Couldn't grip.' The boy licked cracked lips, continued vaguely: 'She fought me. Then she . . . I couldn't . . . I had to do it.' He slumped on to his side, gripped his knees, and shook his head.

'Do what? What happened?' Gil repeated.

Veins stood out in the boy's neck, forearms and hands. He began to moan. Vee looked at Gil again, silencing him. She bent down over the boy and said, 'It's okay.' Then, very gently, she asked, 'Is your stuff on the beach somewhere? A towel? Clothes?'

The boy nodded.

'Where? What should we look for?'

His eyes now seemed full of confusion. After a pause he said, 'Canvas bag,' and turned towards the flags, along the beach.

Vee said, 'We should go get it,' to Gil, who took the hint and set off in the direction of the boy's vacant gaze. He walked past Anna again, now wired to the machine, and deliberately didn't look. Nevertheless, he overheard chanting: 'Three, four, five, *breathe.*' The brightness and heat made Gil feel dizzy. He walked through the wave-hem, right to the lifeguard station and back, staring at the sand above the high-water mark. A siren blared; the surf hushed it quiet. The waves seemed smaller close up than they had from beneath the pines. Though Gil searched the beach above the water-line methodically, he could find no canvas bag and returned empty-handed.

Back at the scene, he saw that a crowd had gathered. It looked like someone had pulled the jet-ski and stretcher further from the sea; in fact, the tide had retreated. He stood with the other onlookers, staring at his wife's back. She was still bent over Anna, her shoulders already pink with incipient sunburn. After a time Gil saw her glance at one of the lifeguards, and thought the look she gave him seemed optimistic. Although he didn't understand exactly what Beth meant by 'We've got an output,' he set off to tell Vee and the boyfriend this news.

They were not where he'd left them. He turned back into the circle and began looking for their faces among those in the crowd, but was distracted by the arrival of an ambulance at the back of the beach. Two paramedics broke in on the circle and took over from the lifeguards. They wrapped Anna in a foil blanket, blinding in the sun. A policeman joined them. He had a carefully tended goatee and sideburns, and began by addressing the crowd: 'Anyone here see what happened?'

Silence. Gil took a step forward.

'Then take off. If you don't have a statement to give, there's no use hanging around.'

People started to move away, leaving just the lifeguards, Beth, and, Gil now saw, Vee. Gil recognized the jogger as she approached the policeman, who stayed her with his palm. He nodded at the lifeguards.

'Wait up. I'll start by talking to these boys,' the policeman said.

This oversight, the policeman's brushing Vee aside, still angers me. The boy must have been within earshot. Though Vee tried to stop him going, he'd risen to his feet on hearing the siren and, oblivious to the burning sand, begun to stagger barefoot toward the tree-line. Why Vee wasn't more insistent with the policeman I don't know; perhaps she was intimidated, thrown by the sight of so crisp a uniform there, out of context, on a beach. She said later she thought the boy had probably gone to fetch his and Anna's belongings himself and that she imagined he would come back. Either way, she waited her turn quietly while the goateed policeman squinted from Waller to his notebook and back again, laboriously scribbling notes. Gil and Beth also waited, sheltering from the sun in the meagre shadow cast by the lifeguards' pick-up, trying to make sense of what they'd just witnessed. Where the four of them – the lifeguard, Beth, the jogger and Gil – had been united in the moment of the accident, officialdom now held them apart. One of the paramedics said, 'Good job, guys,' to Beth and Waller as they stretchered Anna off to the ambulance, but I was shocked to discover that, apart from those words and Waller's brief nod of thanks to Beth, neither of the Defoes had had anything further to do with him, the medics or Vee after the policeman's untimely interruption.

Though the boy's departure didn't concern the policeman, it has since plagued me. He left Anna in the water. Alone, at sea. Which means he saved himself at her expense. He offered no other explanation to Gil or Vee. While Beth and Waller worked to give my daughter another chance, that boy sat on the foreshore with his head in his hands, mumbling incoherencies. Then, when the ambulance and police arrived, he stood up and walked away. Never mind the obvious inference – that he was running for a reason – the fact that he still had the strength to pick himself up, in that intolerable heat, and make his escape, told me that however hard he'd pushed himself to keep Anna afloat, to save her, he hadn't pushed hard enough.

But to begin with I didn't take in the significance of the boy's disappearance. Jo Hoffman described what had happened – her voice sorrowful in my headset – and I heard her say that Anna had not been swimming alone, that she was with a friend, a friend who had left the beach after the accident, and whom nobody had seen since, but although I understood what her words meant I could not then fathom their importance. A light on my phone display had begun pulsing. I stared at it, wondering whether the missed call might have been something important, and was otherwise unable to think. The doctor went on to say that Anna's friend had nevertheless raised the alarm, that a lifeguard, working with a passing nurse, had done his best to resuscitate her on the beach, and that although they'd managed to start her heart beating again, Anna's brain – starved of oxygen for too long – had shut down. The phone-light kept flashing, reassuringly steady. She had 'technically drowned', was reliant now on a machine to breathe for her, would deteriorate with time. Anna's life was 'no longer viable'. Blink, blink, blink. Though the doctor used different terminology, she was trying to tell me my daughter was dead.

1

I flew first class. Not to spare myself discomfort, but because there were no ordinary seats left. Despite my success with Taylor Blake, I'd never seen fit to waste money on luxury travel. Its frills seemed all the more pointless now. A thick-weave table napkin, canapés, hot china: these extravagances make no difference to the prevailing dry air, engine-groan and disorientation of long-haul flight. And in my state, then? If anything, the superfluous comfort just added to a sense of being . . . insulated.

I couldn't sleep. Jo Hoffman's words kept going round in my head. I forced the cracks between them to open up. Anna had been in an accident, a bad accident, yet the doctor hadn't called it fatal. Death is absolute; no matter what the doctor had said, she hadn't been able to push Anna across that divide. Her injuries were grave, but perhaps she was not beyond the salvation of science.

'Sir?'

A flight attendant was at my side, bending down. Her mouth was smiling but her eyes were serious. She was very young. 'Is something wrong?' she asked.

'No.'

'If anything's wrong, just push that button there and we'll do our best to help.'

'Everything's fine.'

'Good.' Her eyes relaxed now, and the quality of her smile changed, became flirtatious. I fought back an urge to laugh, but unsuccessfully. She appeared to notice: she arched an eyebrow. Not many people can pull that gesture off. It was an unfortunate coincidence that the flight attendant could, because Anna learned to raise one eyebrow when she was six, and the young woman leaning down over me, innocently coy, prompted a startlingly clear and painful memory. I rolled forward in my seat, hands covering my face. There was an embarrassed silence. I only became conscious of the trembling of my shoulders when she put a hand on my back.

The moment passed. I didn't notice the young woman go, but when I looked up she wasn't there, and neither was my dirty cutlery. I found I was no longer thinking of Anna. Instead I reconsidered the arrangements I'd made as I set off on the trip.

I run a streamlined business. Taylor Blake is just me and Penny, my associate: I bought out Justin Blake years ago. Penny handles the backroom, I negotiate deals. In the six years she's worked for me Penny has paid off her MBA debt, moved from Willesden to W1 and holidayed on four continents. Anna thinks she's stiff, calls her Money-Penny, but when she was at home they made use of a whole channel of communication I have never got to grips with, texting, swapping *Heat* trivia and film reviews often enough. Which makes it all the stranger that I didn't tell Penny why I was leaving for Australia.

The wingtip light was a heartbeat, lub-dub, lub-dub, lub-dub. When I stared at it hard enough the glow persisted through the flashes of dark. I wasn't trying to spare Penny's feelings by not relaying the news about Anna: it had more to do with protecting something of my own. I'm not religious, but see a benefit in short-circuiting pure reason from time to time. It's often chance, fate, the imagination that makes leaps where logic fears to tread. Where I look at this wider context, Penny sees reality in statistics. That's what makes her so valuable in our business, and that's perhaps why I didn't want her to hear of Anna's accident on the basis of what Jo Hoffman alone had told me.

We began our descent into Brisbane. I had a midwinter head-cold. The pressure needled across my brow. I retreated to the lavatory and splashed water into my face but its coolness was instantly gone. I looked at myself in the mirror. My skin has always been coarse: the flight and worry seemed to have prised open its grain. I appeared to have been carved from rough wood. The blunt nose, hollow cheeks and square chin didn't help. A totem-pole head, eyes burning red. I turned away quickly and staggered back to my seat.

In wingtip flashes I realized that there had been a deeper reason for my secrecy with Penny. She would have urged me to tell my father what had happened, and I wanted to avoid that. Why collapse his world on the basis of so little information? He helped me raise Anna. When her mother fell pregnant and insisted on having the baby, he stood by me, and he did not flinch when, just months after she was born, Anna's mother walked out on us for good. The old man mixed formula for Anna's bottles and stood next to me in Mothercare as I chose her clothes. I went through college and launched my first business without once hiring a babysitter. He fixed her packed lunches, turned up at school functions I couldn't make, changed her sheets when she wet the bed.

There was no question of me relaying the doctor's report to him without first checking its accuracy. What worked in business held true here: verify the claim first, determine the facts, then react.

I stared out of the window, the pain in my brow now pulsing in time with the wingtip. The flashing light reminded me of my phone console, and my conversation with the doctor came flooding back. My forehead felt as if it might split in two. There was relief, almost, in this discomfort: it was excruciating and intoxicating at the same time. As a greenish dawn rolled to meet the airliner, tears welled in the corners of my eyes.

2

I'm not here to gawp at coloured fish or find myself on the end of a bungee rope. No – to make anything worthwhile I must do as the letter said and let go untethered. Falling without blinking is the trick. The photographs – and writing this – will help me concentrate.

I made a start. I cut loose from Dad's cash. His money is insulation – with it I risk going numb. So I flushed his cheque down the jet-roar loo and landed naked. Half a world away – beyond his generous reach. Without a work visa the opportunities are restricted. A week in and it seems waiting bar tables barely covers my board. Still – self-insufficiency is what my mother made do with and this trip is about making sense of her departure. Necessity mothering invention – so to speak.

And today it does. Nothing unusual to start with – the bar a familiar tale of surf rock on repeat and sporting highlights blinking down from on high. Punters halo-hunting – distracted. I ferry bottles back and forth across this sea. My reflection comes at me from a million mirrors. Brown arms against regulation tight white top. Eyes bulging in an optic. Ponytail pirouetting for a glass.

The first group to arrive is still in late. They're out for one thing. I grin through some grief delivering drinks to their perch but little Pip lacks a poker face. One of them says something to her as she arrives with a tray of beers. Her mouth quivers in the mirror and her cheeks relay from amber to red.

– Pardon? she says.

The man's a Picasso. Sunblock triangle of white nose afloat in a sweaty face. He repeats himself and his mates fall about. Reaches for his wallet. All I hear is – She'd snap it . . . How much?

Pip sways. She's broken rule one – don't react – and now she's trapped. The tray teeters. For a horrible moment I hope she's going to throw it. Then my better side wins. I swim out from behind the bar and into earshot.

– She wants – look. She looks—

– No need to stand on cer—

– She looks hot.

– Just an hour.

– You wouldn't last fifteen—

– Hot – hot – hot.

– What would an hour cost then?

Picasso repeats himself as I arrive. – How much? His ears are red handles framing scrambled eyes. I put a hand on Pip's arm and take the tray from her.

– Who needs a drink?

– Two's company and three's a threesome the man replies.

I try to hold his gaze. One of the others is rattling on at Pip. – Your sister can watch no problem. I ignore him and chance a raised eyebrow at Picasso as I set his drink down. There are many variations. This one is intended to put the great artist and me on the same side. His compatriots' bullshit is beneath us it says. But he's deaf. He opens his wallet on the shelf. Its mouth is bright with coloured notes.

– Like I say love I'm prepared to pay.

The fingers digging at that money are calloused. Pip moves behind me. I look round the circle of faces aware that the song on the stereo a minute ago has evolved into another thumping with the same beat and feel the faintest impulse to smile. This is interesting.

– We're happy to accept tips I say. I glance at the man's wallet then give him the look again. This version is more bashful. One of the other girls has paused beside us. Hands on hips and blood-red hair. I don't know her name. There's a barcode tattooed down the inside of her left forearm.

– A tip the man slurs. I get your meaning.

He winks at me. I dumb-waitress back. His fingers are still blind in his wallet. They fishhook out a green note. I don't think about what happens next – my mother wrote the same about walking out – the idea took shape after the act. I just lean forward and brush against him and breathe – Thanks – into a red-hot ear. Then I slide all one hundred bucks of that note into my pocket and spin away corralling little Pip with me. A delicious what-next half-second passes.

– Hey! The man's voice.

I prod Pip onwards but halt myself.

– What the hell d'you call that?

– A tip sir.

He raises his voice. – That's not what I meant and you know it.

In the mirror behind the man's head my eyes are wide. I gawp at myself for a count of three and then say – You'd like another drink?

Two creases above his white nose deepen. – I meant for—

– Sir. I cut him off. Pulling the wad of notes from my money-belt I unroll a blue ten and place it on the countertop in front of him. – If you've changed your mind have it back. We're not about to take an unintended gratuity.

He swipes up the ten. For a moment I think I've blown it. He's noticed. Everything tells me to fake a mistake. But the fool deserves this and the risk is worth more than dollars. Rigor mortis sets in to my smile while I wait for the man's fingers to ram the note back into his wallet. One of his friends punches his shoulder and laughs. Another is already staring up at the nearest bank of screens. The beat thump-thump-thumps. In the mirror I see the girl with the tattoo watching me. Barcode brocade.

Only once he's shoved his wallet back into his jeans do I ship the smile and turn away.

3

The hospital was small, a single storey beneath a painted tin roof, set among green ferns and behind a picket fence. It looked too picturesque to encompass significant suffering, its gardens too manicured, the sky above it too blue. I stood across the street and watched the entrance for a while, but nobody came or left.

A sculpture of some sort, made of seashells and gull feathers, stood on the reception desk. The cheerful girl behind it asked for my name. Her face clouded when I told her, and she stared at her computer screen as if it were an unfamiliar thing. Then she called a nurse, who ushered me to Anna's bedside. He was tiny, his footsteps mouselike as I followed him down the corridor, with its coloured handrails and doorknobs. It felt as if he was leading me through a nursery-school.

We arrived in a ward, empty except for one patient. I stood in the doorway and watched as the little nurse tucked in a sheet, adjusted pillows and wrote something on the whiteboard fixed to the foot of the bed. I tried to think of something to say to put him at his ease, but before I could speak he stopped what he was doing and turned to face me, his hands nibbling at one another.

'I'm very sorry for your loss,' he said.

Over his head I could see an arm, Anna's arm, strong and

tanned against bleached sheets. I smiled and heard myself say, 'Of course. If you don't mind I'd like to spend some time with my daughter.'

He nodded and stepped past me, looking grateful to leave. 'The doctor will be with you shortly.'

I stood alone, readying myself to approach the bed. No feeling seemed appropriate in those seconds. My hands were sticky. I stepped sideways to the wash-basin in the corner and ran cold water through my fingers. The bed stood behind me in the mirror, its white sheet stretched stiffly across Anna's upturned feet, knees, chest. As I watched, the sheet rose and fell. I turned and went to her side.

In the taxi from the airport I had prepared myself to be shocked by the tubes, wires, monitors and charts, but I needn't have worried. Anna dwarfed all the paraphernalia. Her face, neck and shoulders, framed by the gold fan of her hair, looked brown and beautiful against the bed linen. I stared down at her, smiling at first, until something about her hair unsettled me. She never wears it loose in bed. Ever since she first grew it long as a little girl she's plaited her hair before going to sleep, to avoid waking with it in a tangle.

Strangers had put her here. They had picked her out of the surf, driven her to this hospital, washed and dressed her, laid her in this bed. And they hadn't even managed to clean all the sand off her: grains were visible in her hair-line, behind her ear and, looking closely, between her fingers. The thought suddenly enraged me. I reached for her hand and pressed it between mine.

'Careful.'

A figure stood behind me in the ward. She was tall, Anna's

height, with close-cropped hair, which, in the bright room, seemed purple black.

'There's a drip in that arm.' She smiled. 'Mind you don't pull it out.'

Anna's hand was warm and relaxed. I laid it down. The woman stepped forward to meet me. She wore low-cut trousers and a ribbed black T-shirt, but her handshake was official, firm and quick. 'Dr Jo Hoffman. We spoke on the phone.'

'Yes.'

'I can't tell you how sorry I am about your daughter.'

There was nothing for it but to say, 'Thank you.' And yet the way the woman spoke, as if Anna had not been present, made me resent her. I turned back to the bed. 'Where are her things?' I asked.

'I'm sorry?'

'Her stuff. I don't see any of her stuff here.'

'No. She didn't have any belongings with her when they brought her in to us. The police are best placed to talk to you about the effects found at the hostel.'

Again the word 'effects' divorced Anna from her possessions, making it sound as if she no longer had need of them. I just nodded. There was an awkward pause.

'Would you like me to explain what we're doing for her? What each of these machines does?' Jo Hoffman's face was birdlike: sleek brow, sharp nose, hawk-set eyes. The contrasting softness of her mouth couldn't redeem it. When I did not answer she moved to the head of the bed and carried on regardless: 'The big tube runs to her lungs and is connected to this machine, here, which is breathing for her. This smaller one leads to her belly. We drain the stomach through it, to stop her aspirating any of its contents. The drip in that arm is keeping her hydrated; it's also for medicine. The tube running down beneath the bed there is connected to a catheter. See those wires? They run to pads taped on her chest, linked up to this monitor here, which keeps track of her heartbeat.'

The doctor's voice was soft and implacable, laying down facts like velvet bricks. Was she deliberately avoiding speaking Anna's name? I listened as she continued with a description of the tests the hospital had undertaken to establish Anna's mental and physical state. Acronyms nailed me into my place, the doctor's explanation of their meaning slipping into and out of focus. It was absurdly hard to connect the medical terminology to Anna there in her bed. Her glow made nonsense of the sterile surround. I had an urge to start undoing the leads and wires. Free of them, it would be no problem to lift my daughter up and take her to my hotel. She'd prefer it there, I was sure. If the doctor hadn't been hovering over me I'm sure I'd have made a start. Instead I found myself staring at Jo Hoffman's hands. They moved precisely, their nails sea-bleached white. I could see the long muscles in her forearms turning just beneath her brown skin. She was too lean, somehow: next to Anna's full-limbed perfection she looked mean as she stood there telling me how, even with the machinery, my daughter's physical health would begin to deteriorate. Words jutted up like saw teeth: 'atrophy' and 'bedsores', 'wastage' and 'fail'.

'My father taught her how to swim.'

The doctor stopped talking.

'In the bath, to begin with, when she was tiny. He used to lay her on her stomach in a deep bath, with a hand under her chin and shoulders, and let her kick. She really kicked. Her feet splashed water everywhere.'

Jo Hoffman stared from one screen to another.

'Then he'd take her to the local pool, when she was still little more than a baby. The first time, I went, too. He insisted there was a reflex that would keep her from breathing if we dunked her beneath the surface. But there wasn't. She was too old already. She came up screaming. We looked right idiots: him a middle-aged man, and me barely twenty, publicly drowning a baby girl. Still, it didn't seem to put her off. She learned to swim when she was very young.'

'I'm sure. I understand.'

'No, you don't. What I'm saying is that Anna cannot have drowned. It just hasn't . . . it won't . . .'

The young doctor let me search for what to say next. Then, when I didn't continue, she said, 'I've lived on this coast all my life. I've swum here since I could walk. Believe me, the currents are treacherous, the waves deceptively powerful, even on the smallest of days. Unless you know what you're doing . . . no, even if you know what you're doing, you can find yourself in trouble . . .' she snapped her long fingers '. . . *like that.*'

'I hear what you're saying, but no. No—'

'Yes.' She interrupted me. 'This sort of thing happens. People drown here. It's a fact.'

I watched Anna's chest rise and fall again, turned to the doctor and shook my head. She gripped the back of her bony neck and took a deep breath. 'It's routine to run blood tests on a patient in Anna's condition.'

I shrugged.

'We did so. Anna's results showed significant levels of alcohol and cocaine.'

I looked closely at the doctor. Her eyes, naturally narrow – as if used to squinting against a glare – were nevertheless a deep, oily brown, giving her expression a paradoxical shrewd softness. She held my gaze. In a deal situation, a negotiation, I pride myself on being able to distinguish bluff from the bottom line. Jo Hoffman blinked. Her upper lip was damp with sweat. As when we had spoken on the telephone, I felt a sudden tenderness towards her: the terminology and the handshake and the telling-me-straight were a front behind which she was cowering uncomfortably. She didn't want to have to break this news to me, though as a doctor that was what she had to do. Yet her sorrowful reserve gave away something else, too. I couldn't quite put my finger on it, but it felt as if she was holding something back. Her own suspicions, or perhaps even information, a part of the picture. I found this realization perversely comforting: it meant another gap in which to manoeuvre.

Quietly, almost under my breath, I said, 'She isn't stupid.'

'I'm sure you're right,' she murmured in reply.

'You told me, when you called, that the accident happened mid-morning.'

'Yes.'

'Well, I know Anna.' I explained myself slowly. 'She doesn't drink at breakfast, let alone sprinkle coke on her cornflakes.'

Jo Hoffman nodded, the petroleum sheen of her hair rippling beneath the skylight. 'Nevertheless,' she said.

I took a half-step towards the doctor, and drew myself up straight. Never underestimate the importance of physical presence in even the most cerebral confrontations: I always negotiate important deals face to face. I stared down at the doctor. She moved to the foot of Anna's bed, lifted the whiteboard up towards her lap, and continued, preferring to speak to it instead of me.

'We're losing track of ourselves here. Anna's state of mind at the time of the accident is unimportant in considering her present condition. Her body has suffered an injury, a very grave injury, from which she will not recover. It's extremely unlikely, as in a one-in-a-million chance, that she will ever regain consciousness. Even if she does, she won't be able to walk, talk, feed, even breathe for herself again. Ever.' She paused and turned back to me. 'We have to focus on what she needs us to do for her now.'

She wasn't to know it, but the doctor was unwise to reel off odds at me, because odds are what Taylor Blake deals in. Calculating risk is all the insurance industry does, and reinsurers like us simply do the same with bigger numbers. We gamble, pitting one person's worst nightmare against another person's money, and dealing with remote possibilities as a matter of course. The unthinkable, the improbable, the well-nigh impossible *happens* for us. We deal with it in our industry, all the time.

I did not reply. Instead I picked up Anna's fingers again and held them to my unshaven cheek. They were warm, too hot, in fact. What if she was lying there overheating, boiling up, and unable to tell anybody or do anything about it? I began loosening the carefully tucked-in sheet, pulling it down from her shoulders, exposing the garish green hospital gown they had put her in, and a web of wires and tubes.

The doctor said, 'Be careful,' again and continued talking,

but I wasn't listening and, to begin with at least, she seemed to know better than to intervene. The gown was tied loosely across Anna's stomach. I undid the knot at her waist and pulled it apart. Doing so revealed the bruising on her chest. Jo Hoffman was at my side, telling me something about the lifeguard's compressions and suggesting I cover Anna up, stand back a minute, stop, but it wasn't up to her. I ran my hands over my daughter's waist, felt the firmness of her hip bone, continued down her tanned, downy leg. I stopped. Her inner thigh was scored with three long, deep scratches, a violent red. The doctor's reassuring voice now said something about 'struggle', which I blotted out. I didn't need her rambling guesswork: like the mesh of wires, it was just making things worse for Anna, holding her down. The truth was that seeing these physical injuries helped. They were visible harms and they would heal. What was more, they were evidence.

The doctor had a hand under my biceps and was trying to lift me clear of the tangle. She was wiry and forceful, but I am strong and I resisted. I pressed my face into Anna's stomach. We share the same blood. I wasn't sure whose pulse I could hear, yet I knew a heartbeat that strong was more than enough to keep us both alive. The doctor said, 'Please,' but let go. I stayed bent over my daughter, warmth against warmth, breathing deeply, revelling in the precious smell of her skin.

4

4 January

I sit back in the magnesium flare of Sydney's centre and let the day ooze past. Two girls small-talk on the next table. City centre but bare flesh. One holds up a bag coated in fur with a big plastic key sticking out of the back – Camden Market tat. She seems to know. Her voice is glum answering her friend.

    – It doesn't do anything.

    – But it's unusual. At least it's eye-catching.

    – Catches on bloody everything.

    – It's a conversation-opener.

    – A tin-opener more like. I'm taking it back.

The girl is all belly-flesh swell and low cotton waistline. When she stows the bag a dolphin tattoo surfaces in the lean-forward small of her back. Mirror-glasses flash blankly. She takes them off to scratch an itch in the corner of her eye and her face changes. It's suddenly obvious what she'll look like as an old woman. Worse. She is what she will become. When my mother had me she wasn't much older than I am now. I know I look like she did – Dad's occasional double-takes more than make up for the lack of hard evidence. 'Marian – your mother' is how she signed herself. Plain Marian would have been fine by me. Not knowing her has its advantages – I've not had to put up with the sight of myself on fast-forward at least. When the girl puts her glasses on again and sits back in her chair her dolphin dives for cover.

Tattoos – they're everywhere.

Wiping down the steel bar last night I look up to see the girl with the barcoded forearm standing at my side. Her eyes are unforgiving.

– That hundred went into the jar I say.

– Sure.

– Pip earned her share. Check the kitty if you like.

Laughter thaws her face. I see I've misread her and relax into a smile.

– I'm Sasha she says.

– Anna.

– That was something.

– I'm not so sure. I wasn't thinking. If I had I probably wouldn't have taken the guy's money. But you know how it is.

– Idiot tax. He was eligible. She laughs again.

– Still. If he'd noticed.

– But without the occasional risk . . . She trails off. There's a conspiratorial glint in her eye.

It throws me back to the morning I arrived home early from a sleepover at Gracie's. Dad was showing a woman out of the flat. He made no excuse for her but ground his teeth – the tectonic friction between his separate worlds. I used to think none of those women lasted because of my mother – but have since seen it's as much to do with me. Him worrying I'll see it as betrayal and me wishing I wasn't secretly happy to be in the way. They don't stand a chance those women. Her face over his shoulder as they stiff-hugged goodbye – that dauntless wink. Like Sasha's now.

A pause follows in which her look says she's weighing up a purchase.

– Listen she says at last. – Tell me to butt out if you like. I'll drop it and we'll never have had this conversation. But it seems you can handle yourself and you never know—

Whatever her point is she's skirting it so I cut in. – Interested in what?

– In a way of making some extra money. This is just a hunch. It may not be your scene at all. But what I'm talking about takes front and you seem to have that. They want girls with charm but it's as important that you can turn it on and off. Everything's above board. Provided you stick to some basic rules it's safe enough.

– I don't follow.

She waits while one of the other girls passes us with a tray held high – its skyline of bottles clinking. Then she leans forward. – Escorting. Working as a hostess. It takes more than just pass-able looks. You need something to say. Let me be straight with you. I'll earn a few dollars if I make a successful introduction. But if you take up the offer they'll pay you well too. And you get to meet some unlikely people. Less daggy than the lot in here at any rate.

It's all I can do to keep a straight face. But there is something compelling about this girl – Sasha – which makes me try. She's paying me a compliment. A compliment wrapped in a dare.

– You draw your own line with clients. The agency will help you keep it. They do their best to screen the people you see. We're not talking about hooking here. Understand?

A tic starts up beneath my left eye. It is almost impossible not to rub my face – but that would look nervous. I manage to hold still somehow. She traces the fingers of one hand up and down a thin arm. Grips the slip-knot of her elbow. What would Marian have done? – that's the question. Sasha's fingers reach for her thumb-tip and before the gap shuts I feel myself nod.

– Have a think. If you want to take it further just say. In the meantime keep our chat to yourself.

A police car yowls past the bar. She carries on as if I wasn't there. When I look for her at shutdown she has already left.

Sasha's offer then. With any luck I could make more than money out of it. Marian wanted a bite of world. She couldn't settle for Dad and me – had to get out there and meet whoever there was to meet. What better taste of that could there be for me? When my mother left she never looked back. There's a sliver of ice in my heart too.

5

I checked into a motel in the centre of town, a single-storey building, made of pink bricks; they looked plastic in the afternoon sun. I was exhausted: it struck me I hadn't slept properly since I received the doctor's phone call, some thirty-six hours beforehand. I stripped to my boxer shorts, hung up my suit, turned the ceiling fan on full and collapsed beneath it on to the double bed.

The fan was hypnotic, beating slow circles above me, in time with the carousel in my head. There was a stranger in the sea. He left Anna there. He also left three red scratches scored in the softness of her inner thigh. Then he ran away. There were blue bruises across Anna's chest, too. The stranger fled, but I would bring him back; I'd find him and discover what he was hiding. Red and blue: a siren along the seafront, an ambulance full of secrets. Anna hadn't told me she'd moved on from Sydney, that she'd come up the coast to this place, Byron Bay, with its Toy Town hospital and whip-thin doctor. The woman had insulted Anna with improbable odds and now wanted to stop her breathing. They were all against us. Even the police, who had confiscated Anna's things and were accusing her of . . . what, exactly? Of drinking beer at breakfast. It was illegal to drink alcohol on the beach in Australia, the in-flight magazine said as much. Which explained the jogger, who had run to tell the lifeguard that Anna was breaking the rules. My carved face ran with sap. Then it was tears wetting the grain. But I couldn't let that matter because the issue was the stranger: all the while he'd been trying to suffocate her, clawing at her legs.

I awoke in the small hours. It was as dark with my eyes open as when they were shut. I was frightened: for the first few seconds I had no idea of where I was. Then the pulse of the ceiling fan brought the place back to me, and the truth of what had happened pressed in. My mouth was ash dry. I felt my way gingerly along the wall towards the bathroom. The spartan room leaped back to life when I reached the light switch, and I was startled by a movement. A cockroach ran across the ceiling and winnowed into the fitted wardrobe. I heard its pinprick footsteps as it scuttled through the crack. In the time it took me to cross the room and open the wardrobe door the insect had disappeared. With a shudder I retrieved my suit and hung it on the window blind.

I didn't have a newspaper or book, so made do with leafing through the visitors' information pack. Surf school, dolphin cruises, fishing trips: thoughtlessly pleasurable stuff. As well as the sea-centred activities on offer it seemed that Byron Bay regarded itself as a Bohemian Mecca, although the spiritual sanctuary it boasted had a curiously spiritless feel. The folder of 'things to do' in my motel included glossy brochures advertising Buddhist retreats, yoga training and courses in meditation, all for sale in unlikely, pre-packaged combinations. *Hourly rated self-enhancement; bargain basement karmic states.*

The phoniness of the place was sinister. Why had Anna come here? Her 'projects' tend towards the bizarre at times, but she's not prone to bullshit. My misgivings worsened after I set out into the town to find breakfast. When I'd stumbled upon my shiny motel the day before I hadn't noticed that it sat directly opposite a dishevelled backpackers' hostel. Nothing odd in that, except that the pattern seemed to be repeated everywhere else: the town was all Shangri-las and Travelodges, each pretending the other wasn't there. The inhabitants were equally at silent odds. Infant-beset families of holidaymakers, dripping sunscreen and camcorders, plied the pavements alongside barefoot hippies, all piercings, beads and hemp. Perms sat back to back with dreadlocks in the cafés; the beach-front car park was alternate camper-vans and hire cars, equal parts honeymooner and surf rat. The effect was of repressed conflict, a sense that all could not be what it seemed.

I found the police station easily enough, next to the hospital, back over the railway line, on the edge of the main town. As I do before any important meeting, I steadied myself with a fly-by, a minute to consider my surroundings and collect myself before going in. I saw more picket fencing, a drinks machine to one side of the veranda-shaded front door, and two squad cars pulled nonchalantly on to the forecourt, as if before a mall. I must have stood on the threshold for longer than I'd imagined because while I was waiting a policeman emerged through the double doors, looked at me expectantly, and said, 'Yes, mate, can I help?'

I gave him my name and explained what I had come to discuss.

'Righto, for sure.' His cheerful demeanour evaporated, leaving a familiar residue of awkward solemnity in its place. Quietly, he continued, 'I know about your girl. Terrible, horrible.

I'm truly sorry.' He looked it. 'Come on inside out of the sun and we can have a proper chat.'

I followed the policeman. He had receding ginger hair, cut neatly on the back of his neck. In the brightness outside, his forearms looked red; as we moved into the shade they turned brown, dark against the crispness of his light-blue shirt. *Wet sand, bright sky*. We walked past Reception. He stood to one side and ushered me down a corridor. Posters lined the walls. A smiling wife-beater: *He's a wonderful husband*. A drug identification chart: *stimulants, hallucinogens, depressants*. A chequered rugby ball: *Front-line police, not political footballs.* He showed me into an interview room and drew back a seat.

'Here we are.' The policeman sat down opposite me, elbows planted on the table between us, a triangle of brick arms and ginger head, leaning forward. 'First up, I want to reassure you. You're speaking to the right man. I didn't attend on the beach but, in view of the hospital's findings, I've taken over from Sergeant O'Brien. I'm in charge here.' He chose his next words carefully. 'I'm also a realistic man. In my opinion the . . . potential capital to be made out of Anna's accident is outweighed by the hurt I imagine our publicizing the medical report would cause you. Unless you say otherwise, we have no plans to brief the press. We're not about to make this situation any worse for you than it is.' He sucked his upper lip. 'No. We want to do all we can to help.'

'What findings?'

He narrowed his eyes. 'This is a small town, Mr Taylor. Dr Hoffman called yesterday afternoon to say you'd already been in to see Anna. She said she'd told you the facts.'

'She told me you're holding Anna's belongings.'

'Ye-es.' He let the syllable slide.

'Well, I want them.'

'Of course.' He smiled. 'They were clean. Nothing we need to hang on to.' It sounded like he was doing me a favour: he looked genuinely pleased he could help.

'How did you find out where she was staying?'

'As I said. This is a small town. The hostel she was in put two and two together when her room went unused for a night and gave us a call.'

'Which hostel?' I opened my notebook and took down the name and address. When he saw me begin to write, he left the room briefly, and returned with a brochure, inside which was a coloured map. Policeman gone, tourist-board official in his place: I watched in silence as he took the pen from my hand and marked the hostel's location with an X on the map.

'I have to find out what happened to Anna,' I explained, as he retook his seat. 'I want to know where she was staying, who she was with, how she came to be hurt, *who is to blame.*'

His sympathetic smile faded, but he was still nodding. 'For sure. I'd want to know as much as possible, too, but—'

'So I'd like to read the statements your sergeant took from the witnesses.'

He rubbed a freckled temple. 'They're uninformative, to tell the truth, and confidential in any case. I see where you're coming from, believe me. But I really reckon you're in danger of missing the point here. Pains me to say it, but you should know that Anna is the ninth person to drown on this stretch of coastline – Byron, Watego, Tallow Beach – in the last twelve months. Seven of them were tourists. Four under the influence.'

I hadn't imagined he would give me the statements. Such documents attract privilege. They were less important to me than the people who had made them, anyway: it's always best to compile your own evidence when examining a catastrophe; rely on another investigator's work and you might miss something crucial to the claim. But I'd judged the man well. I knew one refusal would make it harder for him to turn down another request. I studied my fingertips, all *eight* of them flat on the tabletop, so many drowned bodies, and then, doing my best to speak in a conciliatory tone, said, 'Of course. But if you could put me in touch with any of the witnesses, that might help. I feel I need to talk with those who saw the accident happen.'

The policeman leaned forward on to his elbows again, rubbing both temples now, and said, 'The fellow who gave the fullest statement, such as it was, is also a visitor here. English bloke called Gil Defoe. They're staying . . .' he rotated the map on the table-top and drew another X on it, '. . . here. His wife is the nurse who helped the lifeguard resuscitate Anna, as I'm sure Jo explained. Decent people, by all accounts. They did their best to help your daughter. I'm sure they'll be willing to talk to you.'

I wrote down Gil Defoe's name. It was a start. The little room was very quiet; although it was early in the morning the police station was siesta silent. I heard myself draw breath before asking, 'And where are you up to with tracing the guy who left Anna in the sea?'

The policeman sat back from the table. Although slim-faced, he had a paunch beneath his shirt, which he now folded his hands across, calm as a priest. 'Ah, yes. The bloke she was travelling with. We were hoping you might be able to help us there.'

'*Me?*'

'We thought he might have been known to the family.' The fingers across the man's belly knitted together neatly, and can-canned once. 'Obviously not.'

'I've no idea who he was. But surely you must know by now? You found Anna's hotel room. If they were travelling together you'll have found his things there, too.'

'Some clothes, a wash-bag, you're right. But that's all. No wallet. Nothing to identify him. The room was booked in Anna's name. She left her passport details. The receptionist just had Anna's companion down as "plus one".'

The policeman's tone was curiously flat recounting this dead end, almost unconcerned. My thighs began to burn as I pressed my feet into the floor. The lino was scratchy against my leather soles, scratchy because of the fine coating of sand across the interview-room floor. I stared at him. Silence is an underrated tool in business negotiations: in its face an opponent will often start talking, and so, unwittingly, begin to show his hand. But although I stared long and hard at this policeman, daring him not to continue, he remained unperturbed. His ruddy fingers came apart, flexed into a steeple, but his face stayed put, fixed in its expression of sympathetic kindness.

Finally, I was forced to continue. It was an effort to keep my voice steady. 'So, what are you doing to trace the guy now? How are you going to run him down?'

'Run him down?'

'Yes.'

'I'm not sure I'm with you. We've no reason to believe this fella's done anything wrong.'

I found it hard to speak. 'Anna was drugged. Cut,

drowned. Left in the sea by a stranger. A stranger who fled the scene. Of course you have to find him.'

The policeman took a deep breath. 'I understand what you're saying, but think about it for a moment. As best we understand it, this bloke tried to save Anna's life, and he failed. That immediately establishes any number of reasons for him to have moved on. Grief, shame, shock, to name just three. She's an adult, responsible for herself. We found nothing untoward in her room. There's nothing to suggest that she was anything other than a recreational user of commonplace drugs, or that she had taken anything against her will. I've already assured you that we don't see a benefit in publicizing this aspect of the tragedy. We've limited resources here. Our policy is to target dealers, suppliers, not individual users. And, in any case, we're straying way off the point. As I understand it from the hospital, Anna's situation isn't going to be improved by us chasing a witness to her accident God-knows-where. This is a vast country. If, and it's a colossal *if* in my book, he's a reason to hide, it'd take enormous manpower to find him. He'll probably turn up on his own before long anyway.' The man's lips parted over white teeth as his kind smile stretched. 'We've his trousers here, for a start.'

Misrepresentation is the bane of my industry. I'm not talking about the man in the street inflating the value of his lost luggage; global companies do exactly the same. We *all* do to some extent: I'd be lying if I pretended I hadn't scored a few pounds in the interpretative gap between the risks we take on and the cover we secure for them. Most untruths are innocent enough; if I judge them workable I'll structure the deal accordingly. But when my nose tells me I'm dealing with a *liar*, if I still can, I shut the bet down and walk away.

Never mind the sympathetic front: this policeman's position was unbalanced. He had conceded that the boy had been in the sea with Anna and had run away, yet casually classified him as a *witness*?

My legs were still rigid under the table, my palms damp against the wool of my suited knees, my heart galloping in my ears. I looked down at my toecaps, shiny black pools on the unswept floor. The policeman was concealing something. His motivation was not necessarily personal – I was prepared to give his sympathy the benefit of that doubt – but it did not have to be. For whatever reason, he didn't want to uncover what lay behind Anna's accident: he would not pursue the stranger, he would never investigate Anna's case.

'Listen,' he was saying now. 'When the boyfriend turns up, we'll talk to him. But he's unimportant. Trust me on that, if you can. I've seen similar situations before. There's nothing to be gained in beating your head bloody trying to find someone to blame. Go to the hospital. Be with your daughter. Let them help you with the . . . practicalities of what happens next. Jesus, mate,' he was blinking rapidly and his eyes were glistening, 'you've more than enough to deal with there.'

I gathered my papers – the map, my notebook – and slid them into my briefcase. The bag was a gift from Anna, an expensive leather satchel, which, as part of that Christmas's 'performance presents' theme, she insisted came with accompanying, personalized instructions. I saw her long fingers pulling the strap full stretch through the chrome buckle; I saw her bend the satchel forcefully across her knee; I saw her sling it across her back and catwalk the length of our roof-terrace, London's skyline bright behind her. 'Like a record bag. Or shorter, like a cycle courier. *Not* lopsided, like a businessman, all stiff and twee.'

I thanked the policeman for his time. He escorted me back down the corridor and out past the drinks machine on to the steps. With the bag on one shoulder, I walked down them into the white sun.

6

I hadn't expected the manager to be a woman. She's dressed like one of my dad's business associates – charcoal suit – designer handbag – ivory blouse. Though she doesn't stop on her way through the bar – of a flash hotel called W on Woolloomooloo pier – a waiter arrives in her wake with a glass of white wine. She sits down in front of an orange table-lamp and I see a halo of split ends.

– So. She looks from Sasha to me.

– Anna Maggie. Maggie Anna. Sasha leans back in her chair and pokes at the ice cubes in her glass with a straw as if to say her work is done. Her fingers seem steady but the straw between them is trembling. What this woman makes of me will reflect on her. Maggie takes an enormous Filofax from her handbag. Turns to a new page and writes 'Anna' at the top of it. Her handwriting is like the receptionist's at the hairdresser's back home.

– Sasha tells me you're interested in working for us.

I nod.

– What part of what we do interests you?

So straight a question. It makes me want to laugh at first. They asked me the same thing in my art-school interview. Alternative answers flash across the arrivals board – insight – risk

47

– attention – fun. Each is true but – given the woman's nail polish – I suspect they're all flights to wrong destinations. Those nails rattle on the tabletop.

– Cash mostly I say. It's flattering to think men might pay for my company. The bar we work in runs on much the same principle. I've had practice. Encouraging tips while keeping unwanted attention at bay. Sasha says you pay good money. And it sounds like interesting work.

– What are your interests then?

It really is a job interview. I tell her about the art foundation course I'm about to start and the travelling I've done and invent some stuff about an office job back home for good measure. She makes Girl Guide notes in her Filofax – all three-pronged *es* and curly *as*.

– You're English, right?

I nod again.

– Well that gives you a start. Something to talk about. A lot of our clients are international businessmen passing through. She looks at me more closely. What do you think the average businessman wants out of a date?

– I'm not sure there's such a thing as an average businessman.

She turns towards Sasha. A smile passes across her face. With it a mole stands out on the line of her jaw – ragged-edged despite the foundation. This flaw somehow gives me confidence to go on.

– The trick would be to work out each client afresh I think. Attentiveness must go a long way.

The woman's nails stop drumming. – How attentive are you prepared to be?

I'm expecting this question. I look at her and wait for her

to return the favour so that I can say what I've prepared to her face.

– I'll sell my company. No more. Sasha told me you screen clients. I'm happy to accompany anybody more or less anywhere so long as they know that.

– Fine. I don't know what Sasha's told you about rates – but that will be reflected in your earnings – as I'm sure you understand? Eyebrows rise in wooden unison on the word 'understand'. Humourless and belittling – as if to say, you'll soon change. It tips a balance somewhere inside me. Stubbornness takes hold.

Dad has always rated tenacity as a virtue. All he ever wrote with our fridge magnets was *Never Give Up*. Those words made me panic when I was little. Give up on what? *Unlike Your Mother* remained unsaid. I lay awake at night worrying that Dad or Granddad would leave too – and grew superstitious. If I could stretch a foot out of bed and keep it flat on the carpet for five minutes that would stop them going. I used to lie with my leg all cramped until the bedside clock shepherded them to safety. Another night the task might be worse. I'd make myself stand in the hall until the television downstairs was turned off. Or until I heard a siren go past – any pointless deadline would do.

And Dad's advice worked. I knew I wasn't making a real difference by standing sentry in the dark but the fact that I'd managed it somehow proved I could cope. He meant to encourage me to stick at concrete things – homework – front crawl – driving lessons – but what I actually learned was the beauty of random focus – the strange power to be gained by concentrating hard on anything at all. Those nights spent swaying in the dark were my first projects. They were physical prayers and they were answered. Whatever you find yourself doing there's redemption to be had from seeing it through.

Before the manager's face snaps back to genial I say – Of course I understand.

She starts talking business then – telling me the rules on money. Clients pay us direct. We account to the agency – the full amount for the rate they're charging – though we get to keep our own tips. But although I'm nodding and taking her in I'm already thinking of how sticking with this is bound to make good material. Pulling it off will take proper indifference.

– Where are you staying? Maggie asks.

I give her the name of my hostel.

– Well you can't have clients pick you up there. So no in-calls. Out-calls work best from hotel foyers like this one – Sasha will give you the list – or the client's base if he insists. Remember to add your taxi fare on top of the cost of the job. What else? She pauses – head on one side – like one of those Botanical Garden cockatoos. – Invest in a wardrobe she says. – And we'll need to arrange a photograph in due course for the books. Apart from that there's just the usual warnings. We'll do what we can to vet your clients but you're a big girl and the date is your responsibility. Be sensible. If anyone complains about you you're off the list. No second chances. Understood?

I nod back.

Maggie pulls dollars from her wallet and stands up – motioning for us to follow. Then she's walking through the lobby issuing instructions about how I should buy a new mobile. – Because this – she stops on the forecourt to point at her own phone – is the office as far as you or anyone else is concerned. You can reach me on it at any time. Give the number to clients by all means – but we don't have an address so don't bother asking.

I hold up my palms in surrender.

Her hard little face softens. A bottle-green Volvo estate with dark windows pulls to a stop in front of us. The driver jumps round the front of the car to open Maggie's door – but the corporate attentiveness of this gesture is knocked back by his grimy string vest and white-blond surf-mop. Maggie shakes my hand then ducks into the passenger seat. The tinted pane drops for her to speak before the car pulls off. – So long as we're straight with one another I'm sure we'll have a profitable relationship.

7

I realized before I made it beyond the police station's picket fence that I hadn't retrieved Anna's belongings. No matter, they would provide an excuse to return. Gil and Beth Defoe were in my sights.

They weren't in their hotel. My heart clipped the kerb when the teenage receptionist told me so. 'Don't worry,' he assured me, closing his book – a maths text with an unconvincingly lively cover. 'Out but not checked out. I can pass on a message if you like.'

I gave my name and said I'd call back later, then retreated to wait in a café across the street.

The town ran busy now, despite the intolerable sun. I sat beneath a striped table umbrella, huddling within its meagre block of shade. Eric Clapton and Bob Marley took turns with Moby to provide a hopeless soundtrack: songs so familiar I lost the ability to distinguish them. The café was mostly peopled with backpackers. Two boys – in their early twenties at most – shared the table next to mine. One was feigning indifference to a small yellow parrot perched on his shoulder. It looked restless. I watched the bird skip on to his baseball cap and sidestep down the brim. It flitted on to the table and marched back up his other arm, the boy nodding earnestly all the while as his friend explained something about fuel consumption. Then, with a sudden jack-in-a-box predictability, the little bird took off and flew into the middle of the dusty street, straight into the path of a passing pick-up. The boy leaped up too. The parrot somehow made it past the truck and flapped off down the road, the boy flailing after it. From behind me I heard laughter and a clipped South African voice: 'I was sold one of those, too. Same thing happened. Fucker flew away.'

I watched the hotel entrance closely but didn't see anybody go in for hours. Just a procession of holidaymakers, tourists and travellers space-walking through the heat. I made my bottle of water last, yet by mid-afternoon the restaurant was filling up so I was forced to order food. How would a professional have handled this? It meant waiting in line, satchel in hand, with the other, barefoot customers, as they queued to order at the hessian-and-driftwood food-hatch. I kept turning back to look at the hotel. When my turn came I still hadn't found the menu among the food-hygiene certificates papering the wall so asked for the first thing that came into my head – an omelette – and quickly retook my seat. Just as my food arrived I latched on to a sun-stricken couple wading one after the other along the opposite pavement. She paused for him to catch up, then they turned into the hotel lobby. Omelette forgotten, I ran across the road calling out, 'Hold on! Wait!'

Gil Defoe's T-shirt was plastered to his chest; his face was slick with sun-cream and sweat. Beside him, his little wife stood squat and pink in khaki shorts, her hair a saltwater mess, a stripe of sand up one plump leg. Both of them had their mouths open – whether panting or in surprise I don't know.

Two things struck me as I stood before them. First, I was confused: it seemed unlikely that they could have been to the *beach* after what had happened. Second, the moment I set eyes on Beth Defoe's flustered face, a bolt of gratitude stunned me into silence. All the questions I'd prepared left me: I simply didn't know what to say.

'Yes?' Gil Defoe swung his towel on to his shoulder and looked at me expectantly.

In answer – and it was a ridiculous thing to do, I know – I slid a pair of business cards from my wallet and gave them one each. Gil squinted at his, perhaps missing his glasses. Beth put a pink hand to her mouth and said, 'Oh!' Then, as if she were stepping on to a stage, she came towards me, startled holidaymaker gone, a nurse in all but the uniform. She took my hand between her own. 'Why don't you come through and take a seat by the pool? Give us a chance to freshen up, and then we can have a chat.'

Gil worked out who I was as his wife spoke. The red of his face deepened. The pair scuttled off to their room to change.

I waited in the shaded half of the hotel's inner courtyard. There were no tables to sit at, just sun-loungers, spread out around the pool like so many basking alligators. I perched on the end of one, feeling suddenly guilty at having interrupted the Defoes on their holiday. A single swimmer cut lazy lengths before me, barely disturbing the water's surface. My breathing steadied. Beth Defoe was an experienced nurse. It was likely she'd helped at many resuscitations: one more would not stand in the way of her enjoying her time off. Of course they would have been to the beach: that was what they had come here to do. By the time they rejoined me I had calmed down, and was intent upon putting them at their ease. 'Beautiful place,' I said, as we shook hands.

'Yes. We were pleased with it . . .' Gil spoke quickly, avoiding silence. 'This is the honeymoon we never had. We've been saving for years. You can never be sure from a brochure. You know how they are. So, it was a relief to find that this place lives up to the hype.'

Beth sat still. In the pause Gil's bony fingers knitted together again and again in his lap.

'Good weather for it,' I offered finally.

'And some.' Gil squinted at the sky, then down at my brogues: anywhere but at my face. 'Too hot for me, to be honest. But you know . . .' He trailed off.

'How is she?' asked Beth. I turned to her, but could not answer. Her eyes were slow-blinking, pale as a saint's. 'I hope you don't mind,' she continued, 'but I called the hospital yesterday evening to find out. They weren't very forthcoming.'

'Anna's fine.' I smiled back at her. 'As well as can be expected, in the circumstances. Weak, but . . . she'll pull through.'

Gil's hands came apart. He let out a long sigh.

'That's fantastic!' Beth looked from him to me and back again, shaking her head in amazement. 'Unbelievable news.'

I was startled by what I had said, but it was already too late to turn back. Over Gil's shoulder I saw the swimmer reach the end of a length and curl forward into an effortless turn. He pushed off the wall, unfurling like a flag. The ease with which he swam underwater was insulting. I heard myself go on: 'And it's thanks to you, Beth. Both of you. I can't tell you how . . . There's just no way I can repay . . . Thank you for giving her another chance.'

'Goodness,' she said. 'No problem. I mean! It's the life-guard you have to thank.'

'They said at the hospital that you played a vital part.'

She shook her head again, this time in half-hearted denial.

'Yes,' I contradicted her. 'And although I can't repay your kindness you must let me try in some small way.' It may have been Gil's reference to their having saved up for their trip. Or perhaps I wanted to divert attention from what I'd said about Anna. Either way, I found that I had my wallet in my lap, its mouth open, the wad of Australian notes I'd exchanged thick in my hand. 'Please accept this. Treat yourselves to . . . what-ever. It's a gesture, my way of showing how grateful I am.'

Beth had gone very still again. Her pale eyes narrowed. I thrust the bundle of money at Gil. He had no choice but to take it.

Beth found some words. 'We can't accept—'

'Nonsense,' I waved her down.

'There's thousands of dollars here,' Gil exclaimed.

'Please.' I leaned forward, took hold of both his hands, folded them around the money. 'Can we talk about what you did to help Anna through the accident? Tell me about the beach.'

Beth was about to protest again, but Gil spoke ahead of her. He was a wiry man, all joints: knees, elbows, wrists. As he told the story of what had happened he seemed to want to act it out. His whole frame grew animated describing the lifeguard's search at sea; he bent low to pull Anna from the waves, put his hands together to help his wife with the com-pressions, clutched his sides, rocking backwards and forwards, as he told of how the boy had been on the beach. Affected by the memory, Gil's voice grew loud and his eyes flashed. He added details from his wife's point of view – such as how sweat from the lifeguard's brow had wet the sand on Anna's face as he breathed for her – speaking for Beth unashamedly. She watched him throughout with a reserve verging on embarrassment. I let his story play itself out, paying close attention to every detail. I only asked my questions at the end.

'This fellow she was swimming with. You said he looked *unhurried* as he came out of the sea?'

'That's right. There was a strange lethargy to his movements. It was as if he were wading through mud, not water.' Gil checked his wife for confirmation. She nodded and drew breath to speak, but he was still in the grip of the moment, reliving it, and he cut her off. 'It was just so *odd*. He came out of the sea to get help, but without any apparent urgency. He must have been desperate to catch someone's attention, yet there wasn't any frantic waving.' Here Gil flapped both his arms. 'None of that. Just one swaying hand. I mean I saw it – we both did! I watched him wave at us from the sea, and I never guessed! He didn't look panicked. It seemed more of a *greeting* than a cry for help.'

'He must have been utterly exhausted,' Beth said.

I focused on her husband. 'Did he not shout for help, then?'

'No.' Gil shook his head vigorously. 'I don't remember any yelling, not as he came out of the sea, or afterwards. You'd have thought the adrenaline and such would have given him the strength to shout, but evidently not. He couldn't call out. He hardly managed to speak to the jogger or to me once he was on dry land.'

'Shock,' said Beth.

Gil shrugged. 'He just sat there. Shivering and holding his sides—'

'Yet when you returned, after searching the beach for this bag he mentioned, he'd recovered enough to disappear?'

'That's right. Poor guy.' Gil's face bunched at the jaw. 'It's been tearing me up, thinking about him. The moment of his decision. Just terrible, how desperate he must have been to leave your daughter in the sea like that.' He shook his head, took hold of his wife's hand. A smile bent the tight seams of his face. 'But – Jesus. He made the right choice after all. Just think of it now! When he finds out! Imagine his relief!'

The swimmer in the pool rolled forward through another turn, a brown shape beneath the turquoise surface. I watched him crawl a length, pursued by his shadow, which caught up with him as he reached the shallows. Sunlight bored into the courtyard, lying like silver paint on the tiles of the pool's surround, oozing nearer to where we sat, advancing to attack the potted palm that, placed between our sun-loungers, raised its elaborate fronds above us in a hopeless plea for mercy. I stared at the fat trunk of the plant and found that it was moving, bisected by a line of ants. Down the uneven bark they crept, over the lip of the terracotta pot, a black stripe across the floor. The column ran straight between me and the Defoes. It was a boundary, placing them in one country and me in another. I heard a faint 'tap' in my territory and looked down to see a shiny droplet on the tiles, a star with shrinking arms. Another followed. I pulled my feet back from the border, wiped my eyes and turned away.

The silence was broken by the muffled ringing of my mobile phone from within my briefcase. I hadn't realized it was on, or even suspected that it would work in Australia. The noise was an affront, it didn't belong here. I wasn't about to speak to whoever was calling. I fished the thing out of the bag and turned it off, apologizing to Gil and Beth. The apology bled into more thanks, and then I was standing up.

'If there's anything more either of us can do to help . . .' Beth was looking up at me. 'I could speak to the medical staff. We could pay Anna a visit.'

'You've done so much! I'm already unable to repay you.' I held my arms wide, gesturing from the pool to the court-yard and the sky above. 'And this is your holiday. Between us, Anna and I have disturbed you enough. What you've told me today is very valuable. It's a help to me to know what happened first-hand. Believe me, you've given me a means of moving on.' I was choosing my words carefully, trying not to lie yet unable to tell the whole truth. 'I'm sure Anna will want to show her appreciation herself in due course. But for now you'll have to let me thank you on both our behalf.'

Gil had to pocket the money I'd given him before he could shake my hand. He looked awkward doing so, but this was easier to take than his earlier embarrassment in the face of my grief. Beth's watchfulness subsided as we said goodbye. Her mouth relaxed in the softness of her plump face; I had to check an inappropriate but powerful urge to bend down and kiss it.

I retreated to the relative cool of my hotel room, took a shower and lay naked on the bed, staring up at the ceiling fan and going over my findings. The Defoes had confirmed my suspicions, but it would still be necessary to speak with the life-guard and the jogger. She, in particular, might give me details that would help speed my search for the other swimmer. The fan scythed on. I dozed and awoke. The cone at the hub of the blades above me was now a drill tip, bearing down. I rolled out of its way, on to the television remote. One of CNN's blow-up anchorwomen started up, auto-reading something to do with a freak storm that had thrashed the coast of Guatemala. Bodies clung to treetops, a slum vanished beneath a mudslide, animals rolled feet up in the flood. An expert considered the effect of global warming on the hurricane season; the president's face was a mask of concern. Though I stared at the screen the guilt I felt was unrelated.

8

Mr Sambi has tiny feet. He uncrosses them as I approach the low table. I catch a glimpse of purple sock and pale shin. He shuts his paper – thrusts it to one side and stands up – a head shorter than me. We confirm our names. His hand dives for the cover of his jacket pocket and emerges triumphant with an envelope. Bows as he gives it up but undercuts this politeness by looking me over with unblinking eyes. There are grooves at either side of his nose – the only marks on a plump face – where his glasses must usually sit. Nothing wrinkles when he smiles.

He visits Sydney twice a year to develop his company's property portfolio. Always – Maggie explained – the same routine. Drink – business dinner – karaoke bar near Circular Quay – then a walk to look at the opera house before departing – alone – for his hotel. A soft date. All the same – my tongue turns to sandpaper and my legs feel as if they may give way as I wait for his invitation to sit down.

He grins again – beckons a waiter. I try to look like I know what I'm doing. Doesn't ask me what I want to drink – just orders champagne with a flourish then turns to me expecting approval – which I murmur. He sits back and recrosses his little legs. Again

61

the semaphore of beige and purple. I can't help myself. My eyes flick down to his ankle and I find myself speaking.

– You have lovely socks.

His grin splits wider showing yellowed canines. – Yes! These are a present from my wife! He lets loose a burst of machine-gun laughter.

I gamble on laughing with him.

Then we sit in silence until our champagne arrives. I'm searching for clues. Mr Sambi looks from my foaming glass to me to the waiter and then to the room at large – nodding approval at each of us in turn. Face aglow with pride – features set in pre-mapped appreciation. I sip my champagne and touch the costume necklace – a present from Sasha – at my throat. He tells me that he likes the weather. Though he has the look of a man who seldom sets foot outside I agree he must indeed be enjoying the sunshine. He checks his stamp-thin watch and says we are expected for dinner soon. I nod knowingly – as if up on the schedule.

– You like lobster? he asks.

– I do.

– Because we are eating lobster.

– Great.

– We always have a lobster. It is the best food for doing business. Flesh from the same skeleton. It brings a table closer together.

– I'm sure.

He flashes those teeth and tells me a secret. – In Malaysia we eat a lot of seafood.

I widen my eyes.

He drains his glass and stands up. I push mine to one side and follow. My growing confidence is checked when Mr Sambi pauses for me to catch him up during our short walk through the lobby. Is he about to offer me his arm? It would be an insignificant gesture yet physical contact all the same. I might resist – miss my cue. Feel my footsteps about to falter as he raises his hand – but in the end it's just to beckon me forward. He wants me to walk across the carpet in front of him. I lift my chin and head for the revolving door.

I've always looked old for my age. Dad – on the other hand – still looks young. At thirteen I could pass for eighteen – he was thirty-three and looked about twenty-five. Waiters steered us towards secluded tables – men gave Dad the lucky-bastard eye. His refusal to treat me as a child didn't mean I wasn't a reluctant adult. I learned early on that there are two ways of handling unwanted attention. Cringe and you suffer. Stand tall and you can face most people down. So when during our taxi ride – throughout which Mr Sambi sits smiling at Sydney scrolling past – the driver starts leering into his rear-view mirror instead of looking at the road it's second nature to knock him back with a glare. Helps prepare me for the restaurant in fact. I keep calm in the face of Mr Sambi's business associates' twelve-eyed stare.

I'm not the only friend. Of the six suited Malays around the table two others are accompanied by young white women. We glance across one another in non-greeting. The conversation takes place in Malay – with stilted asides – about exchange rates – whaling – and the weather again – to us chaperones in English. The girl opposite me can't stop yawning. The one to my left keeps flicking her hair out of her eyes. We all pause to praise the acidic wine which Mr Sambi drinks more thirstily than most. And there is indeed lobster – though I don't eat much of it for fear of squirting gunk down my one good dress.

I excuse myself after the main course and retreat to the

ladies'. In the mirror there I reapply unfamiliar lipstick and mascara. Makeup – Sasha insists – is part of the uniform. Check to see what my new default expression looks like. Sickeningly modest. Bare my teeth and start pulling fright-mask faces – then notice that one of the other girls has followed me in and is watching over my shoulder.

She stares at me and says – You'll get used to it.

– To what exactly?

Without answering she turns and walks away.

The alcove housing our table has a raised floor and lowered ceiling – supposedly for privacy. In fact it's a speaker-box. The group's noise is being broadcast across the restaurant. Mr Sambi's face has turned from olive to ruddy brown. He's telling a joke – in Malay – waving his hands about like a tipsy uncle. We all laugh when he finishes.

Formality evaporates as the evening goes on. The business deal – if there was one – must have happened at dinner. Nobody's making much sense in any language by the time we reach the karaoke bar. A bottle of whisky arrives at our table. Though I pretend to sip at my glass I'm careful not to let the level go down. Pinch a coaster for posterity – not yet sure exactly what I'll make of this experience but that's a start. The hair-flicking girl is wavering in her chair. But the yawning one has rallied and is now on stage singing 'Summer Loving' with her client. Mr Sambi leans toward me. Nods at the girl and slurs – She loves to take her clothes off in the sunshine!

I grin back at him. Realize as I do so that in his drunken way he's testing me.

He goes on. – All of them! Agreed!

Hoping it's consistent with the demure-yet-unattainable act I cut the grin and shake my head in disappointment. It's as if I've scolded a child. Sambi shrinks back into his seat and sticks out his bottom lip. Next thing I know he's bounced back and is demanding a turn on stage. Wants to make it up to me by singing 'Lady in Red'. I'm wearing black which makes it easier to agree. His voice is impassioned and tuneful and he does not refer to the screen for the lyrics. Sensing we are back on safe ground I join in with the chorus. He's earned that at least.

Though the whisky and synthesizers bear the party onwards it eventually breaks apart. Nobody says goodbye. Before I know it I'm outside the club with Mr Sambi beckoning me onward for the final leg of his ritual. Air-conditioning gone – the evening is muggy and close. We stick out in public. Me tall in heels and an evening dress. Him wheezing beside me – squat and ageless and dressed in a suit. He takes his jacket off by the opera house. Flings it over his shoulder and looks up at me.

– Hold it!

A flash cracks twice. Before I can see properly a card is thrust into my hand.

– Five dollars to that address and the memory's yours love.

Barbed-wire accent – harsh Australian laughter – and a camera lowered by a boy not much older than me. Mr Sambi plays drunken catch-up – hopping from one foot to the other. But there's nobody for him to be angry with. The photographer has already turned and is walking swiftly away. I touch Sambi on the shoulder and steer him through a gate into the botanical gardens. We walk along the water's edge. Speed him past a couple clamped together on our way to an empty bench. Once there I motion for him to sit down. A sickly sweetness – frangi-pani – hangs in the air. Wavelets lap the rocks below. Mr Sambi is still agitated – but he can't quite remember why – and his anger melts into appreciation for the opera house – all spot-lit moon-slivers – sea-shells and sails. He coos at it dovelike – much drunker than I'd thought. While I wonder how to wrap the evening up he takes his shoes off and pairs them beside the bench. Then he removes his socks – grunting with the effort of bending down.

– Purple he says proudly.

There's no point in humouring him with smiles. It's obvious he can't see straight.

He slurs something else which ends in – My wife – then fires off another magazine of laughter. I give up on a tip and thank him for our evening. He starts to snore as I stand above him. I look back from the corner and see his feet glowing milky in the walkway light.

9

I returned to the hospital to chaperone Anna through the night. It wasn't my first bedside vigil over her. When she was ill as a small child my father and I would take it in turns to sit with her, and watching over her now felt exactly the same. It was at such times that I used to resent her mother's departure most, a resentment worsened by my father's apparent ability to rise above it. Once he'd made the decision to head off the woman's custody play with cash he never allowed me to look back. At first he wouldn't even let me repay him, and only consented once our fortunes reversed, after his architecture partnership suffered in the property slump that followed Black Wednesday, and my own business grew successful, when I could settle the debt with relative ease. Turning that corner was a source of relief and pride to me: while Anna is my father's joy she will always, ultimately, be my responsibility.

I remember studying for my insurance exams while I sat with Anna, using two hardships to cancel one another out. I set up a desk in her room once, when she was delirious – with mumps or chicken-pox, I forget which – and sat struggling with probability formulae while she tossed and turned. As I waited beside her bed that night in Byron Bay I fell asleep and dreamed our situations were reversed: it now fell to me to wrestle demons while she must overcome statistics. When I woke up I found myself staring at a patch of drool the shape of Australia on Anna's sheet in the dent where I'd laid my face. She hadn't moved.

It was early morning. While the staff had crept in silently to check on us during the night, I now heard bustle in the corridor. At one point footsteps stopped directly outside.

'The little shit.'

'Yeah, well, I'm better off out of there.'

'But to dump your kit in the car porch.'

'I gave him the ultimatum. At least I know where I stand.'

'Still. That takes a prize bastard. What are you doing for a place to stay?'

'Mum's cleared some space in my old room. I can't move for her cake-decorating stuff – there's paper doilies, piping patterns and plastic brides on every surface – and the sofa's too short, but it'll do for now.'

The doctor reversed through the sprung door and swivelled towards me. I stood up to greet her.

'Oh, hello.' She smiled, gathering herself.

'I've been keeping Anna company.'

She folded her arms. I wanted to acknowledge what I'd overheard, to offer her some sympathy of my own, but I held back.

'It's a good thing for you to have this time with her. I hope it's helping you to see things . . . more clearly.'

I pointed at the window and said, 'I opened the blind.'

Dr Hoffman shrugged.

We stood looking at one another. I became conscious of the breathing apparatus and monitors beating out a rhythm, and the chatter down the corridor, and then those sounds combined again into a background noise behind our silence. I raised a hand to my unshaven chin, ran it through the grime of my hair, and smelt myself, squalid in dirty clothes. It seemed I was wavering on my feet; I leaned out to steady myself on the bed, my hand inches from Anna's knee. The walls were pressing us together. All three of us. For despite the doctor's professionalism I saw, in that moment, that she was becoming a part of our struggle. The clue was in her shrug. In protesting too much detachment it hinted at the opposite.

'Look,' Jo Hoffman said finally. 'Events like this are so hard to comprehend. Would it help if I went over some of the medicine underpinning Anna's situation?'

I felt it would perhaps help her: it was my turn to feign indifference.

'The ward round doesn't start until ten. Some air might help us think straight. I missed my coffee this morning and you look like you could use one.'

I allowed her to steer me down a corridor – lined with preachy posters and optimistic art. We stopped at a coffee machine, then made our way to a shaded bench in the hospital grounds. There were fir trees, palms and eucalypts, and a lawn of thick, rubbery grass, cut so short and edged so carefully that it looked fake. The flowerbed was sculpted in a wavelike curve, which raised a grim smile to my lips. We sat in silence sipping our drinks. A flurry of small parrots, billboard bright, arrowed over our heads. I looked down and saw Jo Hoffman regarding me steadily.

'The other day,' the doctor began, 'I shouldn't have bombarded you with all that information. It was too much to take in at once. I'm sorry.'

I tried to reassure her with a smile.

'Breaking news like this is awful. Far, far worse for you to have to hear it, of course, but it's the hardest part of medicine all the same. It shows us doctors our limits; it feels like admitting professional defeat. And on a personal level I feel sorry for Anna and . . . heartbroken for you.'

I was tempted to press encouragement into her knee, but she was balancing her coffee on the one nearest me so I couldn't.

'I find it hard to keep detached,' she continued. 'Yet it's my job to do the best for the patient, and if that involves giving you the medical facts straight, then that's what I must do.'

I nodded.

'Although her heart is still beating, Anna hasn't breathed for herself since she came out of the water. There was a hope that, once the effects of the alcohol and cocaine wore off, her respiratory drive might improve, but it didn't. When we tried to withdraw support her body couldn't cope.'

The doctor had put her coffee to one side and was explaining herself to her bony hands. I let her go on.

'We've carried out neurological tests to determine what's referred to as a "Glasgow Coma Score", where the maximum a patient can score is fifteen, and the lowest is three. Anna scored three. She does not respond to pain, she makes no sound, she does not open her eyes. To put this in context: we intubate patients with a score of eight or below.'

Her hands were puppets, nodding sycophants.

'Now, there's a state known as "Locked-in Syndrome" from which a patient with no GCS to speak of can nevertheless recover. This is the one in a million chance I referred to the other day. You'll have read about it in the papers, though they mostly confuse it with cases in which a patient surfaces from a shallower coma. You really mustn't allow it to give you false hope.'

The more plainly she spoke, the more emphatically her hands agreed.

'Because we've carried out a further series of tests on Anna, called brainstem tests. These look at the most primitive reflexes of all. For example, we look for a response to what's called the "doll's eye" test. We hold a patient's eyes open and rock their head from side to side, to see whether the eyeballs track or stay still. Anna's eyes stayed fixed. Another of the tests is known as the "calorific stimulation" test. We inject ice-cold water into the outer ear, and check for any eye move-ment at all. Again, in Anna's case, nothing. Nothing at all.' She lowered her voice. 'This means that Anna is technically brain dead.'

I couldn't help myself. Icy water in the ears! A doll's head! Even the doctor's hands had stopped their hopelessly affirma-tive dance. I threw my head back and laughed out loud.

Jo Hoffman stared at me. 'Are you okay?'

'Of course. Don't worry. Please, I understand you. You needn't worry at all.'

Drawing two syllables out of the word, she said, 'Good.'

'She's had the best possible care, right from the start,' I said. 'To think that there was a nurse waiting for her on the beach, ready to get her going again. Then the paramedics, this beautiful hospital.' I pointed at the flowerbed, then turned to look at the doctor. '*You.*'

'We've done our best.'

'You've done better than that. Against such odds, too.'

The tip of her tongue moistened her mouth. 'I don't understand.'

It was difficult to know where to begin. I found myself copying her, my own tongue snagging on dry lips. 'You care too much,' I said finally.

'I don't think that's possible.'

'No, you care too much to give up.'

She bent forward and put her head into her hands, a palm against each dark eye.

'It's fate that Anna came to you.'

Her voice was muffled. 'If you want a second opinion—'

'No! There's nobody but you that's capable of making her well again. At first I thought you were hiding something from me. I thought it must be some medical mistake, a failing, something grave. It was a stupid thing to assume and I apologize. Yet you *were* trying to keep a secret, in a sense. You were trying to hide your hope.'

'Mr Taylor, have you not heard a word I've said to you?'

'Please, it's Wilson.'

She shut her eyes. 'Wilson, then. Has what I've explained made no difference?'

'Of course it has. You've made yourself perfectly clear. But it's not me you're trying to convince with your tests, it's you.'

She rubbed her face, then opened her eyes again. They flashed filmy black. 'What are you saying? That you do understand, or you don't?'

'I understand how much you care for Anna.'

'I do care. It's for that reason, I think you should . . .' she dug for the right words '. . . have mercy.'

'You mean give up. The most merciful thing I can do for you is to give you the strength to carry on.'

'Not mercy for *me*, for Anna.'

'You can't give up without my consent.'

'Not true. We – *I* – don't want to have to do that, but—'

'And I'm not consenting.'

'Please!'

'Because you and I are in this together. We both have our burdens. We must both carry on and beat *all* the odds.'

She shook her head, whispering, 'What are you talking about?'

'It's your job to unlock Anna, to make her well again. And it's my job to find the person who hurt her, to hold him to account for putting her in this terrible state.'

'Mr Taylor. I think you should consider seeking professional help.'

'You're my help. I entrust Anna to you. I put my faith in you and I know you warrant that faith. It's instinctive. My most valuable instinct is a sense of who I can trust. You won't fail us and neither will I: I have the wherewithal to track that guy down and unearth the truth. Just watch me.'

'Track who down?'

I looked at her. 'The boy who drugged Anna. The swimmer. The fellow who left her to drown.'

She shook her head again. Then she stood up and threw the remains of her coffee into the flowerbed. I got to my feet beside her and did the same. Brown pearls clung to the nearest leaves, slid together, dripped into the chippings below. A mutual *what else can we do?* Jo Hoffman was breathing deeply. I allowed her to collect herself.

'I can arrange a counsellor through the hospital.'

'There's no need. You have more important things to do.'

She drew breath. 'It may take you a while to appreciate

the truth of the situation, but you will. In the meantime, you must feel free to spend all the time with Anna that you want. I'm sure that doing so will help you come to terms with what's happened.'

The kind smile was in place again. She was back on script and I respected that.

'In the meantime, of course, I'll report our conversation to my colleagues. The hospital has to consider Anna's situation in context, you understand, and do what's best for *her*.'

'Of course. I know you will.'

The doctor explained that it might be necessary to contact me at short notice. I took the hint and offered her one of my cards, careful to do so without looking at the photo of Anna frozen in the window of my wallet. The thought of turning my phone back on made my head throb, but the ache subsided quickly, soothed by the knowledge that Jo Hoffman would be able to reach me at any time in the days ahead.

We walked back into the lobby. The doctor explained she was needed for the ward round. Moving on to the rest of her day.

'So,' she said, 'if you're in with Anna later on, I may see you. Otherwise—'

'Your landlord,' I interrupted. 'I overheard you explaining difficulties. He's thrown you out.'

'Landlord?' Her neck stiffened, head bobbing back.

I saw my mistake, but there was no way to retreat, so I pressed on. 'You have to move in with your parents. There's no room.'

Her lips set.

'Cake decorations,' I offered. 'Short sofa.'

'What are you getting at?'

'You mustn't . . .' I trailed off. She had taken offence.

'I mustn't what?'

'You need proper rest.'

She stood still, head cocked to one side.

'I think you should check yourself into my hotel. You have to be at your best just now. Proper sleep, and you need to eat well, too.'

She laughed, and put a hand to her mouth.

'I'll pay,' I clarified.

She touched my shoulder lightly, as if to reassure an animal, then collected herself again. 'That's a very generous offer. I can't accept, of course. It's out of the question. But . . .' she paused, picking her words '. . . let me reassure you that the machinations of my private life will have no bearing on Anna's care. Now,' she glanced at her watch, 'I'm late. Excuse me.'

I watched her stride purposefully away from me down the corridor, fooling nobody. We were connected. I'd sown an idea: though she played barren ground for now it would take root eventually. The same thing often happens in business: people shy away from unexpected offers at first but take advantage given time. The doctor's refusal was as hesitant as her professionalism was sure of itself. She bolstered me on all levels.

Outside again, I found myself squinting up at the white disc of the sun. It did not appear to sit in the sky so much as to have seared a hole in it, through which untenable heat and brightness now poured. I'd hardly been out, but had some-how managed to burn the tops of my ears and the bridge of my nose. In fact, without shade, my whole face felt painfully hot, as if bent too close to a fire. Though it looked ridiculous with my shirt and brogues, I bought a wide-brimmed hat from a shop in town. Then I set off for the beach.

10

Of course I send money to the address on the photographer's card. But I don't expect a reply and am not surprised when a week passes and I hear nothing back.

In fact when the receptionist slides a letter at me I've forgotten that anyone knows where I'm staying and am suspicious he is trying something on. Hand my board money through the hatch and turn to go but the bloke hollers after me – Put your flamin' eyes in love! – his voice sergeant-majoring in the little hall.

It already seems a long time since the date. Maggie called afterwards to say Mr Sambi was satisfied with my performance – but she hasn't yet arranged another client. Each passing day has made the lobster seem less real. This envelope's contents should help bring back its taste. Just holding the thing makes me feel covert again. My heart begins to race.

There are two photographs. No accompanying note – just the images. The first is a full-length shot of Mr Sambi and me bracketed by two white wings of uplit opera house. Caught mid-step descending. We look oddly glamorous. The photographer must have crouched low with his camera. He's added valuable inches to Mr Sambi – who looks dapper in his stark suit. Stocky rather than fat – more media mogul than middle manager. The knife-cut of his trouser-leg flaps above his out-thrust right foot. There's a streetlamp gleam in his toecap.

Beside him my own right foot is thrust forward too. We are walking in step. Above that foot my leg is long and bare to the thigh. I thought that black dress was understated but from so low an angle it looks way too short. Although Mr Sambi and I are not touching the swing of my hips high-heeling down those steps makes a provocative sliver of the space between us. His hand is flung out unsteady behind him but he might as well have an arm round my waist.

Our expressions are caught by the second image. The photographer must have used a zoom for this one – the flash refired so quickly he can't have had time to move closer to us between exposures – blurring the background and slicing us in half at the chest. Mr Sambi's drunk-frozen eyes appear almost bold. The colour is high in his cheeks. He's staring just above the photographer – intent on forging beyond the frame – heroically unconfined. I'm looking at him with a sort of awed fondness – somewhere between attentive and worshipful. Never mind our differences – my face tells the viewer – we're together Mr Sambi and I.

My mobile phone starts ringing. It's Maggie – with the offer of another client. Though I hadn't wanted to give up after Mr Sambi a bit of me would have been happy enough to move on after having gone through with one date. Yet as she explains where and when the next one will begin I'm remembering my mother's line – 'Your dad was only ever in love with one of my performances.' More clients – and more images. What better way to cut a few similar counterfeits of me?

11

The woman at the surf club had a scab on her elbow, a dark island reefed with livid pink. She looked up from picking at it to tell me that the lifeguard in question – Waller – wasn't on duty that morning. I ground my teeth, fiddled with the brim of my hat. She led me to the office and, while I waited, called Waller's home to tell him he was needed. Though she tried to hide it, I could tell from her half of the conversation that she'd disturbed him asleep in bed.

If I'd been thinking more clearly, I'd have asked her to arrange for the lifeguard to come to my hotel: with a sensitive meeting it's best to take control of the venue. The last place I wanted to wait was the beach. Yet before I could intervene she had replaced the receiver and was telling me Waller would be there within the hour.

Though I say I didn't want to be on the beach a part of me, now I'd arrived there, was unwilling to leave. I walked down towards the sea and looked about, breath-taken. Gil Defoe had described the place in detail but I hadn't expected to be so awed by the vast bay with its tiger-striped sand and punishing sky framing the waves. I stood with my eyes scrunched tight, squinting out from beneath my hat at the view.

The low hills inland stretched long, encircling arms from the lighthouse on the point up to my distant right, where the sand was bleached so bone white that the green line of trees behind it seemed black, to the pale blue saw-tooth peaks shimmering in the glare way off to my left. I noticed how the waves, on that day at least, ran into the point at an angle, and bent in concentric rings along the length of the beach in an endless series of split curves, the push of water as much sideways as forwards, break after white-capped break. The sea air smelt more of sap than brine, sweet and clean, and my ears were hushed full of the torn and retorn swell. Witnessing the place first-hand sucked something out of me. I sank down in front of the surf club, leaned forward, dug my hands into the hot sand and raised two fistfuls to my face. As with the enchanting view, the sand was deceptive, not white at all, but every colour close up, a mixture of pink shell fragments, blue-black grit, and specks of crystal, silver and gold. I stared at my fingers for long enough to lose a sense of the sand's whiteness; when I eventually found it in myself to rise up again I was surprised by the pale oval on each of my suit-clad knees.

But I had to stand, because there was work to do. In the aftermath of a disaster there's no substitute for carrying out a thorough investigation of the site; liability often turns on mundane physical facts – the gaps between buildings in a fire claim, for example, or the camber of a road in a traffic accident. At Taylor Blake we take nobody's word at face value: if there's room to doubt the merits of an originating claim we commission our own report. I took my clipboard from my leather case and set off down the beach – in the direction Gil Defoe had described – to discover for myself the distances involved, the perspective in either direction, the truth of who could see what from where.

I was on the front in the middle of the morning, roughly

the same time as when the accident happened. The sun was high, but not directly overhead: though it glared at the waves from the east it was not low enough to dazzle me on the shore; the sea beyond the break was ablaze with light, but so was everything else in the brilliant scene. The swimmers between the lifeguard's flags were distinct in the water: from where I stood at the back of the beach I could make out the seal-like black dots of surfers, even far away in the distance towards the point.

The beach was broad as well as long: the expanse of fore-shore and sky bit down on the sea, clamping it into a thin strip so that the water almost looked shallow. Only the size of the swimmers against the waves gave a sense of the ocean's scale. As I watched, a couple standing together in the white-water were enveloped by advancing foam. One minute I could see the red of the woman's bikini bottoms, the next she was submerged to the neck. Then the spume sucked back again, unveiling the pair, wobbly at the knees. After watching for a few minutes I understood better why the lifeguards' flags were so close together. At first it seemed almost mean, given the enormity of the bay, to confine the swimmers to just fifty or so metres of sea, but I soon understood the safety in overseen numbers. I changed my mind about the likelihood of Anna's having ignored the warnings. She isn't stupid. Given the choice, I'm sure she would have taken notice.

I trudged south, at the back of the beach, in search of the pines where Gil and Beth had stopped to eat their lunch. The sand was soft and squeaked underfoot like powder snow. By the time I reached the spot Gil had described my face was bathed in sweat, my calves ached, my hatband felt tight round my head. I made for the shade the Defoes had sheltered in and sat down to catch my breath.

It was a surprise to see how far I hadn't come. Although the lifeguards' station was out of sight, the flags, limp on their posts at the water's edge, were still visible, as were the swimmers between them. At least, they were at first glance: when I picked out an individual head, a little way from shore, I saw how the incoming waves bore it high as they advanced, then dropped it out of sight as they surged past. The further out a swimmer was the longer this pause took as the passing swell conjured him into and out of view. And this was from my vantage-point up the incline of beach; as I walked down towards the sea, the true break, and the glassy blue beyond it, were masked time and again by the tumbling ranks of white-water, which fell and regrew on their futile march inland.

Before opposing this assault, I sat down to take off my shoes and socks. I wanted to feel what Gil had described: the pain of hot sand on the soles of my feet. I removed my shoes and rolled up my trousers, and the heat wasn't too bad to begin with. Walking helped cool my soles. It wasn't until I stopped and stood still that I could see what Gil meant. The tingling needle-pricked beyond itself almost immediately, shooting darts through the soft skin of my insteps, spreading to my toes, the balls of my feet, even into my heels. It hurt. I took hold of my briefcase with both hands, gripped it tight, strained against the impulse to move.

Just as the pain was threatening to take on a new dimension, the ridiculousness of what I was doing hit home. What was I trying to prove? The sand was burning hot, yet the boy walked barefoot to the tree-line. So what? If I could bring myself to stand the heat for the purposes of my investigation, his fear, his cowardice, his *guilt* would have driven him across it, no trouble at all. I jogged the remaining yards, into and beyond the darker sand, and stood in the outermost wave-fringe. Pinkness turned porcelain white as the water ran cool over my feet.

I retreated to just below the tide-line, where the beach was ribbed and hard underfoot, which made easier work of the walk back towards the lifeguards' station. This was the surface across which Vee, the jogger, had run to fetch help. I tried running for a few yards to test the ground and managed a gentle lope, but couldn't sprint properly, in part at least because I was weighed down with my briefcase and shoes. When I did pick up my pace, one shoe slipped out from under my arm and fell into the water. It filled immediately and was suddenly funny. I saw myself from afar: stiff-brimmed bush-hat, dirty white shirt, woollen suit trousers rolled to the knee. It struck me that I should buy something more suitable to wear. Not then, though: there wasn't time. When I glanced at my watch I saw with surprise that more than an hour had passed since the girl with the scab had called Waller. I was late.

To have lost track of time before so important an encounter angered me. I don't mind being late, so long as the delay is intentional. If not it means starting a meeting on the back foot. I hurried beyond the reach of the waves to sort myself out, unrolled my trousers and bent to put on my shoes and socks. One sock had escaped, but there was no time to look for it; I used the other to brush sand from my ankles as best I could, pocketed it, and – to avoid inconsistency – forced both shoes on to naked, gritty feet. Labouring the final yards, I arrived back where I'd started out of breath and looking like an idiot: one shiny shoe, the other caked with sand, my trousers a creased mess, my shirt stuck to me front and back, my face purple in the shadow of an inappropriate hat.

Waller was sitting on a boulder at the back of the beach. He stood as I arrived, looked me over and nodded an unhurried 'G'day.' The hand he offered me to shake was the colour of my desk at home, flecked with a grain of bleached blond hairs. He turned towards a wiry young woman who was standing with her arms crossed a little way off. 'That's Vee. Raised the alarm. All right if she joins us?'

There was something both implacable and reassuring about the lifeguard. Although I would have preferred to talk with the two of them separately, I found myself nodding. 'Sure.'

Waller fetched three plastic chairs from the surf club and dug them into the shade at the edge of the beach. A group of kids were thumping a volleyball at one another a little way off. As we sat down, the ball careened in our direction. It rolled into a depression in the sand beneath my seat, hiding from further punishment. All three of us bent to retrieve the ball at once. A half-beat of embarrassed stand-off followed. Then Waller scooped up the ball and flung it away, over the head of the boy who had come after it. He blanked the boy's sarcastic gratitude, turned to me and, with more heartfelt directness than anybody before him had managed, said, 'I'm sorry.'

'Thank you.'

'No, mate.' He spoke slowly. 'I'm sorry, as in I apologize.'

'There's no need.' I shrugged my shoulders. 'I spoke to the doctor. The other witnesses. You more than did your job.'

He shook his head and squinted at the sea. 'I spoke with

Jo Hoffman too,' he said. 'She said you're mad. And you've every right to be. All that stuff she told you about the coast here being so dangerous. It's only partly true. I've worked this beach for three years and your daughter is the first person I've lost. Plenty enough people drown up this coast, but not right here, and not on my watch.'

Vee shook her head. There were badger-streaks of premature grey in her ponytail. I didn't know what she was disputing.

'It's true. I failed. Jo said you're looking for someone to blame. Well, it's me.'

A long pause followed, punctuated by the hollow thud of waves, underscored with hissing foam. Eventually I said, 'She wasn't swimming between your flags.'

'Doesn't matter. We monitor the sea either side of them as well. Or at least we're supposed to.'

'Waller,' said Vee. She was still shaking her head. Less in contradiction now, more resigned.

'I've been down the beach, though,' I told him. 'You pulled her free of the water way down there. She'd have been hard to spot. The waves,' I continued, 'they block the view.'

'Spotting people in waves is what we do,' he said.

Now Vee spoke up: 'The swimmer said they got caught in the rip. He didn't say where. They could have gone in down the beach. You try to keep an eye out beyond the flags, sure, but your responsibility is to the people here. It was a busy morning. The water right in front of you was stacked.'

Waller was watching me and saw I did not understand. He leaned forward, smoothed a square of sand in front of us, and drew a line across it. 'That's the beach,' he said. 'Waves come in this way.' He drew a big arrow. 'And all the water has to get back out to sea somehow. It works channels of current – rips – where the water runs against the general flow.' He drew smaller arrows facing the other way, at intervals along the line. 'Rips travel. They shift about. Depending on the tide, the wind, sandbars and the strength of the waves, they multiply, fuse, go weak or tear up strong, run straight back out to sea or at all sorts of bent angles.' Now the sand before us was a complicated mess. 'What Vee's saying is that just because there was a rip near the flags, doesn't mean Anna and her bloke got in trouble here. They could have swum out down the beach and into a current there.'

'Exactly,' said Vee.

I stared at the diagram. Waller leaned forward, smoothed the sand again, and I had a sudden memory of Anna's Etch-a-Sketch screen. There was a time when she took that toy everywhere with her. Instead of speaking to me, she'd draw what she wanted to say on it, the first in a long line of harmless enough 'projects'. She never threw the thing away. I shuddered now, at the thought of it at home, buried in the back of some cupboard.

'But you just said the sea wasn't as dangerous as all that,' I said.

'Statistically,' said Waller.

Vee agreed. 'More people drown in pools.'

'Your average Australian isn't fazed by a rip,' Waller continued. 'There's no magic to them. They don't generally travel far back out to sea. Even if they do, all you have to do is swim at right angles to the flow and you'll soon be free of it. A rip isn't normally that wide. Kids are taught all this stuff in school . . .' He trailed off.

I was still staring open-mouthed at the sand. Vee elaborated. 'There's just one rule: never swim against the undertow. It tires you out. Before you know it, you're worn out, you've sucked down a lungful, and you're still drifting out to sea. Then you panic and then you drown.'

Waller looked at the ocean. Squinting against the sun was his default face: when he did so the pale lines at the corners of his eyes disappeared into the security of deeper, tanned creases. 'Kids here know how to spot danger from the shore, too,' he said. 'See there, where the white-water's smallest, where the waves behind it are folding last. The sea wants to go out there, not in. It's pushing back against itself. That's a rip.'

I looked in the direction he was pointing and thought I saw what he meant, though to be honest I wasn't sure. The volleyball spiked back and forward across the view. All three of us sat listening to the wave-hush and beach-chatter through the filter of our own silence. The pause gave me time to marshal my thoughts. I was just about to ask my first question when Waller folded his face into his brown hands and muttered, 'Fucking sea eagle.'

'What's that?'

He didn't reply. I watched him closely and was startled to see tears dripping through his fingers. He was a big man and he cried solid, heavy tears. One followed another, pocking the sand below. I did not know what to say. Neither, apparently, did Vee. She looked away; I stared at the ground in front of Waller's chair while the craters there multiplied. When he finally looked up again his face was snot-smeared yet unembarrassed, frank as the 'I'm sorry, mate', which he repeated.

Vee handed him a tissue from her crocheted shoulder-bag and said, 'He wasn't at fault,' to me.

'I know that.'

'Bad things happen.'

I watched a slab of blue swell rear milk green and thump shut. Foam boiled forwards. 'Perhaps you can tell me what you saw,' I asked her.

She did. She explained how, as usual, she timed her run to coincide with low tide, when the sand was firmest, and how she had set off on her normal route – the four miles from her place at the northern edge of town to the lighthouse and back. She told me how when she runs she always watches the sea near to her rather than far away, so that the running feels like progress and not a slog into the retreating distance. For that reason, she said, she'd only seen the swimmer's raised arm when she was almost upon him. To an Australian a single raised arm at sea is as unambiguous as the letters SOS. She had paused long enough to be sure that the man was more or less on shore, and not in apparent difficulty himself, so assumed he was raising the alarm for somebody else. She played down her heroic sprint through the heat to alert the lifeguards, only emphasizing that – given the length of that dash – it did not occur to her that they might already have spotted their help was needed. She described how, once she saw Waller leap into action, she went back to help the boy. I listened attentively to her description of how the other swimmer had looked and acted from the moment of her arrival until he made his escape. Unlike Gil Defoe, Vee told her story calmly. Her voice stayed soft throughout, if anything quietening – in embarrassment, not false modesty – when describing her own involvement.

I let Vee turn up each of her cards until no more came: she had the reserve of someone who, had I interrupted with

questions, might otherwise have stopped dealing. My attentiveness was rewarded with one or two details I would never
have thought to ask about, and holding my tongue had a further, unexpected benefit: Waller recomposed himself in the
time it took Vee to peter out. After she stopped, he took up
with his own version of events. The lifeguard's account was
less comprehensible to me; in part because he was still upset,
in part because he used beach-jargon I didn't understand.
Nevertheless, I kept quiet for him, too. Instead of cutting in
with queries, I took notes of things to clarify afterwards. Note-
taking isn't always a good idea in meetings. It can have odd
effects on other people: either it spooks them and they dry
up, or they find it flattering and become over-elaborate.
Useful outcomes in some contexts, but not here. However, I
judged I was safe with Waller, and I was right: he just carried
on talking straight.

At the end I asked, 'What do you mean when you say it
was "a lighter day"?'

'Light. You know. Wasn't a heavy day. Nothing like now,
for example.'

'Not heavy?'

'The waves weren't that big. Three foot. Four, tops, in the
bigger sets. Today's a solid six.'

I rubbed my hands together; they felt sticky with salt-
water, sand and sweat.

'Means the visibility would have been better, for one.
Weaker rips, too. I had more of a chance to see Anna.'

'They were too far down,' insisted Vee.

'And yet,' I said, addressing her, 'you only saw the boy
waving when he was almost out of the water.' She frowned at
me so I went on: 'You always look out to sea when you run,

you said. Not far, I know that – but you'd get giddy staring at your feet. You look a little way out, say, a few hundred metres.'

'I'm not sure exactly.'

I tried another tack. 'You wouldn't look twice at swimmers in the sea, would you?'

'Not really. I guess not.'

'But a person with their hand up is a person in distress.' My head felt hot again with the effort of thinking.

'As I said.'

I tried again. 'So you're jogging. And you're looking out to sea. Not in the distance, just a few hundred yards out. And it's not a "heavy" day. So you see swimmers a way out. But they're invisible swimmers, because they're not waving. You don't notice them. There are no hands up. Not until . . .' She was staring at me intently, an 'I don't see where you're going with this' look in her eyes. I forced on. 'You didn't see the boy hold his hand up until he was nearly out of the water, because he didn't stick it up until he was there!'

'That's right.'

There was a tight band of fire round my forehead now. She was still frowning, determined not to see the point. And I was still wearing the hat, but we were in the shade. I pulled it off and twisted it in my lap.

'Yet when you found Anna she was already face down.' I turned to Waller. 'Like she was looking for something on the bottom. That's what you said. "As if she'd been searching there for ever."'

Waller nodded.

'Don't you see?'

They looked at one another.

'If he'd wanted to call for help, all he had to do was stick his hand up!'

'That kid was just about spent by the time he made it ashore.' Vee's voice was a whisper. 'He collapsed like a shot dog.'

'A strong Australian accent. You said he had a strong Aussie accent. Right?'

'He was Australian,' Vee conceded.

I turned to Waller. 'And Australians know all about rips. You swim at angles. You put your hand up. You spot them from the shore in the first place. Am I correct?'

The white lines round the lifeguard's eyes disappeared again, but he was peering at me, not the glare.

'You know that her blood alcohol was high?' I asked him. 'That they found traces of coke?'

He shrugged.

I turned back to Vee. 'And yet this boy was comprehensible to you! You said, once he got his breath back, he was coherent. After the English fellow stopped asking him questions he made perfect sense.'

'*Some* sense. He was still distraught, but he spoke more clearly, yes.'

'He admitted he'd done it! It was his fault! That's what he told you!'

The woman was called Vee. There was an arrow of grey above her forehead, and now there was a deep notch in the frown above her nose. V for Vee. She was talking. 'He kept saying "Sorry", if that's what you mean.'

I checked to see that Waller understood. He was scratching at the stubble on his chin, looking kindly, sad and confused. Yet he wasn't to blame! Never mind me. It was suddenly crucial that he should see the thing clearly for his own sake. I raised my voice: 'You did nothing wrong!' I told him. 'As in zero liability! You're not to blame!'

Vee stood up and walked off towards the surf club, leaving Waller and me listening to the pointless sea as it stamped and hissed in the distance. There was still no wind. Despite our position in the shade, the heat we were sitting in seemed to have developed a new ferocity. Each scorching breath was effort: at any moment, I felt, I'd cough sparks and the resinous pine above us would burst into flames. Again, this discomfort was perversely gratifying. It made it harder to focus on Vee's incomprehension and Waller's sorrow, and it linked me to Anna, which was good. Still, I was grateful when Vee returned with iced water. Her kindness reminded me of Jo Hoffman. I realized all I'd had to drink that day was the cup of coffee she had given me, idiotic in such heat. I gulped the water down too fast, suffered a bellyful of cold blades as a result. Repeating my thanks and assurances to Waller and Vee, I handed them a business card each. The pain in my stomach made it hard for me to stand up straight, but that's what I did, since stumbling away bent double would have risked deepening the lifeguard's misplaced guilt.

12

I'd looked at the accident from every point of view, and they'd all been useful. Everyone's point of view, that is, except Anna's, the one that mattered most. To complete the picture I had to experience what she had experienced among the waves, which meant swimming out to sea.

I trudged back along the foreshore. When I reached the Defoes' pines I took off my hat, stepped from my shoes and stripped to my boxer shorts. From habit, I folded my clothes. They were damp: the backs of my trouser legs were wet through where I'd sat on the plastic seat. I unfolded them again, trousers and shirt, and spread both out on the sand to dry. The sight was comical: it looked like my clothes were sunbathing. Recalling a trick Anna learned at Glastonbury, I dug a hole a few yards from this sunbather's camp, put my wallet and watch in my briefcase, and buried it. There was nobody within a hundred metres in either direction, but the precaution cost me nothing and lessened a needless risk. I marked the grave with my remaining sock and hot-coaled down to the wet sand for the second time in as many hours.

When I reached the wave-hem this time, though, I kept going. Pale water tugged at my ankles, my calves, the backs of my knees. All around, the sun spread diamonds on the sea's surface, and the diamonds in turn cast a net of shadows on the ribbed sand beneath my feet. I covered yards before arriving at the first kerb of white-water, made it thigh deep before reaching the next. The pull was as much sideways as out to sea. On I crabbed. The next wall of foam, noisy and abusive, ran straight over my head. I leaped up in it and beat my arms to stay afloat. The bottom was useless to me on tiptoes, so I struck out swimming, conscious again that, between waves, I was being hauled sideways by the current, sideways and out, towards the break.

I'm a strong enough swimmer. Anna, however, trained at a London club. I stopped being able to keep up with her when she was about fourteen. If I could make it out beyond the break and back on this 'heavy' day, she would have had little difficulty doing so the week before.

I put my head down and swam. The water roared and thumped, sucked and clung. My stupor was a useless suit of armour: I shed it and, caught up in a different battle, almost forgot what I was doing or why I was there at all. I was occupied enough learning that there was no point in trying to swim in the foam, but that I should dive for the seabed when the white-water hit me instead. This worked. I made progress. Soon the ranks of swell one or two ahead were blue and unbroken.

Blue and unbroken and, seen from here, huge. Each wave sucked up islands of foam as it pondered forward. From my position, bobbing in front of them, the waves did not peel, crest or tumble, as they had appeared to do from the shore. No, up close they smashed shut, each blue mouth growing sudden white teeth. I swam into the mouth. I felt myself sucked forward on to a muscular tongue of water, propelled into the wave's throat. But the throat did not want me whole.

It coughed me into the wave's teeth, which bit down. Waller had explained: a cubic metre of water weighs a tonne, and waves are much thicker than they are high. So a slice of six-foot wave is *heavy*. I shut my eyes, felt myself thrown upwards and forwards, slammed down hard.

There was no point in struggling: the mouth was huge and I was powerless in its grip. A bulldog. No, a crocodile. The crocodile shook me and twisted me and took me down. I thumped into the seabed, all elbows, spine and knees, and lost track of which way was up. When I opened my eyes to look, the light was scissoring meaninglessly in triangles of white and green and black. Still the jaws held me under. My lungs were full of sparks and my tongue tasted of copper. Then my heel struck the bottom again and pushed off instinctively. Both feet began to kick. The light turned strobe-white and my ears filled with lung-feedback screaming, *Breathe*, and one of my hands broke the surface and hauled.

A ludicrous sight: water running uphill. I had time – just – to roar 'Ha!' and then the next mouth clamped down. This time it took me with empty lungs. I struggled and time passed and I stopped struggling. My limbs were girders, my chest had filled with concrete, my head with shattered glass. I smelt exhaust fumes and tasted blood and the feedback in my ears was now screaming shells. My eyes stayed open to watch the explosions. White, blue, black. A dot. I shrank with it and saw the point.

Give in.

Let the sea take me to Anna.

Accidents happen and grant me the serenity to accept the things I cannot change and so it goes and the courage to change the things I can and so be it and the wisdom to tell the difference and give in and – *just – give – up*.

I went deliciously limp and allowed the wave to gulp me down whole. Acquiescence felt satisfying, like a good yawn. There was a logic to this end, a reasonable and pleasing symmetry. I'd wanted to see the thing from Anna's point of view. Well, here she was. My yawn became a stretch and I could feel pinprick bubbles popping in my ankles and wrists and at the base of my neck. The shrieking stopped; my ears crackled full of loving static. The sea's throat worked gently round me. It seemed my own mouth was full of saltwater. All I had to do was breathe it in. I gave the order, repeated it impatiently: *Breathe!*

My body wouldn't comply.

It fought back on its own. Feet, legs, trunk, arms, neck, the whole assembly unwound in one corkscrewing spasm. They were all still flailing when I broke the surface again. I clawed up the next wave, eating the air as I went, and somehow reached the top before it broke. Like cresting a hill on a bike, I slid down the other side of the swell without trying. Everything went shades of blue. Sky above, wave below, bearing me up. Up, and up. The slope became a cliff face. I felt certain I'd be thrown again. So sure that, as the wall reached vertical, I turned my back on it in disgust.

The slope avalanched white beneath me. I hung in mid-air, braced to fall, and watched the general collapse. Yet I didn't follow into the abyss. Instead, the swell lowered me gently again. I rolled on to my back and kicked further out to sea.

Or at least I tried to kick. My legs weren't working properly. They were caught up in my boxer shorts, which the waves had dragged down to my feet. I reached to pull them up, sank, took a gulp of water, found myself choking and pulling and kicking and *laughing* again, all at once. It took me a few moments of treading water to sort myself out.

My head cleared. At the time of the accident Anna was swimming in her underwear too. I had only entered the sea like that because the situation demanded I do so. The pressure of the investigation had forced me into a compromising – if farcical – situation. Imagine if my shorts had been the thing to drown me. Anna, I saw, must have been under some similar duress to have swum in her vest and pants.

I looked back at the shore. The waves lifted and lowered me. In glimpses I saw that I had drifted towards the lighthouse: though I'd entered the water opposite my clothes, they were now sunbathing off to my right. I could also see the flags – just – and people up the coast. Intermittent, but there. And if I could see others, that meant, if I made myself visible, they could see me. *All I had to do was raise a hand.*

I didn't signal for help, of course, because I didn't need it. In fact, swimming back in to the shore was nowhere near as hard as swimming out had been. The sea was doing its best to push me in the right direction. I'm not saying I wasn't exhausted when I finally reached the sand, but that was not the point: the point was that I made it in one piece.

13

I fail to take a single shot until the dog fight. When I do the result is horrible. I decapitate myself and blur the surgeon and am left wondering if a photograph could be worth the risk.

The date passes in agonized indecision until then. We haven't been together ten minutes before I'm losing track of what the guy is saying and having to suffer his bedside manner as a result. He has an unfortunate face. Still young – and bland enough – but with a problem. Whatever expression it aims for ends up shadowed with insincerity. Now the surgeon is signposting concern with frowning eyebrows and pursed lips.

– Are you sure you're okay? he asks.

– I'm fine. You were saying?

– It's not just the hours – though they don't help. It's the nature of the work itself. I'm either in too deep – literally beneath a patient's skin – or else I'm confined to the surface. There's no middle ground.

– Hmm.

– It's started to affect everything. When I meet someone new – in or out of work – I look for symptoms not personality. I can't feel anything about anyone. Can you imagine what that's like?

– Difficult? I venture – clutching my bag to my lap. The disposable camera inside it burns my thigh.

– But with an escort I can at least be on the level. We don't have to pretend anything – both of us know why we're here. It's so fake it's real! He laughs and frowns all at once. – You understand me?

– Of course.

Maggie billed this surgeon guy as another harmless date – and Sasha backed her up. He took her out once too. – Sweet bloke really – she said. – But Christ can he talk. And wear comfy shoes. He insists on walking everywhere.

She was right. We traipse the length of Oxford Street in and out of bars. I can more than cope with the stroll and under normal circumstances I might be interested in what he has to say – but the bulge in my purse makes it impossible to listen to his talk. Until I've taken the photograph all I seem capable of is considering how best to do it.

I could ask him outright. He's so up-front he might agree – we could hand the camera to a waiter and face it together with fixed grins in place. Except that the idea is daft. Even if he were to pause long enough for me to ask I can't think of a way of phrasing the question to make it sound reasonable. He might get angry and report back to the agency.

Better perhaps for me to excuse myself and take the waiter aside. Ask him to snap us on the sly. But I hold back because in the waiter's position I know I'd refuse such a request. It just sounds suspicious. And even if he agreed in principle he might fail in practice. In Dad's terms that's an uninsurable risk.

Best then to stick with the plan of taking the picture myself. Difficult to get us both in the frame – but not impossible. I escape to the ladies' where – locked in a cubicle – I grip the camera in the open mouth of my bag and charge myself up to shoot from within it. With the bag in the right place it might work. I see my reflection in the full-length mirror as I return though and have to fight the urge to laugh. A child with a magic trick. My sense of the absurd vanishes as I catch the surgeon's eye. For an awful moment it seems he knows what I'm up to as well. He puts up a hand as if to call a halt. I swing the bag on to my shoulder and brace myself for the worst as I approach our table – but it doesn't come.

– Look at this. The knuckles he's offering up are skinned.

I shake my head with concern.

– A friend suggested I tag along to his boxing club. – Trust me. You'll soon start feeling stuff! he said. I still can't shut this hand properly. But you know something? It didn't hurt at all when I did it. He was wrong. I didn't feel a thing.

My sympathy turns to surprise.

– I work with my hands the whole time. Idiotic thing to do, eh?

Unsure whether he wants me to agree or contradict him I smile mildly.

We move for dinner – his life story coming at me as we walk. Something about a car crash he caused as a small boy and the subsequent burden of family expectations. It's the telling he's concerned with – not my reaction. Which is just as well because I'm having trouble nodding in the right gaps. During our meal I learn that the surgeon was once engaged to a fellow medical student who dropped him for a radio DJ. My shock is apparently appropriate – if a little delayed. When he starts telling me about the station though I misread my cue and offend him by never having heard of it. I look up to see that the surgeon has a new knot in the middle of his brow.

– You're sure everything's okay? You seem bloody distracted.

I touch his bruised hand. – I'm sorry. Lot on my mind. You know how it is.

– Too right I do! He agrees so hotly I worry he's being sarcastic – but I'm wrong. He stares at my shaped nails and leans forward doing his best to look sympathetic. As if testing a phrasebook he asks – Would you like to talk about it? The effort is worth something. It softens me towards him. I steer the surgeon back towards the safety of himself.

The one opportunity I do have to pin things down comes as we're hiking again after the meal. By now we're up near the top end of George Street – circling back towards Central Station in time for him to catch his suburban train – on our way to one last bar.

A side-street explodes with barking as we pass by. I'm ashamed to say I freeze – but the surgeon sprints toward the noise. Gathering my wits I pull the camera free of my bag. Not twenty yards away two dogs whirl in the gutter. One is tied by a length of rope to the bumper of a flatbed truck. Yet it has the upper hand in the fight and is shaking the smaller dog by the throat. The surgeon dives straight in. He's immediately bitten by the tethered dog – which drops its opponent in the process. More cacophonous barking. I arms-length the camera – aiming at myself and the alley behind me. The flash cracks and I spin on my heel and move toward the action praying that in his panic the surgeon won't have noticed. As the smaller dog ducks back into the fight a shop door bangs open and a man wearing shorts and boots joins the surgeon. He kicks indiscriminately. Swears at the top of his voice. The smaller dog is denied revenge. I have the camera safely in my bag again by the time it flees past me yelping.

The man in shorts yells – Mongrel! – after it then scoops the tethered dog on to the flatbed. Climbing into the cab he says – Onya mate! to the surgeon. Then his truck lurches away trailing fumes.

The surgeon has one hand wedged under its opposite armpit. His face is performing amazement convincingly enough. I feel suddenly sorry for him and oddly sheepish to have given him so flat and distracted a date. As he returns to the main street he unholsters his wounded hand and inspects both sides with interest. I see the bite too – a half-moon of black dents across his wrist – blood in his palm.

– First one then the other he whispers. And not a thing! I'll be damned.

Careful not to expose the contents of my bag I take my handkerchief from inside and give it to him. He accepts only after protesting – apparently astonished by the generosity of so small an act.

When we finally part he offers the handkerchief – stained with concentric contours where his blood has dried unevenly – back to me. I decline with thanks. Despite its shortcomings my picture – in which I stand headless to one side of the frame with a blur of Francis Bacon dog-surgeon in the distance – is the only memento I want.

14

I returned to the hotel and showered. Lukewarm water was as much as I could take: it seemed I'd burned my shoulders, my knees and the tops of my feet. The latter pulsed scarlet on the gleaming tiles below, either side of the plug-hole with its surprising swirl of sand, which explained my gritty scalp, chafed groin and the broken skin between my toes. It had been a long and uncomfortable walk back from the beach.

Naked, sitting on the bed, I set to work with paper and pen. Vee's description of the boy added invaluable detail to what would otherwise have been a vague plea. As it was, the notice I drafted sounded authoritative, stern almost, as if I knew who I was looking for and expected confirmation of the man's identity and whereabouts, as opposed to a first clue to help establish either. Night fell while I wrote: cicadas started screeching in the bushes outside. As I was writing out my fair copy another cockroach clicked through the lattice door of the wardrobe and ran along the wall. I threw my shoe at it but missed. I decided I'd put the hospital down as a contact address after that.

It was too late to call the newspapers when I'd finished. I flicked through the sheaf I'd bought in town anyway, jotting down numbers for the morning. My phone would need charging. I plugged it in and turned it on: a river of messages stood ready to flow. They were all from my associate, Penny, mapping a trajectory from bored to frantic, passing concerned and beside-herself on the way. It seemed that, aside from the hundreds killed and thousands rendered homeless by the Central American storm – named Angela – the hurricane had also laid waste to Guatemala's new telecommunications network, reinsured – for some forty million dollars – by Taylor Blake.

I turned on the television and battled through the satellite circus to find CNN. No news of Angela: a bomb on the Budapest underground was showing today. We hadn't, at least, reinsured that. I listened to Penny's messages again. She was worried about our exposure to so big a risk, insistent I contact the underwriting syndicates immediately, fearful in case any shirked their share of our claim. Playing the messages through a third time I held the phone away from my head, minimizing her voice and the potential importance of what she was saying, until both were little more than a mosquito whine. Gauging it to be morning back home, I found myself performing the one speed-dial command I've mastered, and returned her last call.

'Wilson! Where in God's name are you?' I hadn't even heard the phone ring. Never mind no satellite delay, Penny was shouting at me from inside my head.

'Calm down!' I shushed her. 'I'm here. I picked up your calls.'

'Then why didn't you—'

'Angela, eh!' I heard myself whistle. 'Such good business, G-Com, too, while it lasted. Crying shame.'

'The phone's melting here, Wilson. We need to placate

some people, hold our ground. I've had ten plus syndicates claiming misrepresented risk—'

'Nothing new there, then.'

'Not this fast. Reports have the total loss at double the insured value, and they're saying the chain breaks with us. Safety precautions weren't properly in place.'

I whistled again, and made another mosquito of Penny's response. Most of it, at least; when I returned the phone to my ear I caught 'just fucked off'.

'Of course they're angry,' I whispered. 'Nobody likes to pay out. Yet we'll all accept a premium happily enough.'

'I'm talking about you!' she yelled. 'I'm going under here. No word. *Where have you been?*'

I should have worked out an answer to that question before I called: it mystified me that I hadn't. I felt suddenly heavy, slumped there on the edge of the bed. The earpiece swelled with unexpected static, exactly the sound I'd heard when held beneath the lid of the waves. I thought fleetingly I might tell her the truth. But truthfulness is a form of intimacy, and in dealing without the latter I have learned to be sparing with the former, too.

'New business lead,' I said.

'What?'

'Huge account's come up. I'd have explained, but they've demanded a stealth pitch. We're holed up offshore. I can't say where. I've signed more confidentiality undertakings in the last—'

'Non-disclosure? From *me*?'

''Fraid so. This is more a poaching exercise than a straight proposal. Trust me. If I succeed we can forget all about Guatemala.'

There was a sharp intake of breath on the other end of the phone. It brought a picture of Penny to mind. When she's angry she bites her lower lip. The expression gives her face a compressed, impish look. Femininity drains from it: you're left looking at a petulant boy. What she lacks in physical presence, though, Penny more than made up for with her strength of mind.

'What's wrong with you?'

'I—'

'Why've you really run away?'

'I haven't, I—'

'Because if you're expecting me to patch up the holes this hurricane has torn – is tearing – in Taylor Blake, you've got another thing coming. I can't do it on my own. We need you out there. You're our face.'

'And I'll be back there sorting it out later.' I kept my tone deliberately light. 'You can hold the fort in the meantime. Trust me.'

'Pah! Right now I need to know what you're hiding. There's something suspect about our cover, isn't there? You cut some corners. I can damn well feel it.'

I employ Penny for her analytical scepticism, but was in no mood to suffer it myself then. The trouble was, she had part of the picture right. The Guatemalan business, like all real business, was more dependent upon relationships than contractual wording, and the relationships in question were ultimately dependent on me. It wasn't so much about cutting corners as playing to strengths: the deal had been difficult to secure. To make the margin worthwhile I had smooth-talked some of my Lloyds contacts, secure in the knowledge that if a claim materialized I could speak the same language to them again. The policies themselves needed more than Penny to back them up.

I understood all this as she spoke, but that didn't help. It felt like I'd been woken early: I preferred to roll into my pillow rather than rise and deal with the day. Added to which, Penny seemed to be forgetting something. Though I seldom have to pull rank, it's my company – she works for me, not the other way round. I was struggling to think of a way to remind her of this fact without sounding like an idiot when her voice, gentler now, buzzed in my ear again. 'Or is there some other problem?'

'Such as?'

'*Such as?* Such as anything! To disappear in the face of a crisis is so profoundly unlike you it makes me think you must be fighting some other battle.'

'You're half right,' I reassured her.

'Well,' she paused, still struggling to keep calm, 'give me the other half.'

'As I say, the details are confidential. All you need to know for now is that I'm working on another opportunity.' I laughed under my breath, intent on clawing back some ground. 'You're good, Pen, but you don't always see the bigger picture.'

Her voice started up angrily in my ear again, so I turned the phone upside down – its hinged face bent beneath my chin – and spoke over her into the mouthpiece: 'And what I'm asking, no, *telling* you to do in the meantime is to continue as normal. Placate the syndicates, buy time with G-Com, commission the usual investigation. Trust me, you can cope.'

I snapped the hinge shut and switched off the phone. Doing so made me feel better instantly. It was as if my flung shoe had hit the cockroach. Never mind the source of the infestation, I'd killed off its immediate manifestation and for now that was satisfying enough.

The call, on top of my time at the hospital, with Waller, and in the waves, had tired me out. Or perhaps it was jet-lag and the sun. Either way, I don't recall lying back on the bed to sleep. The next thing I knew a member of the hotel staff had turned her key in the door and was stepping into the brightness of my room. I'd been dead for fourteen hours, was resurrected naked, mute, scrabbling for the sheet. CNN was still preaching to the evil wardrobe. In the time it took me to find the remote and switch off the television the maid had yelped and beaten an embarrassed retreat.

Those critical of wealth often confuse it with materialism. If, like me, you've visibly sought the former, you grow used to the suggestion – whether implied or made outright – that you are guilty of the latter as well. I don't much care. To an extent the accusation is valid. I have some expensive things, my flat, artwork Anna has persuaded me to invest in, a flash car, and I've spent a lot on restaurant bills and holidays in the past, too. But I haven't worked to become rich so that I could own a lot or move round in comfort. Those things are a by-product, not the object of what I do.

No, for me, it's the *facilitating* itself that is important. Money gives me a capability that others lack. I like the fact that I can take control in situations where I would otherwise be reliant on outside help. Such power brings peace of mind, happiness almost. Flexing my financial muscle that morning in Byron Bay, after such a good night's sleep, was a grimly pleasing reminder of why I work as hard as I do.

I placed advertisements throughout the Australian press. In each case the staff at the *Melbourne Age*, the *Sydney Morning Herald*, the *Australian* and other big papers were reluctant at first to take seriously the size of ad I wanted, suggested smaller notices would be preferable, and finally tried to deter me with their rates. As against the waves, I pressed on. It took all morning, speaking to assistants, advertising bosses, bosses of bosses. Since time was precious, I didn't negotiate hard on price. I'm sure I could have beaten the cost down with my clinching point, which, in each case, I delayed for effect: I wanted consecutive editions of the paper to carry my notices until I called a halt, which would be when I had a lead. This request invariably resulted in my being referred further up the management chain. I stayed patient, calm in the knowledge that my bank details would talk louder than I could. Which, in the end, they did.

By lunchtime I'd secured space in Australia's primary papers. After that, I moved on to the local publications. Starting with the *Byron Bay Advertiser*, and spider-webbing through the recommendations they and others gave me, I placed the same ad again and again, in coastal and inland rags. These smaller papers took much less persuading: the *Byron Shire News* even stretched their copy deadline to run my notice the next day. Encouraged, I honed my spiel, knifed through the crop.

By now it was late afternoon. I needed a proper meal and some time away from the hotel. But the job wasn't done yet.

I still had to send Anna's photograph through to my newspaper contacts. It was a central clue in the hunt for the man who'd drowned her, although of course my missing-person's notice did not refer to him as that. Though it pained me to describe him as such, I'd judged 'travelling companion' innocuous enough. Armed with a list of email addresses and the picture in my wallet, I set off for one of the town's ubiquitous Internet cafés to pre-empt the question 'Travelling companion to whom?'.

Outside, a storm was gathering. Early-evening sun slanted pale yellow through towering purple thunderclouds out to sea. There was even a faint, briny breeze stirring the palms. Down on the beach the wind might have been audible, but as I skirted the burial mound of backpacks on the pavement outside the hostel-café-communications-centre, it could not compete with Janis Joplin.

Entering the place, I again became conscious of my appearance: convict stubble, ruined suit trousers, surrender-flag shirt. Yet the assistant gave me barely a second look, just glanced up from her reading and waved me in the direction of the scanner. Although I could probably have worked the machine – we have one in our office, I watched Anna go through three toner cartridges for her 'pavements' project – I didn't want to look at the photograph, so played dumb. The girl at the desk took pity, cast her book – by the Dalai Lama – aside and set to work. Watching her quick fingers I decided to offer her twenty dollars to type in the addresses I'd transcribed. The task took her less than ten minutes and, combined with her smile of thanks and the cold beer I drank while I waited, was more than worth the fifty I gave her as I left.

Force one step and another becomes possible. I emerged from the café feeling younger, strong again. I swung my arms as I walked. The air about me hummed with the electricity of anticipated change. It smelt of gunpowder. I'd fired the first shot in a battle. That was enough, for the time being, to prove to myself that I could fight on. I stopped to look at myself reflected among mannequins in a shop window and found I was smiling.

Then the shop-front jumped white, blanking out me and my smile. When the reflection reappeared it seemed I was shivering. In fact the whole window was alive with thunder, thunder that shook the ground I stood upon, then rolled lazily away down the street. I looked up at the sky: the clouds were brown, swollen with dust. The first raindrop slapped the back of my hand as I reached to let myself through the door.

At first glance the shop seemed full of wetsuits, skateboard pads and Hawaiian shirts. The wearable clothes were all but hidden. Thrash metal poured down from speakers in the ceiling; TVs in all corners showed pratfall stunts on a loop. I turned to watch the rain dashing against the Tarmac, then sensed a presence. An assistant had appeared at my side. She was wearing a T-shirt with tiny print stretched across her breasts. I couldn't help reading it. The logo said, 'You can fuck me but I won't kiss you.'

'Noah's left his door open,' she said. Her tongue was bubble-gum pink.

'Pardon?'

She nodded at the street. 'Cats and dogs. Elephants. Two of everything coming down.'

I was confused, hadn't yet recovered from the shock of her

T-shirt. She thought that funny, glanced down and rolled her eyes at her chest.

'So, what can I do for you?' she asked.

I meant to excuse myself, but said, 'Clothes,' instead.

'Good for you, you've come to the right place.' She turned into the main part of the shop. I followed her flip-flops. By the time I'd caught them up, I'd regained my senses and was about to tell her to forget it. But somehow I couldn't. At first I thought it was about not being fazed by the logo, but in the end I realized I wasn't leaving because of something to do with Anna.

Aside from my Jermyn Street shirts and suits, I don't buy many clothes. Anna has a better idea of what I like than I do. We have a deal: we go shopping every month or so, she picks out clothes for both of us and I pay.

I found myself explaining this to the shop assistant, who screwed her eyes shut in concentration, then decided I was joking. She laughed again, led me to a changing cubicle, and began ferrying clothes back and forth.

I was in no hurry. After a while the logos shrank, the clothes started to fit, and the hand thrusting them through the curtain of beads could have belonged to anyone at all. I watched myself changing in the mirror. It was plastered with surf-stickers, within which the grain of my reflected face seemed to have been sanded by the sun. I looked less wooden, more alive. I let the girl bring me alternatives long after I'd chosen enough clothes to tide me over. By the time I came to pay the thunderclaps had faded to distant applause.

Warm rain still fell. I ducked from awning to awning to avoid it, and bought more supplies – underwear, shaving kit, a towel and sunscreen – in shops down the main street. Something in me resisted the idea of a rucksack. I consigned these new things to a kitbag, which I bought from an old man wearing shorts and knee-length socks, whose shop sold army-surplus gear and air-brushed paintings of breaching whales, nothing in between.

The old man had been eating his supper behind the counter. His half-finished plate of food made me giddy with hunger. I took a seat in an open-fronted restaurant across the street, slung my new bag beneath the table and prepared to order.

It was a long wait. The one waitress on the restaurant floor seemed also to be in charge of the bar, and wasn't on top of either job: she carried herself clumsily, like a child in an adult's body, spilt drinks, dropped a bowl of fruit salad on her way up the rattan steps. I would have moved on, but she caught my eye not long after I'd sat down, brought me a bottle of beer, and kept casting me apologetic looks as she loped back and forth to the kitchen. She was already besieged by complaints: to have left would have been an act of desertion. When I finally did order, my food took a further three beers to come, and the waitress and I had turned the restaurant's failings into a private joke.

I'd started on a bottle of wine. It was still half full after I'd finished my meal, but I turned down the offer of a cork and poured myself another glass. The front of the restaurant was slung with plastic lanterns, bright now against the charcoal sky. I watched moths the size of robins batter themselves senseless from one light to the next. The futility of their attack was funny and sad at the same time, as was the wine: each gulp of happiness had a lonely aftertaste. When the waitress poured me another glass I steadied her hand and she did not pull it away.

The last customers left, which made me sadder and happier still. I asked for my bill. The waitress brought it and hovered. Then she slumped into the chair next to me, smiled and leaned back heavily, exhausted, offering up a fleshy white throat. I stretched across her, intent on kissing it.

She jerked upright, bringing me to my senses. I raised my hands but she was already on her feet. I shut my eyes and braced myself, opened them again when the expected blow turned out to be a gentle touch on my shoulder. Her smile was still in place. 'I'd love a drink,' she said, 'but not here.'

While she finished up, I waited, calmed by the prospect of a reprieve from solitude. The moths sustained their attack overhead. I felt strange: not guilty, but uneasy. Why? I don't broadcast this aspect of my life to Anna, yet neither do I try to keep it from her. She knows the score. We are not threatened by such trivial encounters. That would only be the case if I pretended to her that they didn't occur, or let a spark grow into a constant flame. Why the odd feeling, then? I would be spending the morning with Anna. What did it matter how I got through the night?

The lanterns went out. The waitress reappeared. She'd undone her ponytail and changed her clothes. Her face looked heavier with her hair down, more equine, and the low-cut top unnecessarily dramatized her chest. Yet something about her, something uncomplicatedly available, was still there. We bumped shoulders – me unsteady with my kitbag, her still clumsy – on our way down the steps, which helped recapture what I'd felt before. I surrendered myself to it. I took hold of her hand, led her staggering through the clear night air, past emptying bars, towards the front.

A live band was playing flamenco in the foyer of a pub hotel. We paused in the street as others had done before us. The waitress wasn't listening, though: she was talking to someone else, a girlfriend. My hand was still in hers, hot flesh against flesh. I looked up, up, above the terrace, until I was staring straight at the night sky, punctured by needling stars. My mouth opened: the skin at its corners stretched to let loose laughter intense as crying. An upholstered hip knocked against mine. I turned to look at the waitress but my gaze snagged half-way. Jo Hoffman, brown arms folded across the driftwood rail of the terrace, was leaning out above the street, staring down.

15

I spend two days down by Circular Quay sitting on the hot steps and giving in to the overpriced café and yo-yoing to and from the botanical gardens – all the time scouring the crowds. No sign of the photographer. Begin to wonder whether I will recognize the man even if he does appear. Every other person seems to be carrying a camera of some sort to capture much the same memory – origami opera house – Meccano harbour bridge – sun-squint smiles. I spend so long staring at faces on this conveyor-belt that I start to see them sympathetically again.

It's not until late on the second afternoon with the sun low and yellow that I look up to see the boy ambling towards me along the walkway. He's wearing faded khaki trousers and an open-neck shirt with the sleeves rolled above his elbows and a waistcoat full of pockets – the sort anglers and war reporters wear. Plus he's trailing a glossy black dog. The pair of them walk past me and then the boy jumps up to sit on the harbour wall. Neither of his cameras is in a case. He swings one forward on to his lap and reaches into a pocket for a roll of film.

My shadow falls across him as I approach but he doesn't look up from what he's doing. I too watch his hands. Work-raw palms and cracked fingertips. Nevertheless those fingers work precisely

116

threading film on to tiny teeth. I step closer. He snaps the back of the camera shut and winds it on. Clicks through three or four frames of oatmeal knee.

– Remember me?

His head tilts back eyes blinking slowly. Wets his lips to speak.

– Japanese uncle. Yes.

I feel myself colour.

– Did you not rate the pictures?

I shake my head. – No. They were good. That's why I'm here. I have a proposition for you.

He strap-slides the loaded camera behind his back and says – Oh yes? with his face giving in to a smile that does not show his teeth. Wolfish – embarrassed – relieved – I'm not sure which. Something about the expression unnerves me. I nearly abort there and then but in one easy movement he pushes himself from the wall and motions for me to sit – so genuinely polite I am taken aback. Waits for me to settle then joins me. – Go on he says.

I tell him what I want. He doesn't look at me while I speak – just crosses his forearms and inspects the concrete walkway beneath his dangling boots. I'm still nervous – but once I start the strangeness of what I'm describing takes over. I keep it simple. Tell him I'm earning money as an escort to put myself through art school – and want the pictures as evidence for a piece I'm planning to do once I'm there.

– Two birds with one stone he mutters.

– If you like.

– And these blokes – they're happy to take part in your . . . collage?

– That's the point. I'm not sure. We have to work on the assumption that they're not.

– We?

I smooth my skirt towards my knees. – If you're interested of course.

He shifts beside me on the brickwork. The cotton of his trousers is frayed at the pockets and knees. The dog leaves off sniffing at the wall to lift its wet-eyed face to the boy who leans down and scratches it under the chin. I try another tack. – But perhaps you're not. Snapping frazzled tourists may be more your photographic thing.

– Who's saying I don't have my own project on the go?

– In which case you'll see the point in mine.

There's a strange quality to his silence. As if – when it descends – he goes elsewhere to think. Somewhere vast. His quiet is not hemmed in. The effect is comforting. While I wait for the boy's decision I remember the hush of my grandfather's study where – as a child – I'd stay up late into the evenings drawing at my table in the corner while he worked on plans pinned to the angled plane of his architect's desk. It was never an effort keeping quiet in there. Silence was part of the treat.

– Look. I appreciate this is a bizarre thing to ask. There's no need to make up your mind right—

– I'll do it.

– You will? I sit up straight.

He nods. – It's a fair deal. Fifty dollars is as much as I make in an average night here. You give me the address on the day and I'll make sure I'm there ahead of you. One good shot is what you'll get. If I can take it immediately – good. But don't worry – I can be patient. If the chance doesn't come along until later in your date then I'll just sit tight and wait.

A ferryboat lets loose a long horn-blast behind us. Gulls above scream back. When the noise dies down the boy gives me another of his thin grins. – Fella did the groundwork for that beaut – he nods at the opera house – never saw the thing completed.

I nod slowly. – And?

– So will I have the chance to see your masterpiece once it's done?

Again I have trouble working out what he's getting at – a joke – a put-down – or something more sincere?

16

Thankfully, I awoke alone, beached on my hotel bed, still dressed, but in unfamiliar clothes. *You can fuck me but I won't kiss you.* Bit by bit, the evening came crashing back. I rolled over and was both relieved and disquieted to see the kitbag slumped in the corner between the wardrobe and the wall. A comatose thing, sleeping in its clothes, too.

I ran a basin full of cold water, lowered my face into it and drank. Then I dragged the kitbag away from the wall, opened its mouth and poured the contents on to the bed. No use. Even deflated, the bag troubled me. I turned on the shower and began to undress. With my T-shirt off I noticed a large red label still attached to my new trousers. The sight of that, and of my body – cadaver-white apart from the pink punctuation of my face, shoulders, knees and feet – made my head throb and spin. I threw up, showered, drank again from the basin, staggered back to the bed, swept the kitbag to the floor and lay staring at it.

Anna's belongings. I'd not yet retrieved them. My stomach lurched again at this callousness, guilt magnified in the aftermath of drink. Though I'd have preferred to face authority with the armour of my suit, it was filthy, so I made for the police station in my beach clothes instead.

To reach the station, I had of course to approach the hospital. Once on my way, the prospect of another encounter with the doctor did more to wilt me than the heat. The memory of her face above the rail was like the sun that morning: impossible to look at directly, manifestly present regardless. I shrank beneath the brim of my hat to avoid confronting both.

Steeling myself to meet the duty sergeant proved wrong-headed, for it diverted my attention from the issue at hand, which was retrieving Anna's stuff. They'd wrapped her ruck-sack in some sort of Cellophane. There seemed a nasty parallel between our luggage: mine, earlier, passed out against the wall, hers mummified here. The policewoman, misinterpret-ing the tremor of my fingertips, offered to help me set the bag free. I let her. The scissors she used had red handles and rounded blade-ends, exactly like those at Anna's primary school. Though I was impatient to open the rucksack, this detail made it impossible for me to do so where it stood. I shouldered the thing – it was surprisingly heavy – intent on heading back to my hotel.

The ginger-haired policeman I'd spoken with about Anna arrived just as I was leaving. This unsettled me, but I managed outward calm. He greeted me as if I were an old friend, open-ing his arms wide: had it not been for the pack I think he might have thrown them round me in a hug. Such bonhomie put me on the defensive at first. I put down the pack to deal with him unencumbered.

'Wondered when you'd show for that.' He smiled. 'I went through it again after our chat, and the boy's stuff too, just in case we'd missed anything. But I'm afraid we didn't. Nothing to lead us to your daughter's friend.'

'I'm sure you're right.'

'He'll turn up, eh?'

I shrugged.

'And if he doesn't, perhaps you'll get a response to those ads. Something to satisfy your curiosity.'

I was taken aback. Part of me had been sure that the police, when they heard of my initiative, would think I was meddling. The papers had only been out a few hours. This officer's vigilance, and his apparent ability to take what I'd done in his stride, shook my former opinion of his reluctance to investigate. I held my ground, nevertheless, saying simply, 'If I do, I'll be sure to let you know.'

'Righto.' He looked confused. His eyes dropped from mine. I could tell which ground he was making for, but was too slow to head him off. 'In the meantime,' he said softly, 'I hope the hospital are keeping Anna—'

'Sure, sure.' His voice was so resigned, I had no choice but to interrupt. 'They're doing a great job. I'm off there now, in fact, to return this' – I wobbled the pack at my feet – 'to its rightful owner.'

The policeman nodded doubtfully. I focused on the back-pack. As I looked at it, two ruddy hands gripped the straps. I almost reached out to tear them away but realized, as the policeman lifted the pack on to his knee, that he meant to help me put it on. His kindness was hard to take. I managed to mutter thanks for it, shrugged into the straps and made for the door.

I'd surprised myself by telling the policeman I was taking Anna's rucksack to her, but had to concede, once I'd regained the street, that that was what I really ought to do. Never mind my reluctance to see the doctor again; the sooner I did so the better, in a sense, and my greater responsibility was to Anna in any case. She had been without her belongings for too long. Who knew? Perhaps reuniting her with familiar things would jolt her from her trance.

Her little room had been invaded. An old man lay in the bed opposite Anna's, his bony hands intertwined beneath his chin. He was utterly still, a marble saint. I stepped closer. Only the gentle vibration of hair in his nostrils let on that the man wasn't dead. That, and a vase of flowers, which stood on the table beside his bed, all yellows and oranges, clashing and immediate. Why hadn't I brought Anna flowers? I bit down on the inside of my lip and turned towards her bed.

With the curtain drawn round us there wasn't much space for me to unpack. I don't suffer from sentimentality as a rule, yet had to force myself not to be unduly emotional about what I unearthed from Anna's bag, in case doing so blinded me to something of potential significance. To enforce a gap I turned up a fresh page in my notepad and made a list as I went: one pair of jeans, a New South Wales guidebook, two pairs of cotton trousers (one with a drawstring, the other buttoned), four sleeveless tops, five T-shirts, three blouses, a pair of board-shorts, a sweatshirt, five pairs of cotton knickers (two in a separate laundry bag, three clean), two bras, two vests, two skirts, a summer dress, four pairs of socks (again, one dirty), one pair of trainers (their soles sandy), one pair of high heels, a sun-hat, a book of matches, one towel (salt-stiff, also in the laundry bag), a coiled mosquito net and one of my old wash-bags.

Checking the rucksack for hidden pockets, I found a further compartment in the lid. It was empty save for a paperback novel entitled *Leviathan* by a writer called Paul Auster. Though I shook the spine, nothing fell from between the book's pages.

I gave Anna a running commentary as I worked. Her eyes stayed shut. Such relentless naming of objects reminded me of teaching her to talk as a child. She started late, at three years old, with a warning that I'd not locked the front door. If as much time must pass before she talked again, so be it: at least I could count on her speaking sense when she did.

With her things now piled neatly on the chair I dug further – inside the wash-bag. Doing so felt more of a violation than unpacking her rucksack, but I judged my actions justified and I was right. Among the wash-bag's contents (shampoo, conditioner, a toothbrush, toothpaste, mascara, tweezers, travel-wash, razor, un-perfumed deodorant, tampons, sunscreen and foundation) was one thing among them that stuck out immediately: a stick of crimson lipstick.

To my knowledge Anna had never worn lipstick. Mascara, yes, foundation once in a while, lip-gloss less often still, but never lipstick, not when she went clubbing, not to my cousin's wedding, not even for the hammed-up sophistication of her sixth-form ball. Her mouth is as emphatic as her mother's: she doesn't need to point it out. So the lipstick was a clue, though to what I had no idea. I stood it on the bedside cabinet – a single bullet – and asked Anna some questions. I expected no answers now, of course, but wanted to give her something to think about.

Checking the other items against my list, everything else appeared unexceptional: the guidebook was unthumbed; the matches had no name or number scrawled inside their flap; the shoes were both empty, as were the pockets in Anna's jeans. Even the novel was unmarked: no corners turned down, nothing written inside the front or back cover. In fact, the ensemble was *exceptionally* unexceptional, full of gaping holes, absences that spoke louder than what was there. Anna is a record-keeper, always has been; there's a tea-chest full of memorabilia – labelled *Anna's Annals* – in the loft at home. So where was her sketch-book, dense with ticket-stubs, drawings and diary scrawl? Why were there no camera, no photographs? Where were her wallet and passport, for God's sake? These things must either have been in the bag Gil failed to find on the beach, or somebody had removed them from the rucksack before the police picked it up. Without them, the policeman was right, there was apparently nothing to go on here, nothing aside from the lipstick, which would have made no impact upon him. How could it? I was smiling. Though I had no idea what they were saying, it pleased me that Anna's belongings, mute to the authorities, were trying to speak to me.

An extraordinary noise swept the grin from my face. The man in the bed opposite was laughing. I'd already decided to ask the hospital to remove him – or Anna – to another room, but now determined I'd make them do so, come what may. As I rattled the curtain back to tell him, the old man's laughter cut out. He lay as still as he had done before. I approached the bed. His hands were still clasped together on the white linen sheet: a sword in their grip and he'd have looked the part on a medieval tomb. The act was so convincing, in fact, that I began to doubt what I'd heard. Bending low over his face, it seemed he'd even managed to still the white hairs in his nose.

'What's to laugh at?' I asked.

He didn't reply. Fine: if he wanted a stand-off, I was prepared to wait. I was suggesting as much to him when Jo
Hoffman strode into the room. Her hair was wet and slicked
back in sharp tongues, giving her the look of a seal. Startled,
I tried to meet her eye, but she was already looking over my
shoulder. She flowed straight past me, intent on the bank of
monitors above the old man's head, and yanked his cubicle
curtain shut from inside. Show over, I was left with nothing
to look at but the doctor's feet, slender and brown in
open-toed sandals, square-dancing briskly round the bed.
Two nurses then arrived, one after another, but I didn't have
a chance to tell either of them about the old man's routine
either, as they slid straight backstage too. The delay turned
out for the best: while I waited more laughter started up, only
this time it was clearly coming from outside. Through the
louvred blind I saw the bird responsible: some sort of malevolent, outsized kingfisher, dark eye gleaming, beak ajar.

I knew then, of course, that the old man was dead, and I
was sorry. But as the hospital staff busied themselves behind
the sky-blue screen, detaching leads, kicking the brake off the
bed, meaner thoughts encroached. I wondered whether they
would leave the flowers behind, and if it would be easier now
for me to ensure they kept this ward for Anna alone. I felt
relief, too, at having made it through an encounter with the
doctor: when next we met this episode would surely be fore-
most in both our minds.

To give the staff some space I retreated once again behind
Anna's curtain. This time, my guard was down, and her
belongings caught me unawares. The sight of her trainers set
neatly beneath the chair made me stumble as if I'd missed a
step. Anna always preferred to go barefoot indoors. Those

shoes belonged on the rack in our hall. But they hadn't been there for a long while, they'd been elsewhere, and that 'elsewhere' was suddenly hateful. I felt a sickening regret at not having kept a closer eye on Anna in the preceding months – not to police her, but so that I might better have understood what she was going through. 'Where have you been?' I asked. No response, for the time being. I'd have to wait to find out. The same, of course, applied to the bigger difficulty. *Where was she now?* I did not trouble her by asking that question out loud.

17

The photographer has a nerve – our double date has barely begun before he marches up and stabs his tripod into the sand. Close enough for me to hear its whir over the white noise of traffic and sea. That and his dog's panting at my feet. He calls it away as the lens pans from headland to headland and keeps going – swivelling through one hundred and eighty degrees of Bondi – sea and shore – then us. His eye is screwed to the viewfinder but the shutter stands in for it. Blink blink blink.

Thankfully only I notice. Rob is too busy telling Sasha that he and the other American boy – Benny – are in Australia for just two weeks.

– One night in Sydney he drawls. And today's Benny's birthday. So I'm thinking we need to have ourselves some fun.

Sasha presses her elbows into her stomach. Rubs her hands together and leans forward over the barcode tattoo. Suitably gleeful – yet in the bus not ten minutes beforehand she was bent double beside me with period pains.

– Yeah agrees Benny distractedly. He has catalogue looks – glossy hair – clean jaw – racehorse physique. Twenty-fiveish – yet he's wearing chinos and a monogrammed shirt – clothes even Dad wouldn't choose. He's been checking his mobile phone since we met. Now he slots it back into his hip pocket and repeats him-self. – A good time – yeah.

That this pair could have picked up a couple of local girls without difficulty makes me wary. My lips stick to my teeth when I relax my smile. I try to reassure myself – Maggie spelt out what they were paying for and Sasha – today at least – would not otherwise have accepted the date.

Though it's Benny's big day Rob's in charge. We've met at sunset armed with swimsuits. He wants to start the evening with a dip but they're more interested in showing off than swimming. After five minutes in the sea Rob spends ten preening in the shal-lows. He's from New York – it's January – yet he has a deep tan.

We head back to the changing rooms at the top of the beach and Sasha promptly curls groaning on the shower floor. But only for a minute. She won't hear of giving up. I press painkillers upon her. She pops two before refixing her smile for our second act.

They want cocktails. Sasha hails us a cab to a hotel in The Rocks and we take a lift to the top floor. A tall building – I feel the pressure change in my ears on the way up. Yet I'm unpre-pared for the view through the bar's glass walls. The colour has all but drained from the sky. Just a few burst blood vessels remain – fading among inky Rothko clouds. Down below Sydney is stretched in all directions around the colossal harbour – a nega-tive shape hemmed by lights – boats stitching to and fro. Neither boy pays much attention. Rob says – Neat and summons a waiter. Benny slumps opposite me with his back to the window and checks his phone again.

– So where were you last birthday? I ask him.

He thinks for a moment and says – Vegas.

– Did you win or lose?

His frown of concentration ends with a shrug. – You know. I can't remember.

There's a little bowl of Japanese crackers on our table and our cocktails are served in odd-shaped glasses. Mine is shallow as a petri-dish – Sasha's is long and thin like a test tube. Laboratory chemicals – anaesthetic. I find myself stifling a yawn – catch Sasha glaring at me – force myself to reboot brightly.

– I have a theory about gambling I say – It's that losing has as much allure as winning. Winning's no challenge. The thrill is in the risk of stuff going wrong.

Benny's silence forces me on.

– I saw a programme once about a guy who bet everything he had on one spin of the roulette wheel. Sold his house – his car – his clothes – even cashed in his endowment early – then walked into a casino in a rented tuxedo to spend the proceeds of his entire life on chips. Took the whole stack to the table where his family were assembled. He hadn't made up his mind which colour to pick beforehand and spent ages deciding – the choice playing havoc in his eyes. Finally he plumped for red. The camera looped from face to face as he placed the bet – his mother wiping away tears – his father blank as a wall – brother giving in to a malicious little grin. The wheel started spinning. A hand sent the ball whizzing the other way. The guy's life hung on double-or-quits for ever – the camera cutting back and forth from the ball in orbit to the gambler and onlookers – until finally eternity ended – on . . . red. The family went berserk. Mum squealing like she'd seen a mouse – brick-wall Dad collapsing at the knees – brother all grimace. What struck me though was the look on the gambler's face as the ball came to a rest – because in the half-beat before he erupted there was this flash of disappointment in his eyes. It was as if in the winning moment he realized that he'd somehow failed. Winning undercut him you see. What he'd really wanted was for everything to be stripped away – but now he had to go on – carrying twice the load.

There's a pause in which I see Rob and Sasha have been listening to this story too. Finally Benny reaches for his phone again muttering – I like to win.

Were it not for the flash of humour in Sasha's eyes I might have given up at this – but more cocktails arrive and before we start on them she engineers us a trip to freshen up. A crop of suits at the bar turn like sunflowers as we pass. She drags me into the calm of a cubicle. – My turn to administer pain relief she says. Chops out two lines of coke on the marble cistern. I'm game.

The date fast-forwards after that. When I next pause to look at the view through the window the city lights are stretched taut beneath a sky filled with stars. Makes me feel suddenly close to Sasha – whose eyes glitter against the backdrop – and when the boys slide into their own world for a moment I find myself leaning into her side with my lips hot to her ear – trying to explain how it's all worthwhile because of the pictures. She asks what I mean. I begin talking about beauty and currency and art – and a real boy taking photographs – and only stop when I sense her stiffening beside me – the ear pulling away. Someone's lit candles on the tables – her eyes are now full of flames. I come to and begin blurring what I've said with *as if* laughter. Rob distracts her further. He grips her arm and repeats the mantra. – Everyone's having a good time. Yeah.

She turns away to agree with him.

Although Benny nods too he seems to slide further beneath the surface of himself as the evening goes on. Perhaps it's the drink. Apart from checking his look – in the mirrored wall of the sushi bar and the black glass door of the club – he simply stops taking notice of what's going on. I stop drinking. The coke has long since worn off. If not for a needling sense of regret – to do with Sasha and the fear that I might let her down further in some way – I think I would have walked. As it is I try harder to understand what this Benny boy might ever find interesting – what his idea of a good time could possibly be.

18

The receptionist stopped me on my next visit to the hospital and went to fetch two packages, which she said had arrived that morning. Though she bobbed up and down expectantly I wasn't about to open anything in front of her and set off to find Anna immediately. We had her room to ourselves again today. I put both packages on the foot of her bed and shut the door, then took more deep breaths in time with the machinery, allowing her presence to slow me down.

One of the parcels was bulky, the other flat and small. I took up the big one first. It was blank, apart from my name and the hospital's address, both scrawled in pencil on the front. No stamps: delivered by hand. Inside was an old canvas knapsack, empty save for a note, also in pencil, written on a small square of paper.

The note said, 'He got wallets a camera and some clothes but they are gone now. From the beach. Sorry. I did get this back. He does not deserve any reward.'

There was no signature or sender's address. I plumbed the words for a hidden meaning, but couldn't find one. I slid the scrap of paper into my wallet and rechecked the bag's pockets for anything small I might have missed. Fluff and sand. My heart sank.

Unwilling to move on to the smaller envelope in case its

contents also proved fruitless, I turned the bag inside out, shook it angrily, then tossed it to the floor. Only as I sat, head in hands, staring at the useless thing, did I catch sight of a grey mark inside the canvas lid. Stretching the fabric taut, the mark became part of a letter, faint but visible: *B*. I held the flap up to the light. Anna's Etch-a-Sketch toy came back to mind. Though you wiped the screen, the imprint of old drawings sometimes persisted. Like now: next to the letter *B* I made out more faded letters, *A-m-i-s,* and beneath that another line of writing, *Broken Kill School of Despair.*

B. Amis was a person. I stepped closer to the window and raised the blind, hoping the square of brightness that cut through the pane might illuminate the odd words beneath the name, but was disappointed. Again my sails sagged. The phrase 'Broken Kill School of Despair' sounded sinister as I repeated it aloud. Perhaps the clue to these words' meaning lay in the other package. The envelope was backed with cardboard, stiff in my hands as I turned it over to reveal a businesslike label typed full of my name and the hospital's address. A Sydney postmark showed yesterday's date. I opened the back flap, slid my hand inside, and felt the smoothness of photographic paper with my fingertips as I withdrew the envelope's contents.

Blink, and your eyes open to the possibility of a different world.

A washstand stood in one corner of the ward. I went to the basin and ran it full of water. My hands were shaking. I reached for the soap dispenser bolted to the tiles above the basin, but pulled too hard on the long metal tongue sticking from beneath it. A jet of pink liquid shot from the nozzle down the front of my trousers. I dabbed at the stain half-heartedly and saw that I was shivering. My back felt clammy, sweat had started out across my brow. I splashed coldness into my face and plunged my hands deep. Fingers fought one another under water: knuckles, white and yellow, apparently trying to poke holes through my skin. I sat down on the floor.

When the doctor appeared at my side my idiotic concern was that she would misinterpret the dampness smeared down my inner thigh. She had dropped to her knees on the tiles beside me and was repeating her question: 'Are you all right?'

Leaning forward over my crotch I fought to pull myself together.

'You look pale.'

'I'm fine, just a bit faint.'

She put a hand on my back. It was more tender than her tone. 'Well, you're right to put your head between your knees. Don't get up until it passes.'

The photograph was face down on the foot of Anna's bed. I had no wish to deceive the doctor, yet secrets are a burden: it's long been a policy of mine not to trouble those who don't need to know a thing with the pressure of keeping it confidential. Assuming she hadn't already seen the evidence, I had to distract her from doing so now.

'What do you make of this?' I scrambled to my feet, retrieved the knapsack and thrust it at Jo Hoffman. Her eyes, more ringed with tiredness than I had seen before, narrowed. I folded the bag's flap back and pushed it into her hands. 'There,' I said. 'What does that mean?'

I turned my back on her while she inspected the wording, and managed to slide the photograph among Anna's bed-clothes. Everything inside me wanted to scrunch the hateful thing into a ball, but I didn't. When I spun round again the doctor wasn't even looking at the bag. She'd put it down on a chair.

'Anna's no better.' She crossed her slender arms, nodding at my daughter's bed.

'The words beneath the name,' I said.

'The nursing staff are doing their best to prevent bed-sores,' the doctor murmured, more to Anna than me.

'The bag came in response to my notice,' I explained.

'But she's growing more dependent on this machinery, not less.'

I picked up the knapsack again and shook it. More specks of sand fell to the floor. The doctor, ignoring me, went on unfurling statistics, describing new factors affecting Anna's condition.

The photograph showed my daughter splayed naked with a man.

Her lungs, according to Jo Hoffman, were suffering: every breath the machine took for her made her less capable of breathing on her own.

Though I'd only glanced at it, every detail of the picture had scored itself on my mind's eye: the man's pale knee pressed into the couch; his hand hauling on her shoulder; the fact his face wasn't shown; and the way they'd somehow forced her to smile.

Jo Hoffman described how Anna's muscles, unused, were already beginning to waste away; 'atrophy' was the word she used.

And yet the leering shadows cut strong curves out of my daughter's body – from the dipping small of her back to the swell of her calf and ecstatically curled instep. The couch she lay on was stabbed full of cigarette burns, but no sordid backdrop or vicious pose could diminish Anna's *radiance*, any more than the doctor could now, with her talk of cruelty and kindness, and how I should not think of it as giving up, but as an inevitable step that I had no choice but to make. 'Otherwise,' she explained quietly, 'the hospital will have to take matters into its own hands.'

A typed sticker stood on the back of photograph, its message simple: bank details, web address, threat.

Sometimes, to break deadlocked negotiations, it's necessary to pretend you're prepared to concede ground which, in practice, you have no intention of giving up. I let the bag fall to my side and allowed the doctor to restate her case, feigning interest all the while in what she was struggling to say. My defeated act must have been convincing enough, for when she finished her spiel her face softened and she took the knapsack from me again.

'This,' she waved the bag, 'wherever it came from, is irrelevant to what you have to do for Anna. But, if it helps, I'd say the satchel belonged to someone called B. Amis. I had something similar for school too. Broken Hill is way out west. A lame joke, perhaps, to go with the kiddie-slang. I've no idea, otherwise, why you'd need a book bag to attend the School of the Air.'

I was still worried that the doctor, poised at the foot of the bed, might start rearranging Anna's sheets and discover what lay beneath them. So I stepped forward, took her by the shoulders and steered her away a few paces, towards the window. The gesture was immediately inappropriate, heavy-handed. Embarrassed, I improvised, and turned the frogmarching into a hug of thanks.

Despite her tan, she coloured. A triangular scar on the side of her neck showed stark white against the prevailing red. Though the memory of her, wire-stiff in my arms, had yet to fade, the gratitude I felt was as complete a sensation as that of sliding beneath the surface of a warm bath. Despite herself, she cared. Not only was she looking after Anna, now, effortlessly, she'd set me on the path to discover who had done this to her.

It's what I do: determine liability and arrange compensation, make good and apportion blame.

She turned away, pulled a chart from its holster at the end of the bed, scrutinized its contents. I, in turn, retrieved the bag. The clipboard, gripped hard, pressed into the firmness of her stomach. I felt for her.

'Listen,' I told her. 'I know you're right about Anna.'

She looked up. The scar was already fading again.

'All I'm asking is for a little more time.'

She nodded slowly.

Though it pained me to continue the charade, I said, 'You told me yourself it was a million to one chance she'd recover and I know the longer she doesn't improve the worse those odds get. Yet she's comfortable now; you're seeing to that. What harm will a few more days cause?'

'It depends on why you want them,' she explained. 'If it's to contact the wider family, make arrangements, come to terms with what's happened, then I understand, of course. But our responsibility is still to Anna. She's our patient. We can't prolong her – state indefinitely. And my fear is that each day that passes is making it harder for you, not easier.'

I shook my head, careful to do so gently, in control. 'All I'm asking for is time to . . .' an ally, she must know '. . . to track this guy down.'

'Why?' she whispered.

I struggled to regain my composure. 'When disaster strikes,' I said, 'we don't pay for it, not ourselves, not when somebody else is to blame.' Folding the bag in on itself, I went on: 'This belongs to the person responsible for Anna's accident. I have evidence.' I took the illiterate note from my wallet and handed it to the doctor. 'Somebody stole what was inside the bag, but it doesn't matter now, because you've cut through the fraud to the thing itself, you've decoded what was left behind.'

'But—'

I waved her down. 'A name, a town, a school,' I told her, my hands held wide. 'I'll find this person, uncover what happened and *make* him responsible. I'll—'

Now she interrupted me. 'But what good will it do?'

The answer was so self-evident it did not bear putting into words. I exuded it instead, smiling simply, and I'm confident she grasped my meaning. She sat down on one of the hospital's padded chairs – the plastic squeaked – and considered me from its comfort, her chin in her hands.

A calm descended. The chair stood at a distance, so the doctor was nowhere near the photograph, not now. Covered up, the image could do no harm. In fact, ignoring the horror of what was depicted, the photograph's existence buoyed me in those moments. It meant I was right. Somebody had been persecuting Anna, and now – *pay or I publish* – they were blackmailing me. She and I were still connected. They'd tried to drown her and failed: their attempt to profit from me now would be their undoing. Though it wasn't the response I'd hoped for, my notices had worked.

A nurse I did not recognize barged backwards into the

room, carrying a tray of wipes, creams and cotton wool. When she saw us her assuredness evaporated; a tube of something bounced to the floor as she put down her tray. She was young, and looked it, laughed a nervous hello to the doctor, skittered sideways in her attempt to greet me, as if, by ducking left and right, she could make herself less painfully there. To put her at her ease I asked if she knew what the malevolent laughing bird I'd seen the day before was called – though I already knew, Anna's guidebook said it was a kookaburra – and, while I listened to her schoolgirl answer, I returned to the foot of the bed, retrieved the photograph and dropped it into the canvas bag.

The doctor, meanwhile, reholstered her chart, amended the whiteboard next to it, and made for the door. I followed, giving the nurse space to work alone. The tendons on either side of the girl's neck disappeared from view as I stepped past her. I quickened down the corridor after Jo, but needn't have: she whirled to face me and stopped.

'Dig round in Anna's private life and who knows what might turn up?'

The statement stunned me. The skin inside my mouth tasted suddenly animal: I kept it shut.

'Whatever she didn't tell you – about who she was with or what she was doing – she may well have not told you for a reason.'

My front teeth bit down on the inside of my top lip and met, freeing a thread of skin.

The doctor took hold of my arm and said, more gently, 'She doesn't need you poking about in the past, Wilson. How can I convince you that it's the here and now you should be concentrating on?'

Anna's mother taught me that it's possible to love and hate a person at the same time. When I looked at her I used to see both things at once. Now the doctor stood before me similarly cross-hatched. Though I knew it to be impossible – the envelope had been sealed – a part of me feared she had already seen the photograph or, worse still even, that she knew ahead of me where it had come from, what it meant. The hate in me wanted to thrust the evidence into her face and demand an explanation, but the love, refusing to believe she could know, held me back.

'You don't get it,' I heard myself mutter. 'Her mother left. She was flawed. But Anna is perfect. I can't let her go, too.'

Jo Hoffman said nothing. Her silence chimed with a truth my heart understood but could not allow. She swayed before me, seaweed under water, tugged this way and that by the currents of love and hate. I stared into the space above her head, at a strip-light, dead flies silhouetted in its plastic shade. The love prevailed.

My voice steady again I asked, 'Are you still lodging at your mother's?'

She folded her arms and took a half-step backwards.

'Because, if you are, you must bear in mind my offer,' I explained. 'It doesn't have to be the hotel I'm using. I wouldn't recommend it, in fact. They have a roach problem.'

'Mr Taylor—'

'If you're concerned about the money, don't be. What better use do I have for it?'

'There's no question—'

'Just until I return,' I cut in. 'I won't be gone long, but while I'm away Anna will need you even more. There's no point in making life harder for yourself than it need be. Any hotel. Or a new place entirely – a deposit, a down-payment. Neither is a problem.'

She uncrossed her arms and smoothed her white vest top down to her hips. A brown stain expanded in the ribbed material at her side; blood from another patient, presumably. The sight of it checked me from insisting further.

'I left a message for you yesterday,' she said, 'with the number of one of our counsellors here. I still think it would be a good idea if we arranged a consultation.'

I seemed to be losing my grip on negotiations, so put a different deal to her. I would make an appointment if she would allow me to help with her accommodation.

Still staring at the hand on her hip, she gripped the bridge of her nose between forefinger and thumb. If it was an attempt to look thoughtful, she failed: I could tell she was fighting exasperation. So was I. There were things I needed to do.

'Think about it, anyway,' I suggested. 'You have my number.'

Now I saw that the doctor was in fact checking a pager hooked to her belt. Looking up again she said, 'Sure,' and, apologetically, 'Please excuse me.' Then she set off down the hall.

It was still early morning yet the hire car's plastic steering-wheel was almost too hot to hold. I wrapped the photograph round it, keeping the blackmailer's account details in view. Ten thousand Australian. There was something almost satisfying in knowing that the man could have succeeded with a much higher pitch. Looked at from the right angle, I was up on the deal. In the time it took me to battle through my bank's automated system and make the payment I had reached the blacktop beyond the edge of town. Time bought, I wiped the wetness from my phone's earpiece, stowed it in the dashboard and quickened my pace inland, fleeing the sun.

It was noon before it occurred to me that I'd begun my journey without wishing Anna goodbye.

19

I had no idea how to talk to Anna when she was tiny. At twenty, and with no experience of babies, I told myself such a failing was to be expected. But it wasn't inexperience, or even the embarrassment of learning baby-talk that hamstrung me, more that when she was very small my love for Anna was cut with fear. The midwife saw as much in my face. 'Relax.' She chuckled. 'She has no teeth to bite you with yet.'

Maybe not, but she had a crocodile grip on me from day one. I hadn't banked on a baby being so wilful ahead of her developing reason, but Anna knew exactly what she wanted from her first breath. With her channel-jamming screams and tiny cracked fists she tried to tell us so at once. That I couldn't understand her, that she couldn't know I was trying, was as desperate as it was obvious. I almost gave up.

Despite herself Anna's mother helped me overcome my fears. When the baby wailed at night she feigned sleep, the covers taut over her turned back. I came home from college more than once to find Anna sodden in a cot stained mustard with neglect. Having refused a termination Anna's mother won the stand-off over the baby's care as well, her lack of interest outbidding my incompetence at each turn. Too proud to let my father take over entirely, I had no option but to shore up the gap.

Still, to begin with, I didn't know how to speak to her. Squealing, motherly repetitions, which Dad somehow managed to ape, wouldn't come for me. Not knowing what Anna understood, I found it impossible to stay at the appropriate level. I would start sensibly, by naming something for her – 'That's a chair' – then add detail – 'See how it's wooden, brown and hard' – but, before I knew it, would find I'd begun talking nonsense over her head – 'We say chairperson now; throne is a slang word for toilet; in Texas they still wire up some chairs to the mains.'

If my inability to talk down to Anna delayed her speech, it didn't do lasting harm. As I've described, when she did finally speak she'd skipped a stage and went straight to talking sense. 'It's like a switch just flipped,' enthused Dad, but if not-speaking had been a conscious choice, so was its opposite.

Having accepted her wilfulness early on, I continued in the same vein with Anna, our relationship mercifully free of the choreographed wars her friends waged against their parents. Most such battles seem to be fought over condescension. I kept on as I had started, talking to her as an equal, and she's always repaid the compliment. In not giving her anything to rebel against I've lucked out. She tends to fight on my side.

The hire car, which I'd rented at Brisbane airport, was equipped with an inadequate map. It detailed the eastern seaboard and a hundred kilometres or so of coastal strip. By the early afternoon I had driven off this map's inland edge. I was also low on fuel. In a market town among rolling fields I filled up and bought a proper road atlas. Looking at it my spirits slumped. I'd come less than a thumb-width from the sea. The hand-span between where I stood now, staring at a hillside studded with cows, and the town of Broken Hill – itself barely a third of the way from Brisbane to Perth – mocked me on the open page. The map told me I was now in New England. It might as well have been Surrey. The drive ahead would take longer than the flight from London. I slapped the book on the car roof, prompting a flock of pink and grey parrots to lift as one from the field behind the garage. At least that sight was foreign. I returned to my seat and carried on.

The distances between towns lengthened with the shadows. I'd climbed higher than I thought, which explained the relative cool on the garage forecourt. As the afternoon wore on the road spilled down from the tablelands on to a vast hot plain that seemed to have been beaten flat by the sun. The trees shrank. Like the livestock they now stood in distant clumps. Continuing further west, the horizon flared red and tightened to a ruled line. Another line stood just above it: the lower branches of faraway trees all seemed to be at the same level, drawn into defensive ranks and underscored with black shadow.

Dusk fell. The radio station I was listening to died and my search for another proved futile. Aside from occasional truck thunder – vast, grille-fronted cabs pulling wagon after wagon after wagon – the road ran eerily empty, with just the drone of the car's tyres on the Tarmac to emphasize the quiet. I drove into the darkness. When headlights appeared on the horizon my windscreen glittered with smashed bugs. On I went. Hugging the hard shoulder past another blinding road-train, my hands tight on the wheel, I bounced in my seat to a deafening horn-blast. Before the shock had become annoyance the truck was gone, leaving a shape in the darkness behind it, which I swerved to avoid too late. I turned my head and braced myself, felt the car slashing sideways, saw fence-posts flickering past, and was still waiting for the impact when everything came shuddering to a halt.

The truck roar faded, overrun by the hire car's air-con hiss.

I don't know how long I sat there doing nothing, the car pointing back the way I'd come, but my heartbeat was still hammering in my ears when the shape I'd missed became a kangaroo, its eyes two angry coals, hopping towards me in the headlight beam.

Frightened, I hit the horn. The animal stopped, glanced over its shoulder, limped away. It looked like it had forgotten something and would come back. I put the car into reverse, made a three-point turn, then continued on my way.

In under a mile I'd come to my senses. The road was empty – juggernauts excepted – for a reason. I nosed in among the scrub beyond the edge of the road and trickled to a halt, finally cutting the engine.

True silence, immensely deep. I was treading water far out to sea, and the sky above was so thick with stars I had to cover my face with my hat to sleep.

I awoke at dawn aching with cold, and drove on to discover I'd stopped just five miles from the next town, which I know would have made Anna laugh. More than double the distance I'd come still lay between me and Broken Hill, yet with so few roads on the map it struck me that the owner of the satchel might well have fled along this very route, stopped to refuel here, stood at the same till. I stacked bottled water on the counter and asked for one of the advertised steak sandwiches. The woman serving had bottomless eyes, which conspired with her mouth to give me an oddly intimate smile. I was tempted to look over my shoulder for the friend she must have seen.

The more space there is around people, the closer they stick together.

You don't leave a person to drown at sea.

I found myself wondering whether the woman wrapping my baguette in greaseproof paper might know who B. Amis was. The scabby little towns from here on into the desert were fists raised against its endlessness, after all. I nearly asked her. Only a premonition of how absurd the question would sound, and the inevitable answer – 'That's hundreds of miles from here' – stopped the words in my open mouth.

A knot of fly-bitten ponies watched the hire car chase its shadow out of town. It turned out they'd built here on a meagre rise in the plain. The blacktop ahead sloped all the way to the horizon. Fence-posts, enclosing paddocks on either side of the road, had by now retreated to a safe distance – why hug the hard shoulder with all that room? – and, no longer flashing past, ticked off my progress at a stately pace. The landscape simply mocked my attempt to hurry. Through-kill, in every state of decomposition – bloody to bone-bleached – became, now that I was alive to it, another monotonously familiar sight. I turned off the air-con, wound down the windows and gave in to the wind-rush and road-hum.

At midday a figure appeared in the distance, floating above the road glare. I drove toward him for a long time before realizing it wasn't just his being there – so far from a town or junction – that was odd, but the fact that he was walking. Why bother? Easing off as I approached I saw an outstretched thumb and found that I had speeded up again. This journey wasn't for sharing.

The hitcher lowered his arm and swung round to carry on. He looked resigned. My foot came off the accelerator, the tyre-pitch dropping. Alone at sea. I opened the door while I waited, to reassure the man I wasn't about to drive off.

Two things struck me as the hitcher climbed into my car. First, that despite its now filthy interior, he paused to kick the dust from his feet. Second, that until we set off, he didn't so much as glance at me. 'Home,' he said simply, having settled into his seat, clarifying, 'North of Quilpie,' when I asked where that was.

His shoulders hadn't straightened when he took off his pack yet, though slow-moving and stooped, he wasn't, I guessed, much older than me. His palm felt cool and dry in mine, his clean-shaven cheeks looked as soft to touch. I didn't want to explain myself to him and hadn't the energy to invent a lie. Our routes diverged at Bourke, a hundred or so miles west. I hunkered down to take him there.

Yet the quiet, magnified by all that space, soon became a heavy silence. I found myself shifting in my seat. The hitchhiker pulled an orange from his bag and peeled it, his sunglasses all the while pointing straight ahead. His fingertips read and stripped the pith; fruit-tang filled the air. My mouth began to water. He offered me the first piece, sighed and said, 'I trained in London, you know. At the Royal College. Fine art.'

I nodded, fighting the temptation to admit to Anna's forthcoming foundation year.

'Of course, I've had to evolve.'

I understood then, and felt a pang of pity. I don't know much about art, yet in the past few years I've tried to take an interest, for Anna's sake. 'Figurative, abstract?' I ventured. What sort of thing would a blind man make?

'Ceramics mostly now.' His fingers worked the top of his bag again and emerged with an exhibition flyer. 'Some installations. I've been putting up a new piece in Sydney. Kings Cross.'

I looked at the leaflet as I drove. A gallery front, glossy against the steering-wheel. From beneath the banner a host of elongated figurines stared up at me, spread in chess-set ranks upon a marble floor. They all had the same shocked expression. As often happens when Anna shows me art she's interested in I foundered, saying, 'Nice, but a long way to walk.'

'I'm no longer allowed to drive.'

'Of course.' I tapped my head. 'Isn't there a bus?'

He sighed again; the tyres droned. 'What there isn't is a rush.'

The thought of being unable to see in the middle of such a horizon made me uneasy. 'Hitching,' I said. 'Way out here. Is that safe?'

He laughed. 'You're not way out anywhere yet, mate.'

On we went, reeling in the Tarmac between nowhere and Bourke. It turned out the sculptor had lodged in Borough, where I live in London, and knew my street. His father once owned a glazier's business. To support himself through art school the hitcher had cut and fitted glass. We worked out he'd put a cat-flap in the back door of my local pub.

'What are the odds?' he breathed.

'Well—' I nodded my agreement and left it at that.

The coincidence somehow allowed the patchy scrubland to flash past in a more comfortable silence. At least, I thought it did. An hour or so later, as we rolled into Bourke, the hitcher leaned forward and ran a hand over the radio controls.

'Reception died,' I explained.

'Long-wave between towns,' he said. 'FM'll do here.' A heavy-metal ballad thrust us among the first buildings, and then we listened to a radio announcer sceptical about the prospect of forecast rain. 'Don't get excited,' he warned, 'only a storm-shower or two. But here's hoping you get under one.' I wanted to offer the blind hitcher help finding another ride, but while I tried to think of the right way to do so houses gave out to store-fronts and, as we paused at a set of lights, he said, 'Quarter of a mile on should do it. Corner of Anson and Richard.'

I pulled over when I reached the junction. He felt for the door handle and released it. The radio announcer now segued from a piece about competitive tractor-dragging into news from the current WTO summit. I shook hands with the hitcher and watched him retreat beneath a shop-front awning to adjust his pack. After a few seconds of my not moving he urged me on with a precise, traffic-cop wave. The newscaster informed the town's residents that their efforts to keep the local library open had succeeded for the time being. I found myself on another garage forecourt. In the same cheery tone the radio told me that, following hurricane Angela, Guatemala was suffering its worst flooding in forty years. The government was pleading for international aid.

The petrol pump rolled its eyes at me.

I asked it, 'What?' while I waited, but already knew the answer. You can't leave a person alone at sea.

Unusually for Penny, the phone rang and rang. I only considered that it was the middle of the night in England when she picked up.

'Yes.'

'It's me.'

Blurry laughter.

'Sorry to wake you. Just checking in.'

I heard bedclothes shift as she sat up. A fly landed on the back of my hand. I shook it – and the phone – and missed what she said next.

'Everything all right with you?' I asked.

'Sure, fine.' Her laughter slid into a cough. 'Never better.'

'Good.' I breathed out with relief.

'It's not my company, after all.'

The fly touched down on the tip of my ear. I brushed it off and swatted at another, also circling my head. I've been inside Penny's home. Scrupulously organized at work, the clutter in her flat surprised me. Clothes spilling from the wardrobe; a bed buried beneath cushions and throws. It seemed I was across a border again. My scalp began to prickle.

'What progress have you made with the syndicates?' I asked.

'Progress?' she repeated. 'I suspect I've made about as much headway here as you have with your secret negotiations.'

More flies had joined those zig-zagging round my head.

One landed on my eyebrow. I decided on a new tactic: I would not flinch, not even to blink. 'Glad to hear it,' I said. The insect crawled in search of moisture.

'Of course, it's not strictly the underwriters I've been talking to, more their lawyers. One or two have returned my calls.'

'Penny,' I said.

'But to be honest, I've not spent as much time with them as I'd have liked. I've been too tied up fielding calls from Guatemala. I thought you might be someone from there now. Or that journalist from the *FT* again.'

'There's no confidential client pitch,' I admitted.

'Really?' More laughter.

The fly had tiptoed to the corner of my eye. I could see it, blurred by my lashes, but still I had not blinked. In revealing the truth to Penny I'd give the horror an extra dimension. And yet, although I still didn't want to tell her what had happened, I seemed to be trying to do so.

'I've not been straight with you.'

'Just me? There's others here would dispute that . . .'

A second fly landed on top of the first. I couldn't help myself. I slapped them both away with the phone, shuddering, shaking my head, prompting more to rise from shoulders, chest and back. They were everywhere. And the petrol gun didn't cut out automatically. The tank overflowed as I stood there swatting the air. Fuel pooled round my feet. Penny's voice disappeared. I found myself gagging – on flies, truth, fumes – I don't know which. Wedging the phone back between shoulder and ear I heard indignation ahead of sense and cut her off: 'I've not told you everything because I can't.'

'Everything? Try *anything*.'

'It's a lot to ask, I know, but—'

'Too much, I'm afraid. I'm not standing in for you. Unless you tell me what's going on you'll have to find yourself another fall-guy.'

'I can't. It's a personal problem.'

She laughed again. 'No, it isn't, it's public now.'

The flies came at me again, landing on my neck, shoulders, the back of my head. I stood on the forecourt flailing at them as Penny said things about non-disclosure and a haemorrhaging of goodwill. Taylor Blake couldn't meet the Guatemalan claim itself. My brow was oily with sweat. If the syndicates refused to pay, we'd go under with our client. I understood what she was saying, but the deeper meaning of her words refused to settle. Or, rather, there was no deeper meaning. The furore didn't resonate here. What did business matter when set next to a blackmailer's photograph and Anna all but drowned? I thrashed at the air with the fuel gun, spraying droplets of petrol left and right.

She was still talking. 'My reputation's at stake, too, you know. Wherever you are, you must come back. Without you, I can't—'

'I wish I could, I honestly do.' I let the fuel hose slip through my hand and pirouetted, lashing at the cloud of flies with the outflung nozzle, narrowly missing an approaching attendant.

'Whoa!' His raised hands were enormous.

'I'm sorry.'

'Not good enough, Wilson.'

'No phones by the bowsers, mate!'

'I have to go.'

'You've got to pay first.'

'Don't think about hanging up on me again.'

The attendant advanced saying, 'Steady.'

'I'll call you.'

'I'll not stand by, I'll assume the worst—'

I tossed the phone on to the back seat, let the hose hang limp and reached for my wallet.

With the fuel gun safely stowed the attendant beckoned me inside. His shoulders shook with laughter as we made it into the cool. 'Struggling against the inevitable only makes matters worse,' he said.

I gathered up my change.

'They seem to like the hassle,' he went on. 'The more you flap at the buggers the more of them you'll attract. If you must, knock them off gently, like this.' A royal wave. There was a blue mark on the back of his hand. A vein, an ink reminder? 'But putting up with them is your best bet.'

I returned to the car and set off again. At its vanishing point the Tarmac shimmered with a mirage brighter than the sky, a notch in the horizon, dead ahead.

20

12 February

This latest client is called Fraser. He's short and stocky with a broad forehead – above which his hair is pulled forward in eager highlighted tufts. We meet at six in a Pitt Street bar. There's an underwater theme – the place is awash with whale music and paintings of seaweed. He chooses us a table in front of a picture window. Through it the office workers returning home are tinted aquamarine – a ready-made frame for the photographer who hasn't yet appeared. Fraser climbs up on to the stool next to me. Sits with his legs apart – square knees straining against his jeans. I find myself wondering whether he hemmed the turn-ups himself. He swivels the seat from side to side and looks round.

– Swarming suits eh. The horror!

I agree it's busy.

– I like being here from time to time though. Makes me thankful I don't have to come more often.

I take the cue. – What is it that you do then?

– Me? A shrug. – I'm an academic.

I widen my eyes.

– Social theory. He looks over my head as he says these words.

I play along. – Social theory . . . of what?

He takes a breath and starts to speak. Louder than necessary. I notice heads at other tables look up. He doesn't expect me to understand. Before phrases he's particularly proud of – *meta-convention* – *moral-normalcy* – *endemic-deviation* – he spreads his stubby fingers wide. His cheeks enthuse red as he talks. There's a book in the offing. Fieldwork is a strength – he confides – tugging at his hair. He doesn't say it outright but I'm supposed to understand that's why he's here – for research. I could shout without him noticing so keep quiet. He expands upon a chapter he's considering about the phenomenon of speed-dating. I sip my drink.

I met Sasha for lunch today. Though they'd forecast temperatures to top a hundred she had a silk scarf wrapped round her neck. I wanted to ask her what it covered but didn't. She had a message from Maggie about photographs the agency needs. At first I wondered whether this was an opening – Sasha seemed to be watching for my response – but I haven't mentioned the photographer since our double date and didn't do so then. Whatever they want – I agreed. She didn't elaborate. Just offered to go with me to the studio when the time came.

The squat academic is talking about evolution and ambiguity and how marriage as a social contract is now void. I smile and nod and keep an eye out – but the boy still hasn't turned up an hour later and by then Fraser has decided it's time to go on to another bar. Excusing myself a moment I slip down from my stool. He hops to the floor too and squeezes my arm. – Don't be long he says.

When I was sixteen I slept with a teacher on a school trip. He had the same insistence as this bloke – but I did it because there was something considerate about him behind the bluster – harmless even – eager to impress. Part of me also wanted to prick

Dad's bombproof tolerance I think – but I couldn't betray Mr Sparks in the end. He kept apologizing afterwards and I felt sorry for him. Unlike this client Sparks was handsome – Whistlejacket next to a pit pony. I wasn't the only girl who allowed herself to be seduced.

Returning from the ladies' I spot the photographer in an alcove – a tank full of tropical fish above his head – and feel suddenly light on my toes. As Fraser walks me to the door I see the boy rise up and follow.

Hot wind blows grit and paper down the street outside beneath a sky all overdone purple with storm clouds edged silver and black. The client walks us the direction of Glebe. There's something in this photographer watching over me that I like. Since the double date he's taken pictures of me with six other clients – including a Finnish oceanographer who broke down in tears and a wheelchair-bound old man who – rules are rules – I refused to let hold my hand. The boy hasn't failed to intercept me yet. He's burnt a lot of film – I've caught him clicking away at the opposite ends of the same date. Excellent evidence – yes – but it's not just the photographs he's taken I value. There's a calm in the boy's watchfulness that inspires confidence – and having an audience gives my performance an added point.

That's what she called it in her letter. 'Giving birth to you was my most polished performance' – she wrote. Went on to apologize but still. It was never me she needed forgiveness from.

We arrive at a darker bar. If the boy followed us inside I don't see him. Yet there's enough light for me to make out a vein throbbing on one side of Fraser's brow. It seems he started early on the drink. Again he touches me – this time to steer me to my seat. I stare at his hand on the tabletop between us – but he's too busy answering his own questions to notice.

– Company is a commodity too he says. – We all know that. The pauses he leaves are not for talking in. They feel more like gaps left in which to take notes. – A variable in the time–money equation that's all. He goes on and on – flecks of spit elastic in the corners of his mouth.

My grandfather handed over the letter unopened. Said he hadn't the heart to burn it. She knew him – after all – and must have guessed as much. A hand on the nape of his creased neck wringing at his conscience. No – he didn't have a right to keep it from me now I'd turned eighteen. Yet you don't miss what you never had. I never knew a mother – might even have pitied the woman had it just been me she left. If I can't it's only because of what her bailing did to Dad. She's still a dead thing blocking his road yet I feel guilty for holding him back. What's that about? He's never spoken a word against her to my face.

– You're even prettier in profile the client whispers. It's not so much the change of subject that catches my attention as the change in tone. Having talked himself to a crescendo he says this all resigned.

– So when will the book be done? I ask.

He pulls on his beer and regards me steadily. – Fuck the book he says.

A current leaps through me but I keep calm laughing. Come on. You don't mean that.

Beneath the table I feel his hand upon my knee. – You've not been listening to a word I've said.

I start to stammer – Of course I have. Some of it was beyond me but I've been doing my best to keep up.

– No. I paid you to listen and I'm not getting my money's worth.

– I've heard every word. I—

He waves me down. – That's the thing about women. Good for—

– Why don't I fetch us some more drinks? I try to slide my leg sideways but he holds it in place. I want to yank the knee free and I'm sure I could – but I don't because a part of me won't move. Fraser's brow is alive now with Keith Haring veins – quotation marks throbbing either side of his face.

– Good for one thing he slurs. – I'm going to make you give it to me.

– I'm sure you don't mean that.

– Sweetie he says. – You've no idea what I mean at all.

I'm oddly calm. It's not just anger the inverted commas frame but desire – which is want – which is a weakness. I think of Sparks. I think of my mother's letter too. Her plea was miscalculated – about the only thing I inherited from her was the ability to ignore it. We stare at one another long enough for the drunkenness to drain from his face.

– You're going to have to give me my money's worth he mutters – the conviction ebbing from his voice.

I take a breath to steady myself and pat his hand under the table. – Perhaps I can help with this book of yours somehow I say. Still smiling I remove the hand from my leg.

– This fella bothering you? A figure looms suddenly beside the client.

– What the? Who the? I'm— Fraser bobs up and down in his chair.

I jump to my feet. A camera is bound to the photographer's hand. Slivers of wrist crisscrossed by the strap on high. Fearing he's about to club the client I hiss – No! at the lens. Close enough to see the shutter scissor open and shut.

– No? Loathing turns to confusion in the boy's face. The

situation is so cut through with anger and misunderstanding and relief that I can't speak. I reach out instead to steady myself against him. Too late – he's already turned and begun to walk away.

I want to follow him but wrestle my attention back to Fraser. Tufted head in shaking hands beside me. – Your research I say again.

His face is ashen. – Listen he says. – I didn't mean—

I hold up my palms to reassure him.

He pulls two fifties from his wallet and offers them to me. Dad's solution. When I refuse he drops the wallet on to the table and presses the notes into my hand. A plastic window reveals a photograph of an old woman cradling a cat. He snaps woman and cat shut muttering – Sorry again. I'm not sure whether it's the picture or the sight of him stumping defeated across the floor that prompts the thought but I find myself dwelling on his turn-ups after he's gone.

21

The road stretched taut between increasingly distant towns. Each one I passed through seemed more meagre than the last: tin roofs, security grilles, dust. Every now and then – and for no reason that I could guess – a small island of green would show at the roadside, just enough to underline the extent of the surrounding umber flatness. Together with the dead kangaroos and fence-posts, these improbable flashes of colour were my journey's only punctuation. Other vehicles grew fewer and further between. Their drivers began saluting, waving, flashing lights as they passed. I stopped to check the car twice, but could see nothing wrong. Further west still, the sun turning blood-orange above an intimidatingly empty horizon, I gave in to the impulse and began waving back.

When Anna was eight we were burgled. It was summer, a hot night. The thief climbed a drainpipe and came in through Anna's bedroom window. He stole the wallet from my bedside table as I slept, drank a glass of orange juice in the kitchen, let himself out of the front door – taking the keys – and drove off in my car. I couldn't bring myself to tell Anna about her window, but should have done. She knew I was hiding something. Much later she told Dad she suspected her mother had come back that night. Who else would have a set of keys? Hide the truth and you risk creating a worse lie.

I made Broken Hill at sunset. The School of the Air was already shut. I was too exhausted to search for whoever ran it that night, instead rolled the hire car to a stop outside the first hotel I saw on the main street, then parked nose-on to the kerb and checked in. Four Aborigines were drinking from bottles in paper bags on the pavement. The eldest wore his trousers with one leg rolled to the knee, an angry wound yellow on his shin. For some reason that detail made me retrieve my kitbag and take it up to the room. Bar noise – laughter, a juke-box, even the click of pool balls – kept me awake long enough to notice the mosquitoes. I slapped three dead with a Gideon Bible before pulling the sheet over my head and finally falling asleep.

It's amazing how quickly the middle of nowhere becomes somewhere once you're there. Make for a distant dot on the map and, when you arrive, you'll find yourself at the map's new focal point. When I awoke the following morning – early, famished, my ankles and feet alive with insect bites – Broken Hill was no longer the embodiment of remoteness but a town I'd come to and slept in, a spot where, for the time being at least, I belonged.

The place I'd chosen to stay in turned out to be more pub than hotel. The bar doubled as a breakfast room and was still heavy with the smell of smoke and stale beer. I went in search of a café instead. Unlike the towns I'd come through to reach it, Broken Hill seemed prosperous and shiny. Walking down main street I passed a sparkling car showroom, shoe-shops brimming with Nikes, and a town hall that would not have looked out of place in the Cotswolds. A crocodile of schoolchildren waited patiently at a pedestrian crossing empty of cars. Even the flies seemed orderly, taking turns to dog me one by one.

Like the street, the café was all but deserted. I sat in the jet wash of an enormous fan considering my next move. Haste seemed pointless in the middle of all that space; who-ever B. Amis was, if he'd fled back here he wouldn't be going anywhere else in a hurry. While I waited to be served I con-sidered what I would do if I found him. When the burglar broke in through Anna's bedroom window I was worried he might come back to harm her. I fantasized about lying in wait to catch the man and tear him limb from limb. I took out the canvas knapsack and tried to whip up similar thoughts of revenge in the café, but could get no further than a question. *Why?* When the boy had answered that I'd know what to do.

A waiter backed through the kitchen doors and pirouet-ted, his face cracking into a grin when he saw he had an audience. He wore a fitted T-shirt, boot-cut black trousers and square-toed shoes, and he had a footballer's Alice band in his hair. Though I'd decided what to order and told him unam-biguously, he seemed determined to have a conversation. Asking me where I was from was an excuse to clarify himself.

'Ah, mate, I started out here originally, school and all that, but I'm not really *from* here!'

Unsure what he meant, I nodded anyway.

'First chance I get and I'm leaving again. I only came back to visit my mum. That was eighteen months ago and *I'm still here*! Can you believe it?'

I supposed not with a shake of my head.

'You see, round here it's all thongs and board-shorts. I'm not interested. Fashion is my thing, and that means south, somewhere cool enough to wear clothes, not just pull them on.'

I turned the bag over on the chair beside me. 'You say you went to school here, though.'

'I've tried to put it out of my mind.'

'I'm hoping to catch up with someone who may have been a contemporary of yours, as it happens. Perhaps you know him.'

The waiter framed his brow with his fingers. 'Shoot.'

I cleared my throat. 'A fellow called Amis. He was a pupil at the School of the Air.'

The waiter's grin returned. He slapped the table and winked at me. 'Nice one!'

I smiled back, lost again.

'Here's the one place pupils there *aren't* from.' The waiter patted my arm. 'You've narrowed it down to half a million or so square miles.'

'Ah,' I coloured, despite the fan.

'The name doesn't ring my bell, but if there's an Amis that tuned in to that school the staff will know where he came from. It's not like they're inundated.'

This reassurance did little to lift my spirits. I looked out of the café window and, seeing endless sky instead of the street beneath it, felt panic fluttering in my chest. My mosquito-bitten feet began to itch.

By nine the sun was pitiless. Beneath it the town's metal rooftops flashed brightly. Sprinklers stood guard over lawn after manicured lawn lining my route to the school. The woman who met me on the forecourt there assumed I was a tourist and wearily told me the tour did not start until later. Her centre parting looked almost painful, a knife-cut nodding as I explained myself. I'd hoped she might be pleased I'd come not to gawp at the school but to ask after one of its students, yet her expression didn't soften. She showed me through a door with apparent reluctance. It was probably the change in lighting, but the anger of her scalp seemed more pronounced inside. An officious red line. I wished I was wearing a suit.

The woman lengthened her stride past corkboards boastful with cosmopolitan display work – a Norman castle in cross-section, something headed 'Precipitation' involving empty pie charts – and ushered me into an office full of computer screens and hard-drive buzz. I sat listening to the machinery while she unfolded a pair of glasses, taking elaborate care. Charm wouldn't work with this pedant, and neither would a bribe. Resistance sometimes necessitates force. Yet as I steeled myself for a fight I noticed one arm of the woman's glasses was wrapped in electrical tape and softened towards her. She smiled at me over the top of crooked frames, then asked the age of the student in question.

'I'm not sure, but he's young. Early twenties at most.'

She cocked her head. 'And his name?'

In answer I offered up the canvas satchel. As I did so the improbability of what I was asking acquired a new dimension. The bag looked ancient, the writing on it – feathery beneath the strip-light – belonged to the distant past. Even if the boy had used the bag to carry his and Anna's things to the beach, as likely as not he'd picked the thing up second hand. An image of the stallholder in Byron Bay – army surplus and airbrushed whales – flashed before me, temporarily robbing me of speech. Eventually I whispered, 'Amis, initial B.'

Again the woman smiled at me over the top of her glasses. 'You'll have to narrow that down, Mr Wilson.'

'I'm sorry?'

'Bowey or Brent?'

I chewed my lip and nodded equivocally, trying to look unfazed. It didn't work. She laughed and went on: 'The twins, out at Yellowhammer. Lovely pair of boys, pupils here up until about five years back. Though by the looks of this,' she passed the bag back to me, 'I'd say you're after their father, Bob. He's one of our former students, too.'

My confusion made her chuckle again. It took me some time to come to my senses, to see the miracle for what it was. Three leads were better than none. I wanted to lean across the desk and kiss her centre-parted forehead. Instead I said, 'Three pupils called B. Amis. You're absolutely sure?'

'You doubt me?'

'No, but—'

'Keeping in touch with students is an edge we have over other schools.'

'Of course.' I paused. 'The father aside, how well did you know these boys?'

She shrugged. 'Brent swam for New South Wales juniors. Quite a feat, given he trained in a water tank. I've not seen him for five years, though. Bowey pops back from time to time. He photographed last year's school sports day for the website.'

For a heartbeat I suspected the woman was having me on. But she angled the monitor so that we could both see it and navigated briskly to the pictures in question. Children in floppy hats clutching hamburgers and drinks. The starter's raised pistol. An action shot of a skinny figure taking the winning tape. My stomach began turning as she clicked through the images. The photographer's more recent work was filed in the briefcase beside my chair: unfolding nausea told me as much. In one picture, of a group of small boys crouched comically low before a race, the cameraman's shadow sat squat in the foreground. He was wearing a hat with a wide brim – like the one I'd bought. I found myself pointing at the screen. 'Do you keep yearbooks? Is there a photo of this Bowen boy?'

'Bowey. Sure. Though not in a yearbook, as such . . .'

I'd confused pedantry with professionalism. The woman's joy in the school's technology lit up her face. She spoke of satellite broadband, web-cam lessons and online libraries, her enthusiasm cut with an engaging naïvety – she was genuinely pleased to demonstrate that the boy's details were ready to hand. I felt almost sorry for her willingness to part with such confidential material without asking why I wanted it: my prepared speech about an official investigation into criminal wrongdoing withered as she worked.

Fearful of how I might react when I saw the photographer's face, I looked to one side of the screen when she tilted it back at me, and asked if I might pay for a hard copy of the headshot instead. She waved aside my offer of money. A printer beneath the desk began whirring. Next, and before I'd asked, she called up a full screen map of the school's catchment area, and tagged Yellowhammer, a property many inches to the west, with a tiny electronic pin. I sat mesmerized by the blinking dot on the map as she told me how, ten years previously, she'd taken part in a home visit there. She was full of advice about road conditions in the dry and wet. I had to put the printouts on the desk when she gave them to me; they made the trembling of my hands too obvious. 'The dashed lines represent unsealed roads,' she was saying. I thought of Jo Hoffman and the charts at the end of Anna's hospital bed, then forced myself to concentrate on the tip of the woman's pencil, which was tracing a staccato route towards Yellowhammer. For one of her more recent projects Anna took it upon herself to go for day-long walks round London, noting each street she went down on her way. Afterwards, using a wall-sized *A–Z* map of the city, a sheet of glass and marker pens, she drew the shape of her route, adding each new day in a different colour. I found these walk-lines beautiful. They quickened down long stretches like Oxford Street, Balls Pond Road and Clapham High Street, curled in loops round Regents Park, Aldwych, and Marble Arch, worried themselves into knots in Soho, the City, or residential neighbourhoods. Folding the printouts into my briefcase I regretted not having praised her more openly. I decided to have the walk-line piece framed for Anna. She'd appreciate that.

I thanked the woman again, squinting at her in the glare.

'No problem,' she said. 'If you catch up with Bowey, give him my best wishes.'

I couldn't bring myself to play along with this and did not smile in return, which was a mistake. She raised one eyebrow – an echo of Anna – and, though she hadn't asked beforehand, said, 'What is it you want with him again?'

'I have a . . . business enquiry.'

She nodded dubiously.

'Photographs, an exhibition,' I added.

The centre-parting nodded more slowly still. 'Come back to the office and you can put a call through to the station, to check he's out there. Save you trekking all that way for nothing.'

I waved the offer down and saw suspicion deepen in her narrowed eyes. Why had I mentioned photographs? The half-truth sounded like a lie. She'd make the call herself as soon as I was gone, warning the boy – Bowey, he had a name now – that I was on my way. Without doubt. Alerted, he'd run again. I clenched my briefcase hard and struggled to come up with an explanation that might smooth the situation over, dissuade her from picking up the phone, but nothing came. We stared at one another, me grinning like a lunatic, her weighing me up for a fool. It occurred to me that I could *prevent* her raising the alarm. I took a step closer, stared down at the scored top of her head, my free hand a balled fist at my side, then realized what I was doing and thrust it out – unclenched – for her to shake.

'I can't thank you enough. You've been extremely kind.'

'Not a problem.'

I strode away briskly. Sprinklers laid down inadequate covering fire: I could feel the woman's eyes hotter than the sun on the back of my neck. Leaving the grounds I passed a board bearing the school motto. *Parted but United*, it read.

22

It began to rain.

Not at first, not until I'd been driving a long time, in fact, but midway through the afternoon, as I rattled and jolted along the dirt track to Yellowhammer, storm clouds, which had been gathering on the horizon all morning, mushroomed and split and swept towards me, until a vast cloudbank pulsing with lightning towered overhead. I leaned forward to look up at the sight, and drove into one of the potholes I'd been avoiding for hours. There was a bang. The car slewed sideways, skidded from the track and came to a halt in a plume of dust. The offside front tyre had blown.

I'm not usually very good with my hands. Yet a wheel I could change. It took me a while to unlock the spare from its housing beneath the boot panel – the buckle fastening the jack to the chassis was horribly tight – but I managed. I cranked the car up, its suspension groaning, and tried to undo a nut. Of course, the whole wheel spun. So I lowered the car again and loosened each nut against the resistance of the ground. Flies gathered, but I remembered the petrol attendant's advice and did my best to wave them away gently, thankful for the first raindrops, which hissed as they surprised the dust. I jacked the car up a second time and removed the shot tyre, savouring the fact that *I could do this*, pushing the spare wheel on to its bolts, lowering the car again, rethreading and tightening each of the nuts. Then I returned the jack and the blow-out to the boot cavity and, with the rain now falling in spears, re-stowed my water and kitbag and slid behind the wheel again, buoyed by my own competence, ready to carry on.

The whole operation had taken less than fifteen minutes. By now the rain was bouncing so high from the dirt it seemed to be trying to get back into the sky. Inside the car, steam rose from my forearms. The map told me I was nearly there. By taking this minor track I'd cut off a dogleg of the bigger road. There were under a hundred kilometres left to go. Only one fork to look out for, back to the main track – though 'main', I'd discovered, didn't mean Tarmac. I turned the key in the ignition, flipped the windscreen-wiper toggle – once I'd found it – and stepped on the accelerator.

The wheels spun.

I put my foot down harder.

A fan of grey mud spattered each rear window.

The rain was hammering on the roof of the car. It was also running across the track – grey dust slick black now – towards the edge, where the hire car was . . . stuck. I shifted into reverse and nudged the throttle with my toe. The car rocked backwards just enough to give me hope, then slumped forwards again, mud roaring in the wheel arches. Losing patience, I thrust the stick into drive again and stamped down all the way, until the engine scream was louder than my own anger. The front end of the car settled comfortably into the mud.

I cut the ignition and sat back. To have come so far, to be so close, and yet to be held up at the last by the *rain*. My sides shook as much from frustrated laughter as from thunder breaking overhead. The storm was so heavy now I couldn't see more than ten yards in any direction; the din on the roof was a stampede inches above my head. Yet I couldn't just wait for it to pass. Stripping off my shirt and trainers I pushed open the door and climbed out to look at the problem, to work out how – when the rain eased – I might solve it and carry on.

The front wheels were buried to the axles. I'd need to dig them out, to create an incline which, when the ground dried, the car would be able to climb. Yet I wasn't prepared to wait until then. Nor was I thinking straight. It occurred to me that I might be able to jack the front end of the car up out of the hole I'd created, and then perhaps lever it backwards, pushing the front wheels on to untorn ground. About as hopeful as relying on *feng shui* to resolve boardroom negotiations. Yet this wasn't a business situation. Rainwater was running inside my waistband, pasting my boxer shorts to my legs. I tore open the boot and rummaged to yank the jack free – using a key on the buckle this time – then slammed the lid shut again to stop the boot filling with rain.

I recognized my mistake instantly. Though I tossed the jack aside and dug in my pockets I knew full well I'd locked the car keys in the boot. I could visualize them lying next to the water containers and my rain-spattered kitbag. A snap of lightning showed me to myself and my shoulders began to shake again. I sat down in the mud, leaning against the wheel arch, and lifted my face to feel the sting of the rain.

There are obstacles and there are *obstacles*. The rain was falling more gently now – into my open mouth – and the car's metal wing was warm, pressing against my back. It felt like resignation. I stared at my feet, bare in the dirt before me, as I sat slumped there beside the car, resisting its damnable inertia with all my might.

I prised myself from the mud and inspected the dashboard for a button or switch that might pop the boot. Nothing. My hands braille-walked beneath the front seat in case the designer had put a release button there – but he hadn't. Neither had he seen fit to provide access to the boot from behind the rear seats. The compartment was sealed. My anger mounted. There was no way through that I could find.

Perhaps I didn't need the key to start the engine. Car thieves don't. I wedged myself among the pedals, craning to see which wires ran where. None were visible at all at first; I ripped a thumbnail trying to pull the steering-wheel's plastic housing free, but even when I'd managed that I couldn't reach the clump of cables buried in the recess. I had nothing to cut wires with anyway, wouldn't know which to splice together if I had. Fury spread across my chest.

The jack was still lying at the rear of the car. I worked out the best grip, swung it high above my head and brought the thing down hard on the tailgate lock. A dent appeared. Two, three, four: crease, bite, smile; flakes of white paint flew up, but the catch held. I gave in to my rage, pummelling without hope until the boot was pocked and dented all over, and still locked.

Another car would be sure to pass soon. All I had to do was wait and flag it down. In the meantime, I ripped off the rear windscreen wiper and tried to use its metal root to lever up the boot panel rim, hoping to create a gap big enough for the jaws of the jack. I don't know how long I'd been jabbing at the tailgate before it occurred to me that, since I'd turned off the main track, I'd not seen any other vehicles at all. No traffic in a whole afternoon. I took up the jack again and smashed one of the rear lights to see whether there was a way into the boot through its empty socket. There wasn't. I hammered at a wing in my frustration, finally hurled the jack through the rear windscreen. It lay ineffectually on the back seat.

I returned to my spot beside the car and forced myself to sit still a while, cradling my head in my hands. My face was hot; I licked my lips, tasted salt. No new ideas came. Just blankness, which turned in on itself, recrimination growing teeth. How could I have been so stupid? Anna needed me and I was failing her, again. The mosquito bites on my right ankle were hard as knuckles; I had been scratching at them and now saw I'd drawn blood. Glaring at my feet, white where they weren't caked in mud, something about the sight troubled me. Both heels were underscored with long shadows. I jumped up and ran a few idiot paces down the road, as if the view from there might contradict the obvious. Dusk, the sun a red disc, the sky above it empty to the horizon.

It had stopped raining.

Not only had the storm passed, but the quagmire was already drying out. Gaps in the low scrub were beginning to show tawny and grey again. I climbed the stock-fence at the side of the track and picked my way into the bush in search a of drinkable puddle of water, but gave up after no more than a hundred yards of grit, brush and damp dirt. I squatted down. Ludicrous as it seems, I'm sure that I could hear the ground blotting up the run-off, the parched land sucking the storm down in one long gulp.

The water I'd bought in Broken Hill, like my kitbag and the keys, lay in the boot of the car. Sleep would stop me thinking of my thirst, I decided, but – contorted in the car during that long, long night – whenever I did manage to drop off I dreamed in rivers.

By nine o'clock the following morning I was regretting not having eaten some of the wetter mud. My throat was swollen, my tongue tasted of copper and bone. Already the car's metalwork was too hot to touch. The sun had risen four hours ago. The front wheels were now set in cement ruts. Which meant the road was passable, so about now another car was *sure* to appear. I sat in the passenger seat staring at the horizon and trying to ignore the thirst ringing in my ears and the water in the car's boot and the earth already baked and cracked all around. Stay out of the direct sun, conserve energy, wait: that was the thing to do, yet as the day wore on and nobody came I seemed again and again to be digging at the boot's metal seam with the wiper, a sharp rock, my fingertips.

At midday I opened the bonnet. An engine, I'd realized, must be kept cool. I twisted off the radiator cap and stared at the liquid in the pipe. Black and silver flashes and a reflected eye. I managed to wet the end of my finger but could see no way of sucking the water out of the radiator. Maybe not, but the screen-wash container was merely fastened to the chassis with plastic jubilee clips. I ripped it free and drank, ignoring the chemical taste until it surged up into my nostrils and I was gagging and retching and refusing to be sick, swearing at my traitor tears as they fell into the dirt.

The heat overran me. Inside the car, with no breath of wind, I felt I was being cooked alive. Yet there was no other shade in any direction and the sun's full glare was unbearable. When I braved it to relieve myself my piss was brown and smoked as it hit the dust.

I had followed my shadow in search of something to drink and now stood among scratchy, stunted bushes, staring at a blackened, twisted tree root: a foetus in the flames. I threw up. Soap bubbles burst beneath my feet. Immediately the ground glistened with flies, which made me shiver, which was blissful, yet untrustworthy. The sun was already low again. No car had passed today: why would one appear tomorrow? In a moment of clarity I saw that unless help came I would die by the side of that track, which meant Anna's enemy would go unpunished, which wasn't acceptable.

My phone was in my pocket. I'd already checked there was no signal in the car, yet here I was out in the open, dusting the thing off and dialling Penny's number again. I shut my eyes and ground my teeth in anticipated disappointment, then sat gripped as the phone began to ring, and rang, and rang, until my amazement boiled to dismay as the thing forwarded me to an automated voice, which told me Penny was unavailable. No 'leave a message' even: with a click I was disconnected. This had to be deliberate, a deaf ear in response to my own silence.

Unwilling to risk the one remaining slice of battery redialling her, my thumb picked out the only other number I know by heart.

'The prodigal! Still on for tonight, I hope?' Dad took up cooking when Anna was born. Once a week we still go for dinner at his place. His voice now sounded less than a kitchen's length away. 'Shoulder of lamb stuffed with caramelized shallots, sweet potato mash to go with it, and glazed carrots. Winter food. Pick up a tub of sorbet on your way over, could you? I overdid my meringues watching the test match.'

'Sorbet,' I said.

'Mango would be good.'

I could see him standing beside a work surface, dutifully wearing the Tate Modern apron Anna bought, his steady hands uncorking a bottle of wine, and the image paralysed me. I sat and listened as he talked me through the day's cricket and believe I'd have stayed there until the phone died, had it not beeped a low-battery warning in my ear. I came to my senses and started gabbling.

'Listen, Dad. Anna's in trouble. She's in hospital. Somebody tried to drown her. The doctor thinks they succeeded, but I *know* otherwise. I need you to go to her. Byron Bay hospital, New South Wales. Don't let them switch her off.'

There was a pause.

'Dad?'

'Son?'

'You have to—'

'You're breaking up.'

I repeated myself, leaving speaking-clock gaps between my words. The phone twittered its warning again. Behind the noise I could hear my father's breathing.

'You understand?' I asked.

'Of course, of course. We'll go together. I'll pick you up right away.'

'That's the other thing, Dad—'

The phone cut out before I could say any more, but I felt no anger at this, just relief at having said the important words first. Whatever came of me, my father would stand in Jo

Hoffman's way. Dad and I have the same hands. Square nails, bony knuckles. I stared at mine a moment, at the oil map in each creased palm, happy at the thought that his clean hands would now take over.

Just then I saw something move on the horizon. A column of raised dust in the distance, coming towards me. Another car finally, help. The heat and thirst lifted until I was almost sorry I'd troubled my father, and then the approaching dust pillar checked and veered sideways and seemed to hold still. That it was rising from the road and yet not coming closer made no sense, but neither did anything else. I stared at the horizon, willing whatever it was to move on again.

When it didn't I set off to intercept the apparition. The going was slow. Amid such featurelessness I had to be sure I kept an eye on the spot I was making for, yet the ground underfoot was ragged and strewn with spiky bushes and my feet were clumsy. Within a few yards I had stumbled and pitched forward on to my hands and knees, jabbing an evil, triangular thorn deep into one of my palms. The blood that welled from the wound had no taste, it was just – wet. I wrapped a handkerchief round the cut and watched a red dot grow.

There was still no sign of a vehicle. I began to doubt myself. Why would a person stray from the road in the middle of nowhere? My thirst redoubled, my tongue swelled to a fist, my throat furred up with rust. When I next looked at the horizon it seemed there were *two* dust trails in the air ahead; one nearby, the other distant. Baffled, I made for the closer one, which in turn seemed to race towards me. My spirits leaped again but they were immediately dashed.

No car. The dervish was just a self-propelled vortex of dirt and air.

Before I knew it the dust devil was upon me. Though I shielded my face with my hands as best I could, red grit plugged my ears, my nose, every pore. I lay on the ground, buried my head in my arms. There were no thoughts in my head, just pictures: a bowl of apples strung with pearls of blood; a broken gutter spilling soapy water; an icebox furred with brown frost.

Time passed and then time stopped and then there was just burning stillness.

When I came to the thirst was all but blinding. I could only see in snatches. A line of armour-plated ants marched over my outstretched arm. It took all my strength to rise up on to my knees. The hire car was there, a white dot on the horizon, and then I was looking through a black tunnel and couldn't see it any more. I decided to crawl in that direction anyway. My hand was still wrapped in the handkerchief, but the rosebud had turned brown. I glimpsed filthy fingers pressing it into the dirt and had half an idea, to do with sucking moisture from the cloth, and the radiator's winking eye. Antifreeze, a voice said, and I retched drily at the ground again. Only it wasn't me crowing, but a large bird that had landed a little way off. Oil-black feathers, scrawny legs: a doctor. I crawled towards it. The bird winked its glossy eye and hopped away. I thought of Anna's beautiful raised eyebrow. My head hurt; a jarring nausea overtook me, the back-slam of falling from a tree. What sort of a drawing would my forays from the car inspire? Meaningless squiggles, red dust ghosts turning in the air. Angela was the name of a much bigger twister. I shuddered at the sudden thought of *people* torn apart by that storm. I was somehow to blame, the incandescent sky screamed as much. Accusing me of that and of failing my daughter by locking the key to her mystery in the boot of a hire car. No matter what else, the voice said, I had to follow the bird and make amends.

But the bird and its shadow kept hopping out of reach. I found myself up against the stock-fence at one point, by the side of the road again, and couldn't crawl through. A snake lay curled at the foot of the fence-post next to me. Its mouth opened, revealing tiny curved teeth and a pink, kitten's mouth. I was not afraid. Then I was not looking. When I focused again both the snake and the bird were gone, leaving me alone. Alone, beneath the stiff post, the tight wire. I collapsed in the crosshair of this mean shade and lay still.

23

14 February

Sasha isn't wearing the scarf today. It covered a bruise – yellow now on the side of her neck. Something about the way we are together means I don't comment on it.

– So she says draining her drink. – You ready for this?

The agency has a brochure for clients. We were due at the 'studio' – Sasha's inverted commas – scored in the air with her fingertips – at four. It's now half five but the photographer's assistant is evidently running late. The vodka and tonic pulses in my fingertips as I put my glass down. I've not yet used the lipstick I bought this morning but I will. Paint should give the photos a pop-art touch.

A woman ushers us into the little townhouse in Edgecliff – head bowed. She's painfully tall with a big forehead and deepset eyes. Her shyness somehow excuses the fact that she doesn't tell me her name. Sasha bounces past her in search of a drink. I ask the woman where I should go to freshen up.

There are three long-haired cats asleep one above the other on the stairs. I step over them on my way up to the bathroom. Negotiate a pair of trainers – big as rowing-boats – moored nose to nose on the landing. Through an open door I glimpse a room messy with books and peer closer to read the covers of those on the bedside table. *Unlocking the Next Level* and *Making Your Customer Work for You*. A blank screen sits buzzing on a desk in the corner. Business student – pyramid fraudster – Internet gamer – who cares? In the bathroom a knee-high stack of fashion and photography magazines topped with a book on Japanese eroticism seems intended to create a different effect.

I inspect my face. The light above the cabinet mirror shows up an annoying redness across my forehead and cheeks and the bridge of my nose – I fell asleep beneath clouds this weekend and woke up staring at the sun. Though the lipstick is a useful distraction what passed for blusher this morning now gives me a flustered look. I make pantomime faces at myself for a few moments. When my features come to a rest they – like the red fingernails earlier – no longer seem to belong to me at all.

Which is the point. Ever since Matt Alexander wrote me a poem called 'The Deer Princess' – I was eleven and he was thirteen – he rhymed 'nuzzle' and 'muzzle' and 'puzzle' – I've known my looks and me aren't the same thing. I'm not yet twenty and already there's a blue vein on the back of my left knee. Remembering this now I climb on to the rim of the bath. I have to stretch to see the flaw – the mirror is hung high on the wall. A bang on the door makes me flinch and sway.

– Need back-up? Sasha's voice and laughter.

– Two seconds. I wobble to the floor and open the door.

The woman's living room is divided in half. At one end a pair of sofas covered with cat hair sit before a television overhung by the fronds of a potted fern. It needs a drink more than I do – but I accept Sasha's offer. The other part of the room is a makeshift studio with lights and reflective paper and a white umbrella on a stand. This gadgetry is all at odds with the wall-hangings and waist-high silver candlestick. Next to which a low couch – covered in velvet – sits spot-lit like a dentist's chair. Another cat is curled asleep in the glow.

While the woman fiddles with her equipment I say – So, cats.

She stops what she's doing and shoos the one on the couch away.

– You don't see as many of them here as we have back home I say.

The woman wrings a lens on to her camera. – Non-native animals are vulnerable. A spider bite here can blunt a cat's inquisitiveness. Why don't you take a seat?

I do so. The photographer can barely look at me but her camera does. While her voice – kept soft – perhaps because it is so low – does some of the talking – her hands give the real instructions – motioning for me to look at the umbrella – lift my chin – rearrange my knees. The drink-buzz helps. I feel mentally unzipped. After my fright-show in the mirror upstairs I manage the full spectrum of expressions – insolent to coy – with ease.

Sasha gives me a wave. – You look like a vase of cut flowers she says.

Then she disappears. An R&B track with a doorbell chorus floods the room.

At the Royal College show last year one of the students did a series of giant canvases showing women in porno poses. Once you got past the shock those pictures were beautiful. The models glowed in spite of what they were doing – the ugly posing some-how made sense of their loveliness. I follow more instructions and think of that exhibition and struggle to stifle a bout of hiccups brought on by the icy vodka. The photographer signals we're done. I turn to see Sasha walk back into the room dressed only in her bra and pants.

A man follows her. He is also in his underwear – holding a

neat pile of clothes under one arm. He nods at me and puts the bundle down on an arm of the sofa. I forget myself and hiccup out loud.

I've not seen the agency's brochure but didn't imagine the girls between its pages would be wearing much – and had already decided I wouldn't undress. Now though it seems they're not about to ask. Sasha takes off her knickers and steps to the couch – waving me aside. – The real money is on a different page she says. Her movements are so self-certain each seems a separate dare.

The man joins her. I retreat a few steps towards the open door – which exerts a sudden magnetic pull. But as Sasha starts to pose – confident as a whip – my feet simply stop moving. It's not the shock that holds me in place but the fact that as soon as the photographer begins I might as well not be there.

The man has a weal of white scar tissue on his right shoulder-blade. His bare legs are almost hairless. They quiver with the effort of supporting Sasha as she twists towards the camera. He kneels down now – revealing the sole of a foot – cracked and yellow. Sweat stands out on his brow.

They don't have sex – but that's not the point. What gets me is how quickly the sunglow of my shock fades – how fast what I'm witnessing becomes a bald matter of fact. In no time the nakedness and camera flashes are as ordinary as the stencilled roses that – I notice – run around the room at the top of the wall – even above the wall-hanging at the studio end. In between poses Sasha's face – drained of mock ecstasy – looks every bit as bland.

The woman adjusts the lighting. Adds a filter and clothes the pair in a sappy Degas light. I find myself wondering what Sasha meant by 'cut flowers' and resenting her comment either way –

then soften again catching sight of a purple stain on her inner thigh. How do you get a bruise there? The soft-focus glow doesn't hide the fact that – after a while – the posing begins to take its toll. In the middle of one set of shots Sasha pauses to shake her elbow loose – her breathing quick and shallow.

With all the shifting about they are doing on the couch a corner of the throw has slipped forward revealing a slice of the vinyl beneath. I think it's that sliver of truth – more than the snub – or vanity – or solidarity – or the money – or even the thought that I'll be able to make something of the photographs – which makes me do what I do next. I put the empty glass down – step forward and pull the throw free.

Honest cigarette burns.

Sasha's grin is conspiratorial. – All yours she says.

I take my clothes off and tell the woman I'd like to earn some extra cash too. She appears unsurprised. The music seems louder – my bare skin is alive to the velvet and the vinyl and the air is charged with static. Up close the man's chest is clearly waxed. I find this funny and have to turn away.

The woman gives instructions. I am distracted by the plea-surable realization that my hiccups have gone.

– Here she repeats. Like that.

I am a long way from home.

– Like this? I ask.

24

I dreamed I was Anna, that my thirst was her drowning. Fingers of water thrust themselves down my throat. But the water was warm and tasted of dust. It spread across my chest. Death, at least, would take me to her. Yet she wasn't dead! I gagged and choked and lost the battle and felt the dust-water in my mouth again.

Then the ground was moving beneath me. It was hard-edged and painful against my back. I swayed from side to side on the tray, my head cushioned by seaweed. No, it was rope, and I was being dragged across the ocean bed. The darkness beneath the waves was a comfort, blurring the jolting of my head against tin. Yet every now and then the surface above me split open and I saw a slash of sky, brightness cut by a fishing-rod, a conductor's baton, an aerial, reeling me to the surface, whipping to the beat, signalling my distress.

'I've no idea. Get hold of Mum, though.'

Static hiss. 'You're sure it's him?'

'The state of the bloke's ride!' Laughter. 'Bogged all right, but bent at every corner too. It's like he tried to *kick* the thing free.'

Crackle. 'Poor bastard.'

'Tell her I've done my best to get some water into him. It just leaks out again, though. She'll need to prepare her stuff.'

The sky went black after that and I was back with Anna at the bottom of the sea. A new and dangerous fish circled us on the seabed. 'Might she simply have decided to go for a swim when she was drunk, and drowned?' it asked. No! She wasn't dead. I swiped at the fish and it flitted away. She couldn't be dead because if she was it would mean she had left without knowing true love. Writing a boy's name on the knee of her jeans wasn't enough. And never mind how pink she went with excitement beforehand, neither was a first date – around the London Eye, aged fourteen – with a boy who stood barely as tall as her shoulder. Nothing since had lasted. I never had to give any embarrassing advice about taking things slowly and saving herself and steering clear of serious-ness too soon because it was obvious she'd decided to do all those things for herself.

The seabed jumped and I rattled sideways into something soft and came to for a moment with a handful of warm fur. There was a dog under the tarp, too. It was looking at me expectantly, its tongue hanging pink out of the side of its mouth. I thought again of the tube of lipstick I'd found in Anna's wash-bag and then the pick-up hit another rut and I bounced clear of the tray again. *Where was I going?* I landed with a thump and the answer to that question skittered out of reach

Night again. As a boy I was ashamed to admit that the dark frightened me, but it did. I wouldn't let my mother turn out the bedroom light. That was Dad's job. I'd hear his foot-steps on the stairs and he'd step through the door and pause to do his inspection. 'Wardrobe: check. Under-the-bed: check. Corner-cupboard: check . . .' I'd feel him beside me, bending down. 'Okay, here we are at the end of another day,' he'd say. 'What happens now?'

'Sleep.'

'And research has shown that the optimal conditions for sleep are dark and quiet. So' – he'd turn the light off – 'that's what I've arranged. I've made sure there's nothing here to wake you in the night. Which means you can . . . ?'

'Sleep easy.'

'Exactly. All systems shut down.' His kiss was scratchy on my forehead. It came with an echo of the day's aftershave, metal and heat and strength. 'Good night, my boy.'

My girl. Years later I'd stand outside Anna's door and listen to him going through the same routine with her. It made me feel proud and secure and obsolete all at once. The seaweed moved beneath my head and I had exactly the same sensation again. It was a relief to think how my father would be at Anna's bedside by now, keeping the beautiful doctor in check.

Next, the torn tarpaulin had become a propeller, bearing down. I lay staring at the still point of its centre until it seemed my wish had come true: they'd let me take Anna's place. I knew as much because there was a drip in my forearm secured by a bandage, and a curl of plastic tube reaching up to a see-through bag hanging from a hatstand. I thought of coils and pinprick curved teeth and the pain in my head was excruciating again. Two figures loomed beside me. An orderly, perhaps, and a nurse.

'Should I mark up the strip for the medic?'

'No need for that.' The nurse's voice was gentle. 'I radioed Dr O'Hanlon. He agrees we've made the right start. Let's wait and see how our man here responds.'

'Vic's optimistic anyhow. He smelt out the poor bugger straight off. Licked the grit from his eyes and insisted on riding all the way home with him on the tray.'

'I wonder what this means for your brother?'

'God only knows.'

'If anyone can help us get through to Bowey, though . . .'

I turned my head and saw, out of the corner of my eye, curtains, a window, a flickering screen. Bowey? The readout on the monitor made no sense. I watched for a while but nothing on the screen moved, which raised panic. When I tried to cry out for the nurse, though, I couldn't. The room dimmed again with wasted effort, the voices frayed.

Deaf and dumb. Did it matter that I wasn't good at talking to Anna as a father? Family sticks, but friends drift apart. Was my speaking to her as a friend to blame? Now we were more than equals: we'd swapped places; we were both the same. Yet this was a different hospital, I knew that. The monitor screen was a dead television and Anna's room had a blind, not curtains. You couldn't change one of us for the other and expect people not to notice. We don't even look alike. Spared my blunt features, Anna's beauty is her mother's. They both had the same extra incisor among their milk teeth, for God's sake, never mind the pale, wide-spaced eyes. As she grew up the echo became painful; it brought back insistent memories of nullified love. I'd turn round and catch a glimpse of her taking off a shoe or reaching to put a glass into a kitchen cupboard and find I'd stopped still and forgotten what I was supposed to be doing. Her bare arm stretching, the shape of her neck where it met the plane of her back. In such moments I had to remind myself to breathe.

But now a reassuring sound of panting was coming from

the end of my bed. I propped myself up on my elbow and saw that the light had changed. It was falling directly through a set of French windows in a white oblong. The shape was so bright that it took me a while to bring the rest of the room into focus. A sea of painted floorboards. A baggy sofa, a wardrobe pasted with photos of agricultural machinery, a chest of drawers with no legs, each moored against its own wall. And me, adrift in a king-sized bed. My headache had gone. The panting was coming from a black dog whose tail, as I sat up further, began to beat across my feet.

'Where am I?' I asked aloud.

The dog's tail beat faster. There was still a crêpe bandage round my forearm, and a lampstand with no shade beside the bed, but no bag of fluid, no tube, no drip. I undid the bandage, revealing a red mark on the soft skin of my inner forearm and was still staring at it when a woman with peroxide blonde hair appeared in the doorway of the bedroom. She looked tiny in the huge doorframe. She was carrying a rolled newspaper, and waved it at me, an everyday greeting.

'How you going there, Wilson?' she said.

25

We sat in the kitchen, me at one end of a boardroom-sized dining-table, the woman – Jeanette – at my side, and a boy of about twenty at the far end, partially hidden by chunks of machinery spread out before him on a plastic sack. He'd stood up as his mother led me to my seat but sat back down after an abrupt 'G'day', and was already engrossed again.

'You must be hungry,' said Jeanette. 'We've a barbecue organized for tonight, but what can I get you in the mean-time?'

'Barbecue?' A crack opened in my top lip when I spoke.

'Geoff, the postie, is stopping over on his way through to Mullagar, and we've radioed the stock boys to come in too. Robert's cut his trip to town short. The doctor's on his way back with him, to give you the once-over. At least that's his excuse. That man can eat a heap of coleslaw!'

The boy's elbow was raised as he tightened up a screw. *Brent*, his mother had called him, and it wasn't a coincidence. I'd ground to a halt seventy miles from this enormous farm-house but had already, apparently, arrived at Yellowhammer. I was on their land; they'd been waiting for me. The centre-parted school secretary had done me the favour of calling ahead. In doing so she'd saved me. Jeanette explained: a couple of days after the rain, when nobody had arrived, she'd sent the boys out looking, just in case. 'And it's bloody lucky for you I did.' She laughed. 'We hardly use that track since they regraded the road.'

She was still talking now. 'Everyone's keen to meet our new houseguest, now you've finally arrived. And . . .' here, I'm sure, she lowered her voice '. . . Bowey, of course – he'll be in as well.' Brisk again, she continued, 'Yes, we've a pile of food to get through later, but what do you fancy now?'

I asked for a bowl of cereal, buying myself time. Brent was wearing a sleeveless vest. The muscles in his shoulders worked as he turned the screwdriver. He still hadn't looked up. While Jeanette trekked from cupboard to fridge and back again, assembling my afternoon breakfast, I struggled to think straight.

Brent was the swimmer. The size of the boy! Sitting there, muscle-bound, unable to meet my eye. Bowey took photographs, and there was *the* photograph, and I'd made assumptions. Anyone can use a camera. I licked my upper lip, tasted iron. Brent had saved my life. And one of them had tried to end Anna's by drowning her in the sea. She was a swimmer too, a strong one. It would have taken a *stronger* swimmer to overcome Anna in those waves. My head ached. Why would this boy not look me in the face?

'What happened to the hire car?' I asked.

Brent removed a screw from the corner of his mouth, slotted it into place with one hand and began twisting the screwdriver. 'It's parked out front,' he said.

'Here?'

Now he looked at me evenly. 'I thought, with the rest of the damage, you wouldn't mind me breaking the steering lock.' He wiped a greasy hand through his hair. 'That way we towed it in.'

People with something to hide, in my experience, are best tackled obliquely: they find a straight question easier to dodge. The canvas bag was in my briefcase, which lay in the trunk. If I could show that bag to the two brothers I'd be able to watch their reactions and see which of them flinched.

I aimed my thanks across the expanse at the top of the boy's head. He and his mother had saved me, and I'd repay them, I said. Jeanette laughed. Brent's big shoulders shrugged.

I went on, 'I locked my key in the boot. You probably worked that out.'

Despite the tilt of his head I saw the corners of the boy's mouth twitch. He reached for a grease-gun at his elbow and angled its long spout into the metal block before him. 'I figured you'd lost it somehow. All those dents.' He paused, chewed his lip. 'We popped the back lock, too, to get at your stuff. The keys will still be in the boot, I expect.'

'Oh—'

'Your bags are in your room,' Jeanette called, over her shoulder.

Brent pushed the lump of motor aside, looked up, shook his head sadly and said, 'The water in there as well. I saw that, and I've thought about what it must have been like. Enough to drive you nuts.'

Jeanette made her way back to my side again. She set a huge bowl of cornflakes down before me and smiled. Her hands were pink. So was her face: she had the sort of skin that never tans. I found myself staring at her eyebrows. She'd plucked them bare and redrawn two curved dark lines in their place. Dark fake eyebrows, bright bleached hair. The eyebrows stayed arched when her smile faded and I shuddered, thinking of Anna.

'You do feel all right, don't you?' she asked.

I nodded.

'Good.' She glanced at the bowl and let out a nervous laugh. 'Then make a start. You'll need some practice for what's coming later.'

The air of expectation in the room unnerved me. I bolted the cereal, repeated my thanks, retreated to the cavernous bathroom and stared at myself in the mirror there. The outback had peeled a layer from my brow, exposing raw wood, and my hair had grown out of its short cut, too, softening my totem-pole features: I looked like a tourist flushed stupid with sun. I took a shower. The pool at my feet was immediately brown. I scrubbed and scrubbed. It took me a while to realize that the water was running the same brackish colour from above. The dirt and pipe-rust were inseparable; my gratitude and suspicion were as impossible to pull apart. These people had rescued me, yet one of them was my enemy. I couldn't tell whether Brent was shy or being deliberately evasive. My kitbag and briefcase, paired beside the big wardrobe, did not appear to have been opened, but again, I couldn't be sure. Nobody had asked me why I'd come to the station. Yet a half-memory of something I'd overheard in the back of the pick-up made me assume the school secretary had mentioned the other boy, Bowey, in her telephone call. Combined with Jeanette's hesitancy when she spoke of him, this suggested they knew he was the reason for my visit. That they seemed glad I wanted to see him just made me less sure he was the reason I'd come. The water drummed cool on the top of my head, but as soon as I turned it off I felt clammy again, then hot with impatience. I picked up the knapsack. Until I could confront them both with that evidence I'd be sure of nothing. I had no choice but to wait for the evening to come.

I passed the time with the dog. It followed me from the back door out on to the vast screened porch that ran round the house. Walking was painful: my joints were stiff, as if full of grit. I hobbled beyond the shade of the house, out past the white fence surrounding its ragged lawn – the boundary seemed arbitrary amid such space – and made for the shadow of a tree with silver leaves and a black, prehistoric trunk. Amid the outbuildings stood machinery of all sorts, junked pick-ups, motorbike engines, a tractor without wheels, a digger cowering beneath its upraised bucket. There was solar panelling too, a listless windmill, fuel tanks perched on stilts, and the interminable drone of an engine somewhere, all bracketed by red earth and blue sky. The enormous house looked small in this context; its fake stone cladding, clinker planks and acre of tin roof added to the place's incongruity. I squatted down to scratch the dog's ears but we were soon harassed by flies. The dog snapped at them. The engine noise was coming from a generator. I returned to my room via the defeated hire car and set my mobile phone to charge.

Guests began arriving at dusk. Dr O'Hanlon first, with Jeanette's husband, Robert, in a silver Landcruiser whose exhaust pipe poked proud of its roof. The doctor wore a theatrical cravat and breathed beer over me – there was a crate of bottles on the back seat – as he rattled through his open-air examination, pronounced me fit, and patted me on the back. 'To fall into a nurse's arms and awake with a bellyful of saline! Oh, lucky Lazarus!' he said.

Robert, a towering man whose red wrists looked too big for his shirtcuffs, seemed relieved by this. He set enthusiastically to the task of building a barbecue in the empty shell of half an oil drum. Aside from proclaiming himself happy I'd arrived safely at last, he was all busy platitudes until, and it was as if he could not contain himself, he spun from the flames and exclaimed, 'An exhibition! He'll be stoked.' I was prevented from asking what he meant by a pair of motor-cross bikes, which buzzed loudly into the yard. The façade of politeness collapsed as Robert waved his arms angrily.

'How many times do I have to say it?' he hollered, as the riders dismounted. 'Stop to drop your fuckin' dust!'

Neither man paid him – or me – any attention. Both strode straight to wash at a standpipe in the corner of the yard, and from there went to inspect the hire car. Another vehicle – an armoured truck of some sort – rolled up the track at this point, and a short man wearing a baseball cap stepped down from its door. He walked with a limp. Seeing the stock hands, he joined them by the hire car. The three men exchanged nods. One thumped the crippled boot shut; there was laughter as it yawned open again. The dog's head brushed my knee and for some reason a lump rose in my throat. I reached to stroke the fur on the back of the dog's neck.

More men arrived. Inside the fly-screened porch a trestle-table now stood heaped with platters of potato salad, coleslaw and lettuce, arranged round a vast pile of uncooked meat, pink in its pool of blood. I stared at each new face in search of Bowey, but none fitted the photograph the school secretary had given me. The evening wore on; Robert blackened the beef. Somebody brought me a plate of food at one point, and someone else handed me a bottle of beer. I answered banal questions about what sort of car I drove back home, and how I'd found the quality of light at Broken Hill, but everyone was holding back: I seemed to be the flame round which the party had gathered, but which nobody dared approach. Brent, I noticed, took his meal inside. He was visible through the kitchen window, yellow in the electric light, still bent to the task – his father explained – of repairing a water-pump. I feigned interest as the big man unfurled statistics about the station's irrigation network – twenty thousand gallons pumped up to a hundred and fifty miles away, daily – but the figures struck me less than the distance his son seemed determined to maintain. Darkness overran the purple sky and bats cut across the stars. The barbecue went out. Still Bowey hadn't appeared.

Geoff, the postman, stood before me in the lamplight, a full bottle of beer in his hand. 'So, big-shot. You found us eventually. Or we found you.'

I nodded.

He took off his baseball cap, wiped a streak of damp hair across his brow with the back of his hand, and flipped the hat back on, all in one movement.

'And it's all mate-this and help-you-out-that as far as you're concerned, eh?'

'I'm grateful.'

'Sure you are. And if I came unstuck in Pall Mall, you'd be there in your Lexus to take me for a ride too.'

I didn't have a chance to respond.

'Sure you would.' His smile was as lopsided as his walk. 'This road-train driver I know, he got so fed up rescuing stranded tourists, off road in their toy cars, out of petrol, with their popped tyres, their radiators holed, no water or blankets, he claims he ploughed straight over one once to save his brakes.'

I laughed. Beside me the dog growled. The man's eyes were black and reflected no light.

'No, seriously. And what part of a tourist do you think comes out the back of a road-train? Fuck all. Too many fucking big wheels. Not even a fluttering page of fucking passport, mate.'

The postman swayed before me, dragging on his beer, until one of Robert's massive hands gripped him by the shoulders and spun him away. 'Never mind Geoff,' he began to apologize. 'He's road-tired, drunk.'

Over his shoulder Geoff said, 'So you were lucky, Mr Piss Artist, weren't you? And one good turn deserves another. You won't forget, right?'

As her husband steered Geoff limping away, Jeanette bobbed apologetically at my side, saying something about the toll taken by an eight-hundred-kilometre postal round on Geoff's sense of humour, and I stared at her comic-book eyebrows and said, 'Where is your other son?'

Her mouth opened and shut again, pink face stricken red with embarrassment, or *shame*. It occurred to me that the family might be working in cahoots. They'd dragged me in from the desert, but for what? To keep me prisoner while Bowey, the guilty son, escaped. Saline solution, the doctor had called it, but what else might Jeanette, the former district nurse, have snaked into my arm through that tube? How long had I really lain tethered to the spare bed?

I took a step towards Jeanette and stumbled. Next, she

was guiding me by the forearm to a canvas chair beside the dead barbecue. Though I shook free of her hand I hadn't the strength to object. A director's chair, yet I was rudderless, with no clue what to do next. Wings beat in my chest; my heart did not feel up to the job of keeping blood in my head. While I struggled to compose myself, Jeanette's hands lowered a bowl of microwaved chocolate pudding and custard into the space between my knees.

'He's a long way out. He must have decided on another night in the ute,' she was explaining. 'But, please, my son needs this break. Brent will run you to him in the morning . . .'

'She's all I have!' I bellowed into the nurse's startled face, but my anger was overtaken by a searing heat. I came to my senses, thrust the bowl from my lap and, muttering apologies, stumped away to my room, where a red crescent burn on each inner thigh stood as the only reassurance I had not completely lost track of events.

26

Shortly after dawn I turned the hire car's key to hear its engine churn, fade and die. Above the water-tower a pair of magpie-like birds rose into a pale sky. I'm not sure where I'd have tried to go if the car had worked, yet the fact that it didn't quickened my suspicions. I hadn't damaged the engine: why wouldn't it start? I tried again and the whirring dropped an octave. A figure appeared in my rear-view mirror. Brent, bow-legged, thick arms swinging at his side. Seeing him, the dog turned circles in the dirt. The third time I turned the key the engine just click-click-clicked.

Brent drew open the passenger door. 'Wait, and I'll rejuice the battery from the truck,' he said. His shirt flapped open, a diagonal crease showing across the taut hairlessness of his chest. Until just a moment ago he'd been face down in a crumpled bed, but now he was busy reassuring me he'd mend my car after breakfast, if that was what I wanted, or else get it running when we returned from our trip to meet Bowey, out at the new fence-line, later on. His eagerness was as unnerving as the adjustable wrench clamped between his palm and the ripped denim grinning on his knee.

I could see no alternative to going with him. If the offer was a trick, if the family wanted rid of me and were relying upon Brent to see me gone, I'd have to cope. If he truly was taking me to meet Bowey, I'd face both brothers together, at last. I climbed out of the car and accepted Brent's offer, talking to him across its dirty roof. Confronted directly, the boy's assertiveness drained from his face. He looked down to button up his shirt, saying we could set out before breakfast if I liked. Generator noise frayed the early-morning stillness. I agreed, then went to retrieve my recharged mobile.

Messages had overrun the phone's memory. The first few were from my father, desperate for detail, angry at my silence, then resigned to relay his progress to Anna's bedside. I smiled, hearing him urge me not to give up hope, and turned from the dog's gaze as he told how he'd arrived at the hospital after midnight and spent the small hours watching her dream. His voice snagged, then cut out entirely.

I gritted my teeth, eager for more concrete information. But the next message was a distraction. Penny, anger spent, explaining in a clipped monotone that she was co-operating with a Financial Services Authority investigation. She'd turned our Guatemalan files over and would not be instructing counsel to oppose G-Com's impeding freezing order or go after the syndicates. Neither would she wait any longer for my explanation. She was tendering her resignation. A whining noise – feedback – rose in pitch as my teeth locked tighter. I pressed save and let the last voicemail begin.

'Son, listen. I've met the doctor. She's given me the facts, and they're . . . not good. What's more, she says she's explained the same to you, that you've been out here for over two weeks. She says you were here all that time, and then you just disappeared, in search of a someone you think is to blame. What . . . Why didn't you tell me? Now's not the time! What in hell are you thinking? Phantoms, son, ghosts. You've not returned a single call I've made! The doctor is worried for you. So am I. She says we owe it to Anna to do the right thing. I need you here, I can't do it alone. The doctor, Anna, me. We all need you. Please . . . get in touch.'

He sounded so unsure of himself, suddenly old. Jo Hoffman had undermined him. I was furious with the doctor, my anger exacerbated by . . . intimacy. I couldn't walk away from her. Anna bound us together. I stared at the phone, gathering myself to call Dad back and warn him not to give in, but did not dial. He'd said he couldn't *do it* alone. My silence marooned him on one side of the abyss: call and I might build a bridge. Cruel as it was, not contacting him for the time being would keep Anna safe. I was so close now, so nearly there. He'd understand. Once my investigation was complete, I'd explain.

A noise flared in the yard, tyres slewing to a stop in the dirt. I shouldered my briefcase – with the knapsack inside – and reached for my hat, hurrying as if it were likely Brent might take off into the bush alone. Stepping through the fly-screen door I saw the boys' parents by the pick-up. Jeanette, in a turquoise dressing-gown, was stowing cooler bags under the tarpaulin stretched across the tray. Robert, excited, clapped his massive hands.

'A relief? We're thrilled! Never mind last night,' he said, holding the door open for the dog to jump through. 'Cold snags, a slab of beer! Don't let these boys do you out of your lunch!'

Jeanette thrust a Thermos through the passenger window. My visit would be fruitful yet, she reassured me, eyebrows high. To be blind to the guilt of one of their sons didn't make this couple complicit. My hand was wet with dog lick. I raised it and waved back.

We drove east, into the glare, along a loose track of red and grey dirt. At times the ground was so soft it seemed the pick-up was floating. Then the back end would drift sideways and my heart would leap and Brent would steer one-handed into the slide, feet light on the pedals, until we were straight again. He barely slowed when the track's teeth poked through the dirt, let the pick-up weather the ridges and bumps flat out, only changing course to avoid the biggest ruts. With the windows resolutely down, the wind-roar in the cab blanked out the need for speech. Brent didn't turn from the wheel until some forty minutes after we'd begun, when a gate across the track forced us to stop. He looked at me, an automatic expectation – I'm driving, you get it – plain in his face. I jumped to the ground and let the truck through the gate. This helpfulness pricked Brent to play the host. 'So, there's upwards of a thousand kilometres of fence-line on Yellow-hammer,' he explained, as I retook my seat. We gathered speed past a desiccated emu hanging upside down in the wire. Brent looked at it through his side window and became almost enthusiastic. 'See those metal strips that hold the wires taut without the need for another post in the ground? Spacers, they're called, keeping the fence porous. Which means most of your roos, feral goats, emus and the like, anything with a bit of speed, can run through it. They hit a middle section of wire at pace and the whole thing'll twist flat for a second. Boom, they're over, gone.'

Politeness made me nod. I said nothing.

'But see how he hit next to a fixed post. That isn't moving. It's made of native pine.'

The truck was on the plane, a speedboat again.

Brent raised his voice. 'Bowey's gone lunatic hard at repairing the L-shaped section since he got back.' He nodded to himself. 'That'll be why he stayed out last night, to finish a stretch.'

'You think?'

Brent nodded vigorously, raising his voice. 'Sure! It's not like him to come on all false modest. And he's hopeless at fencing! You'd think he'd have bit your hand off to come in and take a break.'

We crested a rise, not high, but enough to reveal the cambered endlessness. It swamped the cab, killing our conversation. Brent squinted at the sun, put both hands on the wheel, and raced us into the distance.

Two hours and three gates later, when the monotony threatened to erode my sense of purpose altogether, a figure appeared on the horizon. Although we were still a long way away Brent's foot eased off the accelerator. He reached for the radio handset bolted to the dash and blipped the talk button twice. After a while a voice crackled somewhere behind my head. 'You there, then?'

Brent: 'Just about.'

I slid my briefcase from the footwell up on to my lap.

Jeanette, through the hiss: 'Give the man some space. Got that?'

Again the talk-button semaphore. If we hadn't been rolling to a stop I'd have had time to suspect a hidden meaning in this exchange. Give me space? Here! Every nerve felt distinct in my body, every atom. It was as much as I could do not to fly apart at the seams.

'Get out of the car,' I told Brent.

The boy's shoulders stiffened. He looked confused. 'But . . . you heard Mum. Give you guys time to talk business, she said.'

'It's the pair of you I want to speak to,' I whispered. My face was already filmy with sweat. I dragged a sleeve across my forehead. It occurred to me that I was in the middle of nowhere, beyond help, without a weapon. Brent's back was huge, sawing clear of his seatbelt. Why had I chosen to fight on enemy ground? Stepping from the truck I looked down and was further undermined by the sight of my trainers, comically pristine still, marching me through the dust.

Bowey did not look up as I approached. He stood silhouetted in the white heat, feet planted in the red earth, swinging a sledgehammer at the top of a wooden stake. Brent's boots crunched in the dirt behind me. Bowey, impregnable in his solitude, swung again, and again, and again, each hammer-blow – as we drew nearer – louder than the last. A roll of silver barbed-wire shone in the glare at the boy's feet. Once he'd driven the fence-post home, he tossed the sledgehammer aside and bent to unravel the wire.

I imagined the stake from above, as valiant as it was futile, and could not speak.

Bowey was still bent double, unhooking, unrolling, stretching out a tangle of wire. How pointlessly hard this task was, performed alone. Brent seemed to be thinking the same. He walked past me in silence and pulled a tool of some sort – a wooden stick complicated with nails – from the mess in the back of Bowey's pick-up, parked at an angle further down the track. Then he joined his brother.

I clutched my briefcase to my chest, felt my shirt stick to the wet oval of my back, and watched in silence as the brothers tensioned the wire and nailed it to the new post. Beside me, the dog snapped at its halo of flies. When they'd done, Brent took hold of his brother's shoulder, preventing him picking up the sledgehammer again. I walked towards them. Twins, yet Bowey was the shadow of his brother. Wire against a fence-post. He looked worn out, his cheeks hollow, his eyes dark and red-ringed beneath the brim of his hat. The one I wore was identical. I felt suddenly exhausted as well. It took everything I had to remove the canvas bag from my briefcase and hold it out to the two brothers.

'Which of you does this belong to?'

There was a pause, after which Brent said, 'What?'

Bowey took the bag from me, turned it over, limp in his hands.

Frustrated, Brent blurted, 'Tell him about the exhibition!' at me.

The rawness had passed from Bowey's face. His eyes filled with tears. He tried to hide this by looking at the ground. He patted his brother on the back and whispered, 'That ute's front shocks are shot. Seeing as you're here, could you have a look?'

Brent retreated.

Bowey's face was still downturned behind his hat-brim. Yet this was the boy, he was responsible, and he was before me at last. An immense stillness descended. It felt like relief. But even as the sky pressed down the relentless flies reminded me to *hate*. The contradiction was paralysing: I felt like an actor, thrust onstage; I'd prepared for the scene but forgotten my lines. I looked wildly about. A metal tine the length of a broomstick lay next to the fence-line, not five yards away. Before I knew what I was doing I'd dropped my briefcase and the spike was hot in my hands.

Bowey looked up and took a step backwards.

'I've just one question,' I said. '*Why?*'

He was still blinking back tears. 'Because I'm weak.'

'Not good enough. Don't give me that.'

He shrugged. 'It's the truth.'

'It's not the truth. It's an *excuse*. Something worse than weakness made you hurt her, something *deviant*. Admit what it is!' I gripped the heavy spike harder, turned sideways with it. 'She's mine. You couldn't have her, but why did you try to take her away from *me?*'

The dog, having sniffed its way along the fence, now came between us, head down, and pressed its wet nose against the boy's thigh. He kneed it aside roughly.

'Yours? Take Anna away?' Bowey moved towards the spike's sharp tip, shaking his head. 'You and her? She never mentioned anyone else. I don't know what you're on about, mate.' His voice faltered. He spoke as much to himself as me. 'I tried . . . but . . . I failed. I saved myself, I'm weak.'

The thought of Anna's fear in the waves swamped me again: the sea closing over her head, foam blotting out the sky, electric desperation in every limb. Again I felt the fist of water that pushed down her throat, its fingers in my lungs, sharp nails tearing from within. Drugged and dragged out to sea and abandoned by this boy, blind to his own evil, defiant even behind his cloak of excuses.

'And was it weakness that tempted you to blackmail, too?'

'Eh?'

I raised my voice, shook the tine. 'Open the bag, you worthless—'

Brent's voice drifted up from behind the second pick-up. 'Everything all right?'

Bowey said, 'Nothing!' over his shoulder and repeated to me, 'I don't get what you're on about, mate.'

I watched as he opened the flap and slid the contents from the knapsack. Unlike my hands, his were steady. They were also, I noticed, livid with cuts, cracks and calluses. I thought of barbed-wire, axe handles and nails. My own palms felt puffy round the ribbed metal spike.

'Did your cowardice stuff that envelope, too?' I asked.

The dog was squirming on its back at our feet. I couldn't watch the boy inspect his work, so focused on the dog's tongue, flopping grey-pink over its upper jaw. Instead of Bowey's face as he looked at the photograph, I saw the grinning wetness of the dog's yellow lower teeth. A dribble of sweat ran down the back of my right thigh. I heard the boy's sharp intake of breath and stared harder still at the dog, its tail a wiper blade in the dirt. There was a gentle thud as envelope and photograph hit the ground, and almost instantaneously I was on my back in the same red earth.

Blink, and your eyes open to the possibility of a different world.

The boy's weight pressed down: I was with Anna again, our lungs knocked empty of air. He had the metal bar pinned across my chest and I could not draw breath. His eyes were open immediately above mine, bloodshot yet full of light, green irises with amber spokes.

Assuming a game, the dog wriggled excitedly beside us.

Bowey's entire face was quivering. He rolled the spike up my chest. 'Who the fuck are you and where did you get this filth?'

My hands found his and closed over flint knuckles. I tried to roll sideways, pushing up against his weight, but he brought his forehead down hard into my face. It didn't hurt so much as cancel out all my efforts. He had the bar wedged across my throat now, crushing my windpipe. I felt heavy and knew I was somehow wrong to have accused this boy, whose eyes, it was obvious to me now, were full of *love*.

Anna's love; it belonged to her.

My agony was happiness and I had the thought again: *Give in*.

Then the pressure was gone and I was staring at the sky. I twisted sideways and saw the brothers staggering as one, Bowey's boots clear of the ground, Brent's thick arms round his waist. Bowey thrashed fishlike from side to side. Brent lifted him higher. Bowey's face was black with rage. He dropped the spike, but could not break free of his brother's grip.

My lungs had filled with air. I used it to hack out a word: 'Father!'

'Stop! What are you doing?' Brent shook Bowey, his face twisted with confusion.

'Anna's father,' I shouted.

Bowey's legs went slack. The pain caught up with me, a white heat to rival the sun. In flashes I saw that the dog's tongue was streaked with dirt licked from my face.

27

Two men follow me into the bar. The place is almost empty but they take seats at a table opposite mine. When the older man leans back circles of sweat under his arms become a third set of eyes.

Check my watch and think back to the morning. I managed to keep my teaspoon steady watching Sasha click through to my page on the agency website – but its figure-of-eight touched the side of the glass when she laughed at my request to see the other photos.

– God knows where they are now. If you care you'll just have to do a search.

– Surely there's a web address.

Sasha steadied my hand. – An address? There's hundreds. Whoever bought the pictures will have sold them on – and on.

I laid my spoon across its edge of saucer. Tip first then the handle.

Sasha laughed again. – If you're that bothered I'm sure I can get you a copy on disk. But you're better off counting the money I reckon.

The younger of the two men has a shock of surf-white hair. Something about it makes me look at him twice. He's wearing a sleeveless vest taut with belly bulge. Wipes a hand through his hair and then drags it across his chest. A habit – the white cotton there is already grey.

I pick up the drinks menu and recheck my watch. The client – my first since the day of the photographs – is now sixteen minutes late. It's not him I'm looking to the entrance for now though – the boy hasn't shown yet either and he's responsible for the quickstep in my chest.

The backs of my legs feel clammy. I rock from side to side in my chair and suffer a memory of doing the same thing in the school office a few years ago. Sticky legs beneath a short skirt. My heart beating hard in my ears seeing Dad stride through the frosted-glass door. By the time the headmistress had begun her offensive I knew it was the heat and traffic – not anger – that had turned his carved brow red.

– It's not just that she didn't show up for the gala. That's not the issue here. No. The problem is what Anna chose to do instead.

– Cut to the chase and tell me what she's done wrong.

– I think she should do that herself don't you?

– Oh for—

His anger was due to me so I shook my head and interrupted. – They banned Mr Hopwood from hanging Halle's nude in the hall. I organized a protest.

– What sort of protest?

– Anna stole every poster in the main building.

– I didn't st—

– And tampered with the school's art collection. Many of our pictures are valuable.

Dad pinched the arrow above his nose so I let her continue.

– Without the contents of our noticeboards the school's

extra-curricular activities ground to a halt yesterday afternoon. The woman had bloodless lips which puckered as her confidence grew. – And her meddling with the artwork amounts to a sort of vandalism.

– Vandalism? said Dad. – What did she do?

– I vandalized nothing. It was retaliatory censorship. We put the pictures face down on the ground. And we didn't steal the posters. We piled them outside the staff room.

– We? The arrow had relaxed. Now he was rubbing his nose to cover the beginnings of a smile behind his hand.

– A group of girls acted together. But we've established that Anna was the ringleader.

– I see. Dad glanced at his watch and sat back in his chair. – Tell me a bit more about the decision not to hang this girl's nude.

Sasha's promise to produce a set of the photographs put my mind at rest. It's not that I regret what I did in Edgecliff. Any embarrassment – like the thrill – faded with the woman's last flashgun burst. But I do want to see the results. I would have explained why if it hadn't meant telling her about the client photos again. That glint in her eye – which I used to think of as a spark of recognition between us – is at best unreadable now. Occasionally it flashes cold.

– Now you've started – she pulled the straw from her iced coffee and bent it into triangles – where do you suppose you'll stop?

I wasn't about to rise to this.

– You can save that decision for the next time you need the money I suppose.

I sipped my coffee and watched as she tied her straw in a knot.

– I mean photos are a stupidly easy way to cover the rent.

– Yeah – I replied a little too quickly. – It's all about the cash.

She smiled. – Sorry. I know you're not here for real – but I forget.

Walking out to the car park with Dad I felt deflated. The head had excluded me for a week. As much for leading others astray as wilfully disregarding the property and disrupting the smooth running of the school – she said. I wasn't bothered about the punishment. Screwing the woman's thin little mouth tight with disapproval was a victory if anything. But Dad's reaction made the pleasure hollow. He blipped the car's central locking and opened his door – motioning for me to let the hot air out by doing the same.

– The chances of you getting away with that were nil. He shook his head at me across the silver roof. – I mean. You fail to show for a gala in which you're anchoring the relay then wonder why they come knocking on your door.

I blew air up my face and shrugged.

– If it had been me I'd have turned all the posters and notices round. Pinned them face on to the corkboard. That would have looked funnier.

– I should have thought of that.

Knowing I wouldn't mind a week at home he hadn't fought the decision or even bothered to look particularly grave. If I'd glanced his way he'd probably have winked. Where was the rush in that? It hadn't even been necessary to tell the truth. I was no ringleader – Halle came up with the protest idea herself. Her abattoir nude did nothing for me. I only helped out of allegiance to Mr Hopwood – who a week beforehand had turned a blind eye when he walked in on me in a darkroom full of smoke.

Did I start the escorting and the photographs knowing they would snap the elastic of Dad's tolerance? To step beyond his borderless state? I shut my eyes. When I open them it's to see the bloke in the vest wiping his hand across his stomach again. The older man is reading a magazine now – but the one with the bleached hair is still looking at me. String vest – white-blond dreadlocks. For a moment I feel I recognize him from somewhere – but his blatant staring is the more likely source of my unease.

– What made you start doing this then? I asked Sasha, determined to step off the back foot. – And why do you carry on?

She pulled another knot in her straw tight. – The money. I already said.

– Sure but—

– No buts. Everything has a value. Some things are overpriced. There's hard boring work and there's easy cash. The combative glint in her eye softened then and I saw what she was saying at face value and although I merely smiled and shrugged again it struck me that I could have answered her because the novelty of the dates had – for me – worn off. Or rather the project had now changed shape. The news that I had a client for the evening made me happy – but not in itself I understood. Another client meant another evening watched over by the boy.

And it's him I'm still waiting for alone at my table five minutes later when I look over at the man with the bleached dreads again and realize I have seen him before and know where and feel the coolness in my veins turn to nails and fire. Grimy vest and salt-white dreadlocks. Ushering the agency's manager – Maggie – into the back of that dark green Volvo. I'm almost sure of it. Convinced enough that the consequences – inexorable as lava – start to flow. He's not just staring at me. He's watching me. Waiting to see what I do. Which means they must know about the photographs – Sasha must have shopped me. They're here to check if she was right – to see what happens next.

A flame of acid rises in my throat with the fear that the boy might turn up now. And I'm desperate to look up again on the off-chance that doing so could turn my memory into a mistake – Sydney's awash with blond surf-dreads after all – yet before I can summon the courage I sense both men stand and begin to move towards my table and I'm blinking at them with the fire bright now in both cheeks.

The older of the two men is still holding his magazine – a thumb keeping his place.

– Excuse me love he says.

I choke out a reply – Waiting for a friend.

The pair exchange a baffled look. The older man goes on gingerly. – Of course. And we'll leave you to do that. But could you tell us where to find this place first? His fingernail hovers above an advertisement for a Thai restaurant. – We just got here – its owner explains. – From out West.

Whooshing release speeds my voice up as I give the men directions. They thank me in unison and leave. My shivering knees are a convenient excuse to sit still a little longer and wait.

Sticky rain has begun to fall. I step off the pavement to skirt a drunk lying in the doorway of an electrical shop and see myself on the bank of television screens above him – landing ankle deep in gutter-puddle. As I balance one-legged – shaking a dripping high-heel – a hand steadies my shoulder.

– Change of plan?

The boy's camera bumps my ribs as I right myself against him – but it's the warmth of his gentle grip I know I'll remember. His eyes are bright with shop light and reflected relief. I'm still holding on to his arm after I've put my shoe on. Letting go feels an oddly self-conscious act.

– Cancellation. I only came to tell you not to wait.

– Righto. His cheeks are hollower than I remember. No – he's sucking them in – wry. – You got anything else lined up?

I shake my head in disappointment. – No, but I'll give you a call when I do.

– I meant now. He focuses on adjusting his camera strap. – I wasn't planning on shooting any tourists tonight. We could get ourselves something to eat.

In the noodle bar my chopsticks are clumsy. I reach for my beer to steady my nerves and knock an eggcup of soy sauce into the boy's lap – thinking that the performance of escorting does not compare. Does not – did not. Though I'm convincing with the truth – that I'd already made up my mind to stop – the contradiction raises colour in my cheeks. He does a good job of ignoring this – telling me there are more than enough outtake photographs from the dates for me to work with. In fact he seems emphatically pleased. He weighs his words like each one's bought on credit – which makes me gabble idiotically. Only when he's walking me home do I relax enough to stop filling in the gaps.

28

Bowey drove. I sat on the torn seat beside him, Jeanette's icepack pressed to my forehead, watching the countryside roll past. Whereas before I'd just seen sameness, the landscape now was ever-changing. The searing brightness, which had seemed to stamp the flatness with a uniform glare, in fact moved over the land like a ripple across water, raising mirages, bleaching grey scrub pale silver, scorching the red earth of the foreground to a distant, shimmering pink. At dusk on the first day a cloud of white cockatoos erupted from the bush ahead, wheeled towards us as one, and shot upwards over the pick-up. I turned round to follow them but they were already engulfed in our signature of dust.

The boy's rage when I showed him the photograph did more than prove he hadn't sent it. As Waller had claimed, Bowey had tried, and failed, to save Anna at sea. Whoever had sent the photograph had begun by using it to persecute my daughter. They'd entrapped her and shorn her of her senses, humiliated her and driven her into the water by threatening to publish her shame. Which made sense of the drugs, too. Oblivion beckoning, she'd fought Bowey off. Bile rose in my throat. Though I banged the icepack down on the dashboard and opened my door the truck was still rolling as I retched into the dirt.

Afterwards Bowey passed me a bottle of water, apologizing that it was warm. The boy held himself responsible for everything. In the aftermath of our fight, once he knew who I was, he was mortified to have hurt me, and he still looked compressed by guilt. We swerved to avoid a tangle of bleached bones in the middle of the track. I had to tell him, and did. 'Nobody's dead,' I said.

'What's that?'

'I said Anna isn't dead.'

He stopped the car hard. Dust caught us up, fogging the windows. 'But I called the hospital the day afterwards. They said she hadn't made it.'

'They were wrong.'

'No hope of recovering. That's what they said.'

'You spoke to a female doctor, right?' The anger I felt thinking about Jo Hoffman was cut with an inexplicable urge to smile. 'She's a pessimist, but tell me, did she actually say Anna was dead?'

He thought for a moment. 'No, but—'

'No buts.' My voice sounded persuasive. 'Anna's chances of recovery were slight, but the doctor miscalculated. She has no head for odds. I do. Trust me, I know about these things. Improbable things happen and I take care of them. There's always room for hope.'

Bowey looked sideways at me and tightened his grip on the steering-wheel. The determined line of his mouth had relaxed. He drew a breath, as if weighing another question, but let it out without asking me anything, which made me feel happy and worried at the same time. His will to believe was as strong as mine. Yet as soon as I stopped comforting myself about Anna the warm feeling wore off. Reassurance had the same effect as hard drink: each gulp of heat meant a worse chill to come. To stop my shivering I drank again, explaining to Bowey how I'd befriended Dr Hoffman and won from her the promise that the hospital would not give up. He listened in silence.

On our return to the farmhouse at Yellowhammer, Jeanette had been unable to focus further than the bruise spreading either side of my swollen nose. Her fake eyebrows dipped woodenly, no match for the crumpled concern of her mouth. She'd fussed over me with her frozen peas and field-strength painkillers, insistent that it was out of character for Bowey to have lost his temper, pitifully hopeful I'd consider his pictures regardless. In not correcting her assumption beforehand I'd been to blame, so now I merely nodded.

Bowey was in charge. I'd run out of next steps but he bristled with purpose, storming round the oversized house in search of my kitbag and clothes for himself. I looked on through the fly-screen as he dumped our bags into the tray of his battered pick-up and reversed across the yard. There was a bang as the tailgate clipped one of the legs of a rusty fuel tank perched among the workshops, which summoned the boys' father from a nearby door. His consternation had nothing to do with the collision or my black eye, however, but with the thought that we might be leaving without first having eaten lunch. Bowey, ignoring him, kept pumping the fuel. I told the big man we hadn't yet tackled the provisions his wife had packed that morning. He tried unsuccessfully to look as if I'd made a valid point before setting off in search of more cold meat.

Shortly after the explosion of cockatoos Bowey pulled off the road for the night. We rolled to a stop in a clear patch among clumps of needle-sharp grass and he set about building a fire with mechanical practice. I was grateful to his father then, for the woodsmoke instantly hollowed out my stomach, but the boy's expertise with the fire was not matched by his cooking. I watched him char three sausages before offering to reheat the rest myself. The occasional crackling of the embers only deepened the quiet once we'd finished eating.

'I didn't know whether I was chasing you or your brother at first,' I began.

In the firelight Bowey's eyes glowed gold.

'I wasn't sure which of you had been with Anna. In the waves.'

'She'd have been better off with Brent.'

'The sea's no water tank. She's a strong swimmer herself.'

'It's not that.'

I watched him picking at the back of his hand, his knuckles saw-teeth in shadow.

'Growing up round here,' he said, 'you're taught to steer clear of snakes. Most of them are harmless, but some do bite. A nip from one or two is the last thing you'll feel.'

I nodded, with no idea where he was going.

'The boys on the station, though, they'll catch a poisonous snake if they can. There's money in milking them for anti-venom.'

A shooting star speared towards the horizon. I wanted to point it out, but could tell Bowey hadn't finished.

'If the boys catch a snake they stick it in a sack and keep it in one of the sheds until someone goes into town. When we were small Dad would let us watch the sack moving from a distance, because that was safe. The bulging always reminded me of a tongue trying to get out of a shut mouth.'

My tongue began probing my cheek. I looked up to see if his was doing the same but couldn't tell; his face was turned away from the fire.

'There was this older kid on the station, one of the mechanic's sons. He had a thing about snakes. It wasn't enough for him to watch a bulging sack. He would sneak in and unhook the bag and stand it on the ground and slowly let the neck open to see what was inside. We were more scared of what Dad would do if he caught us doing that than we were of whatever stupid snake was in the sack. So we watched through the shed window until one day when Dad was out mustering feral goats and Mum was away in town, and since there was no danger of being caught we went inside with this boy, Stoney, he was called, and stood next to him as he took the sack down and put it on the ground and let the neck flap open and wallop, the snake struck, hit him right on the chin.'

Bowey flicked at his jaw with a middle finger, then shook his head.

'I was out of that shed before the bag hit the floor. But when I looked round I was standing in the yard alone. I ran to the window and saw Brent dragging Stoney wide of the coiled snake, across the cement floor. I couldn't have told you my name just then, but once Brent got Stoney out of the shed he had the presence of mind to go back and shut the door.'

'What happened to the boy?'

'Oh, he was all right. We'd stopped thinking he was dying by the time everyone got back. Dad killed the snake with a shovel later that day. Eastern Brown, and they're deadly all right, but from the look of the scratch, Dad said, it hadn't landed much of a bite.'

I gave a no-harm-done-then shrug.

'That's not the point, though,' Bowey insisted. 'Since then I've always known, deep down, Brent is made of something better than me. I spent ten years telling myself that next time I'd keep my head. But with Anna in that rip, when she fought me off . . . I can't even remember the moment I turned to swim ashore. It was no more my choice than when I ran from the shed, which only makes it worse. I love her, but something buried in me gave up.'

He was talking under his breath. I had to lean forward to hear.

'Then, when I realized what I'd done, on the shore, I ran again. Pointless. Nowhere is far enough away.'

He had begun to rock on his heels – as Gil had said he did on the beach. I wanted to steady him now, but didn't. Though the fire glowed red from a distance, on closer inspection each ember was edged grey, white, black. I believed that Bowey loved my daughter and that he hated himself for failing her. The problem was that I sympathized with both the love and hatred. He hadn't caused the accident, so he wasn't to blame, yet neither had he been prepared to give everything to prevent it, which made him guilty, too.

I tried to change the subject. I asked Bowey how he and Anna had met. I thought I wanted to know, but as soon as the boy started mumbling about a bar in Sydney where – news to me – she had worked, my hands began to worry at one another. A mosquito landed on my upturned wrist. I watched it sidestep on spindly legs and thought of the fuel tank Bowey had reversed into, an imminent mosquito bite being preferable to the thought of Anna fending for herself, alone, in a place I'd never been. I brushed the mosquito away. The boy noticed my attention wander and seemed relieved that I wasn't going to ask him for specifics.

'That's where you and I start looking,' he said. 'I was with her every step between the bar in Sydney and Byron Bay. Nothing . . .' he paused '. . . happened.' He cleared his throat. 'So whoever sent you the photograph will have done so from Sydney.'

I nodded agreement. 'The postmark said as much.'

'There was a friend, another waitress she worked with. We'll begin by finding her.'

Bowey's head-butt had shocked me into seeing we were on the same side, but until now I hadn't allowed myself to think how I'd find out whom I should have been chasing, who our real enemy was. Now, hearing that the boy had a plan, I balled up my fists and ground them against one another, relishing the pressure of bone against bone.

'Who's this friend, then?'

'I didn't meet her as such.'

'But you have a name.'

'I'll know her when I see her again.'

This sounded flimsy, but I resisted the temptation to press him with questions. I sat waiting for him to give me something else to go on instead. But when he began talking again he started on a completely different tack.

'Brent told me you had a hell of a ride out to us. The car getting bogged, losing your keys, collapsing from the thirst.'

I nodded.

'You were never that far from water, you know.' He moved towards me in the firelight and drew a line between us in the dirt. 'That track you were stuck on, there was a fence either side of it, remember?'

I told him yes.

'A fence means a paddock and a paddock means livestock. Livestock need water.'

'I could barely walk a hundred yards. How was I supposed to find a water trough in all that empty space?'

'Think about it, though. The water doesn't spring out of the ground, not here. There's just the one river, and that's a hundred miles away. We *pipe* the water to the animals.'

'Good for you. I don't see how knowing that would have helped.'

'You're not thinking. We have to have access to the pipes, to lay them in the first place, to repair them when they bust. You've seen odd splashes of green all alone by the side of the road?'

I nodded.

'Why do you reckon they're there? Because the plastic pipe buried alongside the road – running alongside just about every bush road – has sprung a leak.' He drew another line parallel to the first in the dirt. 'We spend half our time repairing the damn things, driving the tracks looking for green patches to dig up.'

'There was nothing green near where I was.' I shrugged. 'Not that I remember, anyway.'

A smile filled out the hollowness of Bowey's face. 'You

don't wait for the pipe to break! Find yourself a stick, a rock, use your fingers if you have to, dig a line from each fence to the edge of the road. We don't lay the pipes deep. It'd take a couple of hours at most to hit plastic and crack it open.' He laughed. 'Bingo, all the water you could need.'

I found myself laughing with him. Then our laughter merged and we were laughing together, and I forgot why. But only for a moment. Whether it was guilt or self-consciousness or just that the togetherness cancelled itself out, I don't know, but one of us broke off and we were both suddenly quiet. I stared up at the sky again and saw another shooting star, and then another, and I was glad not to have pointed out the first because, as we both sat in silence again, it seemed I had only to wait a minute or two from one slash of silver to the next.

29

Mid-morning, and Sydney harbour couldn't hold the light. I squinted at the sun on the water and saw television static. We crossed the bridge. The needlepoint brightness below us, and Bowey's certainty, and the fact that I was no longer alone, lifted my spirits. I gave into the sensation, let my heart fill with hope.

So optimistic was I, in fact, that I'd decided to call my father. Perhaps he had good news. Enough time had passed since his message to allow for hope of that, too. And if things hadn't changed, if he was still at Anna's bedside, he'd need my encouragement to carry on waiting. I felt sorry that I'd left him to cope alone for so long.

As soon as I decided to call, I became impatient to do so. I barely noticed the ratty hostel Bowey checked us into, just nodded at the Irish proprietor, who welcomed Bowey back like a lost son. He had two fingers missing from one hand. I thrust a credit card across the countertop and pretended to study a faded map of Sydney pinned to the wall. It seemed to take the man a long time to process the transaction with those fingers he had left. 'Sorry, mate, no go,' he said eventually, giving the card back to me.

I opened my mouth to tell him to try again, then saw

Bowey reaching for his own wallet and gave the man my personal American Express instead.

The room I found myself in was really half a room, divided from Bowey's by a thin wall, in the middle of which stood a connecting door. It felt like some sort of a stage set. The stud wall shuddered when I dropped my kitbag on to the bed. Never mind audible, Bowey's movements behind the partition – kicking off his shoes, puffing up a pillow – were amplified by the hostel's acoustics.

An image of seashells and feathers came to me as I asked the hospital receptionist to put me through to Anna's room. Dad picked up on the second ring and launched right in. 'Will, Jesus! Where in hell have you been?' His anger eclipsed any sorrow, which was good. I felt my chest inflate. He wanted an explanation. I gave it to him, buoyed a little more with each word I said. Of course, I was not so cruel as to tell him everything. I watched myself in the mirror above the wash-basin, describing Jo Hoffman's first telephone call, my meetings with the police, lifeguard and witnesses, my success with the newspaper ad and Bowey's canvas bag. The planes of my face had been softened by something: not just beatnik hair, I saw, peering at the mirror more closely, but a tan. It made me look younger and . . . more vulnerable, warm flesh in place of carved wood. There was no need to burden Dad with the photograph. My time in the outback helped explain away why I hadn't been in touch. Anna had been derailed in Sydney, I told him, persecuted and driven to despair. Since he'd probably know as much from the hospital, I told him about the blood tests. He was on my side, so I could trust him to join the dots. I've noticed as much at work: leave gaps and people who want your business will fill them with what suits them best. When I explained how I'd enlisted Bowey's help to track down our enemy the sound of my voice in the phone's earpiece, echoing back to the rhythm of my father's breathing, was so convincing it made the hair stand up on the back of my neck.

Dad didn't reply. I listened to his breathing long enough to notice that my nape was no longer tingling. Like the rest of me it just felt clammy. I thought of the creases on the back of Dad's neck. When he's worried he puts his hand flat across them and grips hard: Anna says it looks like he's holding his head in place. The phone was still pressed to my ear. I stood there waiting for him to say something, picturing him anxiously kneading red skin at the base of his skull, and realized I was doing exactly the same thing. I let go quickly and whispered, 'Dad?'

'You're in Sydney?' His voice was tight.

'I just got here, yes.'

'That's hundreds of miles away.'

My heart had begun to race. 'How else do you expect me to track the guy down?' I said.

'But, but—' He sounded further away now than he had in England. 'What does it matter, for now, how this happened?' he said eventually. 'Jo – the doctor – needs us to act on where Anna *is*. I don't know what her – state was when you left, Will, but—'

The temptation to silence him with the photograph was almost overwhelming. An image of Jo Hoffman's black hair, slicked back in wet seal-fur tongues, came to mind instead. 'I know the doctor, Dad. You should have seen her to begin with. I can encourage her again – to have more faith.'

I heard him sucking air through parted teeth. 'She has

Anna's best interests at heart, son. I'm here now and I'm convinced of that.'

I've never taken the gift of Dad's help for granted, but gifts can be painful to receive. When she was about seven Anna told us both she needed a costume for her school Hallowe'en play. I was away on business the night beforehand so Dad sacrificed an old umbrella to make her a set of devil wings. It wasn't that I minded binning my shop-bought outfit, but the assumption that I'd forgotten rankled. The certainty of his help both reassured and undermined me, as if I were walking the high wire above a safety net. Dad talked on about read-outs and prognoses but a thought, harsh as a face full of torchlight, blinded me to his meaning. Perhaps I hadn't told Dad when I first heard about Anna's accident to avoid being usurped. Though I blinked, a resentful afterglow persisted. Those devil wings beat in my chest. This was ridiculous! I was shielding *him* from the truth about Anna, not the other way round.

'Tell the doctor we're to hold out for Anna's recovery at all costs.'

'Hold on and I'll fetch her, you can tell her yourself.'

'Dad.'

'She'd want to speak to you. It's not just Anna she's concerned about.'

'I'll be with you soon. The minute we're done here I'll book a flight. I should get on now—'

'No,' he said. 'Wait.' Bowey was washing his face in the next room; the water running from his basin sounded like it was leaking across my floor. 'There's post here for you, Will, marked urgent. And switchboard have put through three calls in the last day. What do you want me to do about that?'

'Bin it, answer for me, what do I care? It's not imp—'
Suddenly I was back-pedalling in mid-air. 'Hold on. Listen,
Dad. This will have to do with my investigation.' I flipped
through the contents of my wallet in search of the hotel
credit-card receipt. 'Whatever you do, please don't open anything addressed to me. Got that?'

'Will—'

'I mean it. You'll jeopardize everything if you so much as
break the seal on that envelope.'

'I wasn't—'

'Redirect the mail.' I read out the hostel's address. 'Give
the caller my mobile number. Promise me now you'll do that.'

There was a pause. Eventually he said, 'Of course,' in a
tone so resigned it almost made me doubt myself.

I hung up.

It seemed farcical to go into the corridor and knock on
Bowey's door in order to speak to him, but that was what I
did. I explained I needed to take a walk. We'd already decided
to wait until lunchtime before going after Anna's friend. The
bar didn't open until then. I'd been happy for the boy to over-
hear my conversation with Dad, confident that news of Anna
would do him as much good as me. But I didn't necessarily
want him in on my chat with the bank. In ten years they've
never, that I can remember, stopped one of our cards. Perhaps
it was being back in a city that made me eager to sort out the
problem immediately, or perhaps I already secretly suspected
the inevitability of what the account manager – who took an
age to come to the phone – was explaining as the street-
sweeping truck ground past the doorway I was sheltering
in. I heard 'unopposed freezing' and polystyrene scraping
cement and 'regret for now' and diesel revs and 'G-Com's

lawyers' and bristles on Tarmac and 'have it all ironed out'. A woman with a shaved head sucking a lollipop walked bare-foot in the wetness of the truck's snail-trail, placing one foot in front of the other with a beam-walker's care. 'We will, of course, act immediately on any order Taylor Blake's lawyers obtain.' The man was easier to hear now; there was even, I'm sure of it, a gratifying frog in his throat. 'But unless there's anything I can help you with in the meantime, I'm afraid—'

'What you staring at?' The girl had stepped towards me, clicking grimy fingers in my face. Abruptly she smiled. 'Relax. I'm just the lollipop girl. You know, the one you've heard so much about.'

I nodded at her, then saw she had hitched her skirt above a bruised knee and I turned away. She laughed happily, repeating, 'The lollipop girl! Remember me.' Though I spoke into the mouthpiece authoritatively the phone buzz told me my conversation was over. I'm not sure whether I was more relieved about that or that when I next looked up the girl was stalking the truck again.

It took me a while to rewind to the hostel: I'd not paid atten-tion to where I was walking and had no mental map of this new city I was in. At home I keep my eyes on the street, but here, every block or so, I found myself looking up. The sky above was offensively blue, the sun painfully bright. It scored the outlines of buildings, lampposts and trees with a blade-sharp edge. At street level everything sparkled: shop-fronts, windscreens and bicycle spokes; café tables, cutlery and bottle-tops; cuticles, eye-whites and teeth. The light was forensic, giving the city a sanitized feel. And yet everywhere

I looked I saw evidence to the contrary. In the middle of a row of gleaming taxis a man with a tattooed face and neck sat slumped on the kerb, his contrasting Scots-white arms hugging his knees, a pool of vomit at his feet. A skeletal Asian girl stalked the pavement in their midst, wearing a bra top and oversized plastic high heels, each step an effort; it seemed she was struggling simultaneously to keep her shoes on and kick herself free. Pausing outside the hostel I saw handcuffs flash on the hip of a policeman stepping from a squad car on the opposite side of the street. Such seediness – made invisible by the cement-dust skies back home – was thrown into relief, exaggerated even, by the prevailing airbrushed perfection here. A film set, it felt like, a backdrop for some sort of performance. Was that also what Anna had seen?

Bowey was pulling leaves from a potted palm in the foyer when I stepped inside. He threw them aside when he saw me and asked, 'Where have you been?'

I checked my watch. 'There's still an hour to go,' I said.

'That's when the bar opens, yes. But the staff have to get the place ready before they let customers in. Our best chance of catching the girl alone is when she turns up for work.'

I allowed him to lead me out past the squad car – the policeman I'd seen was still there, occupied with nothing more sinister than handing coffee through the open door to his colleague – and up the mirror-bright street. There was no spring in Bowey's step as he walked; he had the measured stride of someone used to covering long distances on foot. I fell in beside him and was surprised when, after no more than a hundred yards, he stopped. He pointed out a building opposite, which housed the bar where Anna had worked. The place was unremarkable; a TV-sports bar called Final Score, complete with stumps and rugby-ball motif. I could not imagine Anna wanting to work somewhere like that back home. One telephone call and I'd have sent her more money. The 'Happy Hour' sign pained me. Though it should have made no difference, I could not bear that she had come unstuck somewhere so banal.

'You met her here, then?' I asked.

'Once or twice.'

'I meant the first time.'

He shook his head and said, 'There's a café across the street. We can watch the entrance from there.'

Bowey retreated into the shade of a nearby awning and began repositioning chairs before I could go on. He didn't pick a spot with a clear view, by the pavement, as I would have done, but his movements were so sure of themselves I found it impossible to suggest anything different. Once he was installed I passed him a menu. He waved it away, intent on the bar all the while, muttering that I should order two of whatever I was having instead.

I thought back to Byron Bay, where I'd staked out the Defoes. Alone, then, I'd had difficulty concentrating. Bowey, by contrast, could apparently watch for ever, despite my questions, which, as minutes turned to hours, and the bar's employees gave way to customers, I could not stem.

'You're sure you'll recognize this girl when you see her?'

'Yes.'

'But you don't have a name.'

'No.'

'And you've never spoken to her.'

He shook his head.

'Have you been in the same room as her even?'

'No, not as such.'

'How, then, can you be so—'

His eyes flicked to mine, then returned to the bar's entrance. 'I don't forget a face.'

I picked an ice cube out of the jug on the table, placed it on the pavement, watched the ice melt rapidly and the water shrink to a dot. Before the dot disappeared entirely I gave in to the impulse to voice a fear and suggested the girl might not be working that shift. This possibility had seemed so obvious to me it barely needed stating, but apparently the thought hadn't occurred to Bowey: he was crestfallen.

'Do you know her face well enough to describe?' I asked him.

'Of course.'

'Why don't we ask one of the others when she's next on, then?'

Where lying in wait had suited the boy, the threat of confrontation made him hesitant. 'We might scare her off,' he said.

'We don't have to mention Anna.'

'But—'

I dismissed his further objections by striking out across the road. Sure enough, he followed. Our shadows, striding in unison over the Tarmac, were cartoon-black, like moving paint.

We perched on bar stools before a chest-high chrome table; if possible, the place had less appeal inside than out. Bowey's calm had deserted him. His eyes wove from wall to mirror to television to television to mirror to wall. I couldn't fathom his nerves, not until he turned to look at me and I saw that his face was trembling like liquid in a jolted glass. It was the same face that had stared down at me in the dirt, overrun with rage.

'I can't believe she'd do that to me,' he muttered. 'No way. Not voluntarily.' A girl approached our table. I hushed him but he went on, 'I already showed her to herself, she had no need.'

I'd have asked what he meant, but the waitress was upon us. She raised a pad to take our order. Each of her fingernails was painted a different colour.

Abruptly Bowey snapped free and smiled. 'Two beers, please.'

'Anything else?'

'Yes. You been here long?'

The girl rolled her eyes and gave her watch a 'not already' look.

'No,' I reassured her. 'He means, have you worked at this bar for long?'

She shrugged. 'Long enough.'

'My friend here is a photographer. There's a girl who works here who we want to get in touch with. It might earn her some money.' I forced myself to cast Bowey's baited hook. 'Modelling opportunity, fashion stuff.'

The waitress's face lit up.

Bowey went on. 'Your height, grey eyes, kind of what-you-looking-at face. She's got long reddish hair, dyed, I think. When I saw her she was wearing it up.'

The girl's smile melted and her mouth opened a fraction. She raised her crayon-set fingers to her bottom lip and slowly shook her head.

Bowey's knuckles were bunched against the table's edge.

'Some sort of tattoo on her right forearm. A totem pole or something.'

'Sasha!' The girl gave a little jump and then her shoulders slumped. There was a leaden predictability about what came next.

We had a name, but the girl it belonged to no longer worked at the bar. She'd left a fortnight beforehand. I tipped the waitress for trying, but although she asked the rest of the staff, this Sasha hadn't left a forwarding address. Bowey's face drained whiter than the froth on our untouched beer. He was swaying on his stool. I scribbled down my number for the waitress and hurried him outside for some air.

30

Defending the fortifications on Manly beach proves futile. The kids we inherited the castle from were wise to leave when they did – before the tide turned. An hour later and it's all falling into the moat. Vic doesn't help. Wherever Bowey tries to work – shoring up a burst wall here and replacing a collapsed turret there – the dog digs next to him – literally undermining his efforts. We give up. I pour us each another plastic cup of Bundaberg and Coke – pre-mixed in Bowey's hostel room – and we retreat up the beach to watch the sea do its worst.

We've spent six of the last seven nights together. Still – when Bowey's knee brushes against mine I'm alive to the grains of sand that stick to my calf and those that fall to the ground. Feel the grit and the feathery tumble and the pressure of skin against skin as if for the first time. Bowey reaches down to brush the rest of the sand away and I am captivated by the hairs on the back of his wrist. I see them separately – each one salty and wiry and unremarkable – and together as part of the perfectly unrufflable texture of him.

– So monster trucks I say.

– You don't have to come. But I've promised I'll do it.

– No. I want to. The thing is – I think you're just pretending it isn't your scene.

He points at the back of his head. – Do you see a mullet here?

– Not now but—

– I need the cash if we're going to head up the coast. He puts an arm round my shoulders. – I lost my only regular job you see.

Money-regret surges past when he says this. The truth is – since that last no-show date – Sydney's glitter has palled. I feel a different kind of watched here now. And my memory is playing tricks on me. Can't quite recall whether Maggie's minder had bleached dreads or yellow surf-locks – but all of a sudden there's both everywhere. Each street-corner glimpse of shaggy pale hair makes me flinch. Yes – I want to start on up that coast more than Bowey knows. Something precious means something to lose. If he'd only told me he needed cash I'd have kept some back.

We gather our towels and stagger soft-footed from the beach. An evening breeze raises whitecaps in the harbour. Despite the dog's barking a seagull hangs in the evening air just feet from the back of the ferry – where we stand at the rail. I'm not really a dog person – they've always struck me as sappily dependent creatures – but the other morning I woke up to see Vic sitting before Bowey's shut hostel-room door – waiting for the boy to come back from his shower – and something hopeful in the set of the dog's shoulders made me get out of bed and scratch it behind the ears.

The bus back from Circular Quay takes us past the restaurant I met Sasha in yesterday. She was wearing a long-sleeved top but her wrist poked out of the cuff as she laid the envelope on the table between us – revealing a lipstick-red welt. When I opened my mouth to say something she immediately started explaining how she'd had it with the bar. I found myself sympathizing with that instead. Said she thought a shift there meant more hassle than a night out with a client. I told her I'd already handed in my notice.

– I know she said. – What's his name then?

I raised an eyebrow.

– Your phone goes dead to the agency and you leave the bar and get all panicky about these photographs. Has to be because you've met some fella.

– Maybe I just want a change.

Her smile ebbed to a sneer and back again. – Sure you do.

– Think what you like but not that I'm panicky about these. I put a hand on the package. – I'm just curious. These are evidence. The experience is just a blur of velvet and cat fur without them.

Sasha's fingers closed over mine on top of the photographs. I looked down and saw the mark across her wrist again before she quickly pulled the hand away.

Bowey picks up his equipment and we catch a train north to the suburbs for his date photographing polished chrome. If Sydney is tropical Europe – Californian mall-sprawl is duplicated here. Although we arrive early the air is already heavy with fumes and the metal thunder of engines. Hadn't expected a circus – but that's what we find complete with battered clown cars and hoops of fire and a ringmaster in a top hat. Bowey steers me through a crowd full of denim and ponytails to a caravan hatch. Orders us both a hotdog from a man with a purple handlebar moustache. The PA system pumps a brand of especially tinny surf rock across the arena – enough to prompt a stab of fondness for the bar's comparative sophistication. Mustard drips on to my bare toes. I bend down to wipe it off and feel the ground – my foot – hand – and heart shake. Earthquake revs drown out the ringmaster's announcement as the first shiny lorry drives round the arena. The crowd claps. I bump my head on Bowey's lens and press my laughter into his chest.

Sasha and I sat back from the table – both staring at the package between us.

– Thanks for bringing these anyway I said. And I reached to slide the photographs into my bag.

She grabbed my hand again. – Hold on.

I spread my fingers wide.

– They don't give anything away for free.

– Fine. I'll pay.

– Don't you want to look through them first?

– To be honest – no. I'll take the set either way. How much do they want?

– That's the thing.

A sigh escaped me. Sasha seemed to soften hearing it. – These are businesspeople we're talking about. They sense an opportunity to make money and they take it. You should forget the whole thing. If you're ready to move on then do just that.

– How much?

She licked her lips again. – They want two thousand bucks.

After the first intermission Bowey and I move round the ring so he can take photographs against a different backdrop. Beyond the floodlit arc the sky is cavernous and indigo and full of stars. We skirt the crowd – end up among a row of trailers. Power cables and hoses coil like spilt entrails in the dirt. Rounding a corner we come across a man in a motorcycle helmet and rhinestone jumpsuit – undone to the waist – peeing against a eucalyptus. He shakes himself down and shudders and turns round as he puts himself away. Bowey wishes him luck. I give a little wave. A hornet buzz starts up in the arena. We duck beneath hoardings and rejoin the ringside crowd and cheer as one two three four motorbikes scissor past one another in mid-air.

– Ripper! shrieks the PA.

Bowey is grinning one-eyed into his camera-back.

– Admit it! I yell. – They're for your bedroom wall.

– My brother's maybe. Not mine.

– A little brother – how sweet!

He lowers his camera. Still smiling. – Not little exactly.

Though Bowey tries to keep up his charade I can tell he's listening to the commentary – sucking down the torque and horsepower and r.p.m. I bob to the Van Halen and drink warm beer and when he cranes forward to see a jet-propelled van enter the ring I stand on tiptoes too. I glance sideways again to drink in the sight of his boyish eagerness – all the sweeter because he can't cover it up – and my teeth shut hard as a shock of blond hair ducks backwards behind him through the crowd.

Everything's for sale and all prices are negotiable and life is business and business is poker and in the end it all boils down to a matter of bluff. It makes Dad happy to say stuff like that – but I doubt even he believes it. Whether Sasha dreamed up this extortionate price for the photographs herself or was delivering someone else's blackmail wasn't the point.

– What happened to your arm? I asked.

– Nothing. She plucked at her sleeve.

– The same nothing that hurt your neck a while back?

There was something fragile about the flicker of a smile she mustered but it was gone as fast as it came – hidden behind a stony cool. She licked her lips and said – The same nothing that has to do with you.

– Was it a client?

Sasha turned her gaze to the window. – A client? No.

Her bored-to-distraction look said she was anything but. I told her I'd be back in a minute – made for the ladies' and slipped out of the restaurant unseen. There was a cashpoint down the street. If it hadn't refused to let me have the full amount I wouldn't have had the idea I did before the teller inside – to with-draw everything from my account. All my unspent escort money. There'd be symmetry in giving it to Sasha – perhaps she'd use it to move on herself. This thought lit me from within. Not want-ing to return flustered I shade-hopped back to the restaurant slowly and paused in the entrance's air-con waterfall before retaking my seat.

– There you are. I put the money down in front of her.

Sasha glanced down at the bundle of notes. – Don't be daft she said.

– I've added some extra. Think of it as a thank-you.

Sasha looked at me uncertainly. – A set of prints. She tapped the package. – They're not offering you negatives or computer files or whatnot. The fine lines scoring her lips grew more pro-nounced as her uncertainty deepened to concern. – You can't buy back what you sold. Let it go. Why allow them to take the piss like this?

– I'm hoping to leave town in a few days. To go up the coast. I dropped my voice conspiratorially. – If you're able to pick me up a going-away present before then—

– Sure – I'll score – whatever. She pushed the money back at me. – But I only brought the pictures so you could see them. Take a look and then let me tell her where to go!

We'd emerged from the chicane of her concern in different positions. She'd betrayed herself with compassion for me. I felt the exhilaration of the open road ahead. I took the package and put it into my bag.

– Don't worry Sasha. I want you to have this money. I couldn't care less how much of it you have to hand over to them – or what they do with the originals. Use the rest to put some distance between yourself and the cause of that. I pointed to her wrist. – That's what I want you to do.

– But—

– I'm happy. I laughed and felt the weight of what I'd just said as a warmth spreading through my chest. – As in content and excited and optimistic. Almost as good as the bought stuff. Thank you – I mean it – for fetching me these.

Her eyes narrowed. The flash of light in each of them shrank to a needle-prick. Whereas before I'd seen defiance in this expression she now looked confused and defensive. She didn't believe me but neither did she believe herself. I felt sorry for her.

– Remember that evening with the American boys? I began. – When I told you about some pictures I'd had taken of me with clients? I patted my bag. – I want these for the same thing.

– Sure she said. – Like I took that seriously. You were high. I shrugged. – I was out of it but I was telling the truth.

Sasha leaned forward in her chair. Her brow creased. – Stop bullshitting me.

I laughed – but this time it sounded nervous. She was slipping away from me. I felt the blood begin to lift in my face again.

Sasha shook her head. – Whatever you're up to you're playing with fire. Never mind forcing you to pay silly money for a set of pointless prints – if these people suspect you're messing with the business – threatening clients with stories of photographs – they'll come after you – and your boyfriend. You'll have to be a long long way up that coast road.

Her voice was a muddle of viciousness and sympathy. Worried for me yet relishing regaining the upper hand. It suddenly mattered to me – very much – that she believe what I'd said. More than that. I wanted – of all things – to tell her about my mother – and about Dad. About her heartless performance and his infuriating tolerance. About how this trip was a step beyond them both – and how the photos were evidence of that.

But we were wrapped too close. I couldn't even look at her for any length of time – much less say these things. I was glancing around the restaurant and through the picture window to the pavement with its semaphore of traffic and bright store-fronts – and seeing nothing in any detail. A new fear gripped me. Fear of Sasha – of the truth in what she'd said – of the risk I had taken in telling her what I'd done. She'd spoken of the threat to me from others – but what I now saw was the threat she herself represented. Did I have a baser motive for offering her money? Was I trying to buy her silence?

I'm still craning to see where the bleached bob went when Bowey scoops me on to his shoulders. He's strong – all wire-strung spine and arms – and lifts me so fast I don't have time to protest. From on high there's at least three people the hair could have belonged to. One turns out to be a woman – the second must weigh thirty stone – and the third has a full beard. I unclench my teeth – feel Bowey's head warm against my stomach – his grip firm on my knees.

A light aircraft on a trailer is hauled into the centre of the ring.

Mechanics in tracksuits unfold the plane's wings and position ramps either side of their span. I trace the greasy whirl of Bowey's crown with a forefinger. He pretends to sway beneath my weight. I cup his jaw and rub my palm against the grain of his stubble and a tractor spouting two vertical red flames ponders into the ring – ahead of some sort of beach buggy with ridiculous collagen wheels. The buggy farts back and forth as if looking for a way out. Bowey's shoulders fake-quiver with drumroll. The buggy noses up the ramp and retreats and repeats the feint and the PA shrieks with feedback and drums. I pass a hand across Bowey's forehead – the dampness of his hair-line – then taste the salt on my fingers as I press them to my lips. The air is molten – full of tractor exhaust and raced clutch and hot-brake smell. Bowey has stopped wobbling about beneath me. He is – bless him – straining to see the stunt. The tractor flames turn green and shoot fifty feet into the air and the crowd roars and the buggy accelerates at the ramp. In a blink it jumps the plane. We all cheer. I feel his laughter in my lower back and – forget the fear – know exactly what I'm doing here.

Dad taught me the old adage about there being a winner and loser in every conversation – but I learned for myself the difference between victory and having the last word. Sometimes it's only after the event you can tell who came out on top. Though I did try again to persuade Sasha I only wanted the photographs for myself – the more I tried the less she appeared to believe me. All the softness bled from her expression – leaving a taut neck and a defiant whiteness round her lips. She kept tapping the money with a fingernail. It seemed to have evolved from a gift into an obstacle between us. I needed some new proof to bridge it.

I pulled a pen from my bag and took the top banknote from the pile and carefully printed the web address for my journal across the Queen's impassive face. Sasha's look of confused hostility made handing the details over simple – it's often easier to trust a stranger with secrets than a friend – though she and I shared something we could have no more to do with one another now.

– Have a look at this when you get a moment. It'll convince you I'm telling the truth – that nobody has anything to fear from me.

Her frown deepened. – Whatever you're up to I want nothing to do with it. She stood up from the table. But that didn't matter because as I watched she also folded the address into her purse.

I picked up the rest of the money and followed the twitching flame of her hair. She seemed to know I was behind her – we walked in step. Automatic doors hissed back and shushed us out into a searing world of hot bright concrete and pneumatic-drill noise – dry air and burning dust – and when Sasha turned to give me a nod goodbye it was as if her own harshness could not compete – she was bleached vulnerable by the light. She did not resist me as I took her bag from her shoulder. Said nothing as I slid my money inside.

Without heels she's shorter than me. When I leaned forward my lips were at the right height. I squeezed her arm and kissed her forehead and wished her good luck.

The pictures were still unopened in my bag when I arrived at Manly. I tried to resist – but my curiosity got the better of me as I sat waiting on the beach. Keeping one eye on the board-walk – in time I'm sure I'll tell him but there's no point in scaring

Bowey now – I started to flick through the pack. It took one complete cycle before I could even begin to believe that the girl on the couch was me. Second time through and my heels started digging holes in the sand. The pictures are ridiculous – I couldn't have looked more awkward on crutches. Bland light – stiff poses – clownish lipsticked pout. A step beyond Marian's numbness – maybe – but if it needed proving here was the evidence – I'm not cut out to stand on such unfeeling ground. The bloke's waxed chest makes him look like a shop dummy. I sped through the pictures a third time – digging my feet further into the cool undercrust – pausing to wince only once – at a close-up taken from behind that clearly shows the blue vein on the back of my left knee.

I think of that flaw now – sliding off Bowey's shoulders – smoothing down my skirt. Has he noticed it? If not the mark is about all he's missed. Turns out he sent me only a fraction of the photographs he took. Confessing this the gold spokes in his eyes flashed – even as his face clouded over. He seemed as embarrassed as he was proud of the heavy shoebox he was giving me – unsure whether it amounted to an insult or a compliment. Muttered something about needing to take a shower and set off down the hall.

My first thought was that I'd have many more shots to choose from now.

The second thing I noticed was how lovingly he'd filed the photos. Tied in bundles – grouped by date.

Then I noticed how there wasn't an unflattering picture among them – and wondered how many he'd thrown away in editing the collection like this.

There were photographs of me with clients – but many more

showed me alone – the client either cropped from the frame or not there in the first place. Bowey had shadowed me before dates – following me around from in front – and he'd tailed me after them – seen me all the way home. Hundreds of pictures – too many for me to look at in one sitting. In other circumstances this collection would have been frightening but here – now – it gave me a sense of well-being.

I realized it wasn't being watched that I had relished – but the fact that Bowey had watched over me.

Whatever else – this boy would keep me safe.

31

After the bar, Bowey lost his bearings. I had to steer him back to the hostel, a hand on his elbow, our roles reversed. He muttered to himself all the way back about how he'd failed and was blind and had tried his hardest but missed some crucial event. There being nothing I felt I could say to convince him otherwise, I guided him childlike down the street and up the plywood staircase and into his dolls'-sized room. A night's rest would help, I told him, but sleep was a long time coming. Bowey's mumblings kept me awake. Though they petered out eventually, it still seemed to be his silence that I fell asleep to, and I awoke the following morning to more of the same.

He'd left his door ajar.

I pushed it open to see him exactly where I'd left him, still sitting on the edge of his bed, head in hands, a prisoner awaiting execution. He looked so forlorn I had no choice but to be parentally upbeat.

'This is a setback,' I said, 'but I've been through worse to get here. We'll track this girl down one way or another.'

He shook his head. 'How? She's gone. Means it has to be her. She took your money and fled.'

Though it hadn't occurred to me, he was right: the girl's absence made it likely we were chasing the right person at least. I explained how in business negotiations one of my cardinal rules is that there can be no such thing as a brick wall. He did not react. The space between us seeming to yawn, I tried to shore it up with more words.

'Sometimes you have to take sideways or even backwards steps to go forwards, but if you keep an eye on where you want to end up, and you think creatively, there's always a way through in the end.'

He looked up at me through spread fingers. 'Oh, please,' he said.

Stung, I retreated to shave and dress. The drum-skin wall separating our rooms wasn't enough to block out his pessimism, which threatened to become infectious. I set off to buy us both breakfast. I was turning my hat over in my hands in reception, waiting for the Irishman to double-check I'd received no messages, when there was a tap on my shoulder.

Jo Hoffman stood before me, there in the hotel.

A warmth spread through me, from the soles of my feet to the tips of my fingers. She'd come all this way to see me. It could mean only one thing.

At work I routinely have to pass business-breaking news up and down the chain. In doing so I've noticed a universal trait, of which I'm as guilty as the next man. Good news we love to share immediately and in person, but if the news is bad we use time and space as a buffer, cower behind official words set out in letters, make the ink responsible for any harm caused, distance ourselves from reflected pain.

Before I could check myself I'd reached out both hands for the doctor's and pulled her half a step towards me. The satchel she was carrying jerked from behind her back to the crook of her arm and her eyes widened in surprise, whites bright against her tan. I dropped her hands. She let her arms fall and the bag went with them, strap slithering to the floor. We both looked down. The bag was open. There was an envelope sticking through the zip. She bent down for it and then, as I knew she would, she handed it to me.

Every part of me condensed into one hope: I could not stop myself acting inappropriately again: I turned the envelope over to inspect the seal.

Once satisfied it was unbroken my eyes worked their way back to the doctor's face. Her pained sympathy was now cut with curiosity. An objectifying look. One of my hands rapped the envelope against the other's open palm.

'Business difficulties,' I said. 'I don't want to worry my father, would rather he didn't know.'

I'd forgotten how sharp her features were: the three fine lines across her brow, which passed for wrinkles of concern, looked out of place in the tautness of her face.

'Yes, your father.' She wet her lips before going on. 'He's pretty distressed already. I doubt your business problems will make a difference.'

I looked around the hostel foyer, at the dirty carpet and faded harbour-bridge print, at the potted fern over Jo Hoffman's shoulder, at the dust suspended in the block of window light. Everything seemed yellow, jaundiced, thrown into unhealthy relief by the doctor standing before me. I focused on the imperfection of the triangular scar on the side of her neck, saw the cord of muscle and tendon move beneath the brown skin there as she looked over her shoulder, at the door.

'Of course. But please tell me you didn't come all the way just to give me this.' I tapped the envelope again.

Her attention shifted back to me. 'No,' she said.

I asked if we might talk elsewhere. She checked her watch

before agreeing. Despite the sun, I couldn't bring myself to wear my hat in front of the doctor en route to the café. I felt scruffy enough as it was before her: gone were her pedal-pushers and ribbed vest, she was dressed for the city, in a grey skirt, kitten heels and fitted silk shirt. I led her to the café where Bowey and I had waited the day before. Home turf, of a sort, though the waiter watered down my advantage by blanking my smile of recognition. I pressed a palm against the heat of my brow. Bowey's head-butt bruise had yet to fade entirely. Perhaps that explained the doctor's continuing look of concern. I decided to try to put her at ease by letting her know my own good news first.

'She worked there!' I pointed at the sports bar across the street.

The doctor shut her eyes.

'They both did! Anna, and the girl who's to blame.'

Jo Hoffman gripped her forehead, her fingernails salt-water white. I allowed a moment for the news to sink in. 'I tracked her down,' I said. 'We're very close now.'

Eventually the doctor's eyes blinked open again. She said, 'A girl, now, is it? I thought you set off in search of a man?'

It pleased me that she had remembered the detail. There being no better way to advance negotiations than by crediting the other party with a breakthrough, I told her how she'd been right about Broken Hill School of the Air. I explained what I'd been through to track Bowey down, and how I'd come to understand that the episode in the sea wasn't his fault. Confidence begets confidence: I described how, working together, the boy and I had pinpointed the girl who'd ensnared my daughter, incapacitated her and driven her under the waves. Now it was just a matter of bringing her in.

'So you found the boy she was swimming with. And he knows who Anna bought the cocaine from. Tell the police and perhaps they'll be able to do something. All well and good, Wilson, but—'

'There's more to it than that.'

She stared at me. 'I'm sure there is,' she said. 'But none of it makes any difference.'

I waited while she gathered herself to continue, but the strangest sound, as much a bark as a shriek, cut her off. It came from the pavement down the street. We both turned to look. A woman dressed in a burqa stood next to a kerb-stopped limo, waving one hand in the air and howling at the other, which was shut in the car's rear door. As we watched, the limo jerked forward. A pink trainer flashed out behind the woman in the sun. Then the car stopped dead and she fell against its midnight paintwork and dropped to her knees on the pavement, her hand still clamped in the shut door. In a gap between her bark-shrieking I heard a pneumatic hiccup as the car's central locking unclicked. Then the woman's companion had yanked the door open and was picking her up. Her cries folded into a sustained wail. Passers-by gathered around the couple.

Jo Hoffman's long hands tightened round the arms of her seat, holding herself in place. She winced from the woman to me.

I looked at her expectantly.

'What?' she said.

'Go to her,' I whispered. 'You can help!'

The limo driver had hopped round the front of the car. He was little more than a boy: his suit jacket flapped behind him like a loose sail. But he was ushering the woman back through the open door with authority.

'Hospital, yes!' the husband agreed, again and again.

The doctor's fingers uncurled from the armrests. She shuddered. 'That's got to really sting.'

This feigned matter-of-factness coloured what she said next. She wanted me to believe my father had asked her to drop in on me, while he kept watch over Anna, in the hope that she might at last convince me of the immutability – that was the word she used, as if by adding syllables she could give what she was saying more weight – of Anna's stricken state. It did the opposite. I could tell she was toeing some official line, a line drawn between the twin poles of professionalism and pessimism. The limo tore off; the bystanders melted away. The doctor's instincts mattered more to me than her pretend logic. She'd felt the urge to help that woman, to push herself from her seat. All she'd needed was encouragement – encouragement that I should have given her more forcefully – to keep from holding herself back. Whatever she was now saying, about reality and delusion and accepting the finality of Anna's accident, I was more impressed by the fact that she'd come all this way to talk to me about my daughter. A starving man will live on crumbs: the doctor's very presence in Sydney, dressed so smartly, her knees brown and neatly folded beneath the severity of her skirt-hem, was all the good news I needed. The sun now hit the mirrored bar windows opposite and cut at us from across the street. Jo Hoffman took a pair of tortoiseshell sunglasses from her bag and pushed them up her fine nose with a forefinger. She spoke slowly. 'If you're still unwilling, or unable, to give the hospital the necessary consent, we may have to refer to your father. He's there, he's thinking straight. He says he can put us in touch with Anna's mother if need be. She's also her next of kin.'

A dog wearing a white plastic funnel round its neck yanked a small girl past our café table, the animal's face spot-lit with reflected brightness. Every few paces it turned to snap at a raw patch on its back leg, oblivious of the protective collar, its tongue flinging crystal spit to the floor. I looked from the dog to the little girl to the doctor. Jo Hoffman wore those glasses to mask the battle she was waging against herself. Her kind heart needed protecting. I reached out for her shoulder, my hand closing on the contradiction of silk and bone. Drawing her towards me, guided by religious conviction, I whispered into her ear: 'I have faith you would not do such a thing.'

She started to duck beneath my grip but I steadied her, held her in place. I could resist her resistance; it was helpful, something to oppose. My confidence grew. I leaned further forwards and slid her glasses gently from her face, then laid them on the stainless-steel tabletop between us. It seemed to me that her eyes, dark in the shadow of her lowered brow, were wet. She brought the heel of her hand up – to press against the tears, I assumed – but converted the gesture at the last moment into the reflex checking of her watch. It didn't fool me.

'But you needn't worry. You won't have to decide, because Dad won't put you in that position,' I reassured her. 'He simply . . . won't.'

She lifted her chin, looked directly at me – the dark pools disappearing – and slowly shook her head. 'I'm sorry,' she said. 'I have to go.'

'What?'

'I'm giving a paper. At a critical-care conference in this big hotel. The Westin in Martin Place.'

'Of course,' I said.

She stood up. 'I'm already running late.'

I held her sympathetic gaze for a moment. There was no point in denying the doctor this fabrication. Fifteen years of negotiations have taught me the fruitlessness of tearing down another person's imaginary world. You're better off working to understand its rules and perspectives, then bending them, realigning the projection with reality from within. That the doctor felt she had to make an excuse told me enough. She'd come all the way to Sydney. She stood up and pressed long fingers to the scar on her anglepoise neck. Looking at her I felt red pressure rise up again, warm and lovely in my chest. She cocked her head to one side, checking her watch again, a distracted, beautiful eagle.

I smiled at her, swallowed, wished her good luck.

She gave the briefest nod, and started to turn away.

'Tonight, though,' I called out. 'We'll talk some more then.'

She spun back towards me, beak mouth opening and shutting. She held her hands wide. It looked like she had dropped something.

'Where shall we meet?' I asked her.

'I can't. There's a dinner.'

'Of course,' I said again. I had to stop myself winking at her. 'Afterwards, then. You give me a call when you're ready.' I stood up, took another of my business cards from my wallet, and dropped it into the open mouth of her bag.

'Mr Taylor. Wilson.'

We faced one another across the table. My heart was full of fervour. I wanted to kneel, press my lips to her hand.

She couldn't think of what to say either. Her heels were as sharp as compass points. One left a white mark on the pavement when she turned away. I stared at it so long she was out of sight by the time I realized she'd forgotten her sunglasses. I put them into my shirt pocket where they sat next to my heart: a relic left by a saint.

32

A hopelessness descended after the doctor left. To bolster myself I pulled the stiff-backed envelope out of my trousers, only realizing, as the irritation went away and I lifted my T-shirt to see, that the corners had dug triangle points into the softness of my belly. I knew what was in the envelope, didn't have to lift the flap and slide the contents out on to my knees to suffer what that photograph showed, found myself focusing on the white border, the fact that the glossy finish looked wet in the sun, anything but what was going on in the picture itself.

The headless man was behind her this time. She was still smiling.

I turned the photo over immediately. The information on the back was bearable, in a language that made sense. Bank account, web address, threat. Identical to the back of the first photograph, except one detail, which I only noticed after staring at the print for some time. There was an extra zero at the end of the demand.

I smiled to myself. There was something comforting about the seriousness of the sum. It suggested the blackmailer didn't suspect I was on their trail. By making the payment I'd keep things that way. And although it wasn't the point, a voice in my head told me I'd be more likely to retrieve a proper chunk of money like this because it would be easier to trace.

I took out my phone. One half of me concentrated on the automated bank voice in my ear, the other watched the street. A hearse drew up in the very spot the limo had occupied. The driver checked his hair in the rear-view mirror, smoothing his hands down both sides of his head. I keyed numbers into my handset. There was no coffin in the back of the hearse that I could see. The bank voice asked me to confirm my instructions. Had he just been to a funeral, or was he waiting there before picking up his load? I retyped the numbers. The driver readjusted his mirror. The biscuit tin voice in my ear explained that the bank could not carry out my request.

I ordered a bottle of water to quench my sudden thirst, and set about making the payment by other means, but soon found that I couldn't. My money was in the wrong place. Not enough in my own accounts, and frozen in those held by the company. Creeping frost had taken hold of my legs as well. To shake the numbness from them I stood and took a few paces down the street, turned in front of the hearse and saw the waiter glaring at me from beneath his green awning. I walked back to my table and pulled ten dollars from my wallet. He was my ally and it felt good to wave away the change.

'There are no brick walls,' I said.

He narrowed his eyes but nodded all the same.

And yet, and yet. The facts wouldn't budge. If I couldn't pay, Anna wouldn't be safe from further humiliation until I'd found and stopped the blackmailer in person. How? Bowey's pessimism roared. I watched the undertaker pull on a pair of tan driving gloves and make starfish of his hands before gripping the wheel. Why had the doctor really left me? The hearse started up and rolled implacably away. Anna was still this side of that divide. As the car passed the café its driver gave me a sardonic wave.

I didn't wave back. Not through embarrassment, but because I was patting down my pockets for my phone, which started ringing as the car departed. *Number withheld* showed on its screen. I pressed receive, but before I had a chance to speak a girl's voice with a sharp Australian accent sounded in my ear.

'Who is this?'

'Hold on,' I replied. 'Let's start with who are *you*?'

'Mr *Wilson*, right?'

'No, Mr—'

'Right. Had to be a hoax. Good—'

'Wait!'

'Wrong number.'

'I am Wilson Taylor! Who am I speaking to?'

'Oh.' Canned television applause filled the gap while I waited for the girl to go on. Eventually she did. 'This is Sasha. Do I know you? Are you a client? Because if you are you should know the deal. Book through the agency. You have their number. Stay the fuck away from where I work.'

I could only trust myself to repeat the word 'Work?'

'Final Score. Worked, whatever.'

Excitement creates an impression of weakness: indifference, by contrast, suggests strength. In flat monosyllables I said, 'I'm no client. No. But if you're the girl from the sports bar' – I looked across the street hoping the place's physical presence would give substance to the voice in my ear – 'then my scout thinks you may have the look we want. He could be wrong, of course. We have to see you to know.'

The anger left her voice but the scepticism didn't. 'Yeah, right,' she said. 'Who do you work for? How does your *scout* know me?'

I'd thought to leave my number and I deserved this leg-up. But I wasn't sure of capitalizing on it yet. Something in this girl's voice suggested flattery wouldn't work, any enthusiasm would make her retreat behind the safety of her suspicions for good. I said, 'Listen, I'm too busy to take crap from you. We're seeing people in . . . the Westin Hotel, Martin Place, tonight. We can fit you in between eight and nine if you're interested.' Then – an old trick – I cut the window to half an hour. This worked; she was repeating the time and hotel name to me when I pressed *call end*.

As soon as the phone went dead my false composure fell away. I stood up and walked in small circles round the glinting table and chairs, watched by the waiter leaning in the café doorway. He folded his thick brown arms. What did this man's censure matter? Bowey deserved the good news, not him. I jogged – yes, jogged, in that heat – the short distance back to the hostel, knowing my arrival would transform the boy's day.

Yet Bowey wasn't there at first. Sweat dripped from my nose on to the corridor carpet when I knocked on his door, but he didn't answer and, when I recovered enough to hold my breath, empty silence pulsed through the wall. I retreated to wait in the relative cool of the lobby, fell into a doze, and came to slumped over the sofa arm with my head cricked against the wall.

The boy stood over me. 'It's pointless. I've wandered

round all morning, but I don't know where to start looking. They could be anywhere.'

'They?'

'Any of them.' His jaw worked, eyes on the floor.

My own mouth tasted of cardboard. 'I don't follow,' I said.

'You saw the photos? My note.'

'Of what? Forget photos. We don't need any more pictures. I know *exactly* where to look!'

'What?' He looked up. 'Where?'

'The Westin Hotel. I've set up a meeting.'

'With who?'

'The girl! She called. Who else?'

Bowey stared hard into my face for a moment, looking for something that was not evidently there. Satisfied, he pushed past me and took the stairs three at a time. I followed, heavy-footed, unsure what was going on. I had to catch my breath again on the landing. An imprint of woodchip stood out on my cheek in the mirror there, from where I'd lain slumped against the lobby wall. When I caught up, Bowey was ducking through the partition door between our rooms, back into his own, a shoebox under his arm. I caught sight of a flash of silver ribbon.

'What was that?'

'Not important. Where was the girl calling from? Why aren't we meeting till tonight?' His hands gripped one another. 'Can we call her back? Did you get an address, a number—'

'No, no, no.' I smiled at him. 'That box—'

Bowey ground his teeth. 'You mean to say, you had her on the phone and you just let her go?'

'Trust me,' I told him. 'It's because of that we can be sure she'll show.'

This assurance was genuine, but my confidence ebbed as the afternoon wore on. I tried taking practical steps to prepare myself for the meeting but got no further than my kitbag. Though Jeanette had washed my stuff at Yellowhammer, all I had now was crumpled dirty clothes again. Twenty minutes with a hairdryer wasn't enough to dry the shirt I rinsed. Somehow, in worrying about that, I forgot everything else. Stepping from the bus opposite the stone edifice of St Martin's Square I caught sight of myself in a shop-front and had to turn away: shipwrecked shirt, dirt-pink trainers, hat-hair.

Happily Bowey looked the part, a real photographer in a khaki waistcoat full of pockets, a long-nosed camera hanging from his shoulder by a frayed strap. We marched up the steps and past the uniformed doorman – he watched us but didn't approach – with ten minutes to spare. The lobby smelt of floor polish. It was awash with silver hair and charcoal suits. Bowey strode round the giant floral centrepiece, in and out of pillars, from the concierge desk to the alcove full of brass-doored lifts and back again, moving with the oblivious intent of a boxer before a fight.

I tried to calm myself by thinking of what I'd told Penny after our pitch to Syndicate 12. She was new then, and apologizing for having corrected me during the meeting. I cut her off. 'We're stronger together,' I reassured her, 'tempered by our differences, reinforced by our shared strengths.' I was proud of those words when I came out with them, but later realized I'd read something similar in a business-theory book. That didn't matter now. If Bowey was frantic, I must keep calm. I shut my eyes and opened them again, slow-blinking like an owl, but it was no use. A pair of busboys exchanged looks as Bowey stomped past them again. I cut him off between two pillars, put a hand on his chest and hissed, 'Stay put!'

He was staring past my shoulder, back at the revolving doors. I was close enough to see the gold flecks in his eyes again. Now they looked like knife-tips. He swallowed, his Adam's apple knuckling in his throat. 'She's here,' he said.

He pushed against my palm; I held firm, though it felt as if he was about walk through me. Still in a whisper I said, 'Anna is my daughter. Let me lead this, please.'

He rocked back on his heels. My hand dropped from his shirtfront. He breathed out through his nose and nodded. 'Short dress, long boots,' he said.

I turned round. She was a slight girl, and she looked less substantial still next to the pillars in the reception hall, where she stood gazing up at the ceiling, one leg forward, a hand on her bony out-thrust hip. There was something defiant in her stance, but intentionally so, which undermined the effect. I set out towards her across the marble floor and felt like I was waist deep in waves again. She reached up to push a strand of reddish hair behind her ear, revealing a long tattoo along the inside of her slender forearm, at odds with the petite femininity of her face. She'd made an effort, I saw. I could not suppress a guilty pang as I walked towards her.

'You're Sasha, right?'

She looked me up and down without smiling and asked, 'Which magazine do you work for?'

I pointed across the cavernous entrance hall. 'Let's take a seat, shall we?'

'Shall we. *Shall* we? Mate, I'm going nowhere until you tell me where you're from.'

Politeness is a weapon; easy to ridicule but hard to oppose. 'Please,' I summoned my kindest smile. 'I'll explain, but not in the doorway.' I stood to one side. 'Let's take the weight off our feet first.'

She looked from me to Bowey, who had stopped at a distance. He was loading his camera with film. A simple touch, but it worked. The girl allowed us to lead her through the archway into the lounge, and she sat down at one end of a leather sofa, in an alcove next to some sort of installation made out of cooking utensils modified so as to be useless: holed pans, a whisk without a handle, square-edged rolling-pins. Then she crossed her legs and looked at me expectantly. No, dauntlessly. *This better be good, or else*, her eyes said. The girl's expression reminded me so much of my daughter that my blood thinned as I sat before her; I felt transparent, unable to prolong the charade.

'I need to talk with you about Anna,' I said.

Her face was blank.

'Anna Taylor.'

'What is this?'

'You worked together, you—'

'I know who she is.' The girl's fingers worried at one another. She swallowed. 'What's she gone and done now?'

Bowey, who had followed us through to the lounge, snapped his camera shut and sat down on the sofa. He slid up close to Sasha. Too close; she leaned away and turned to give him an accusing stare. This having no effect, she tried to stand up, but in one quick movement Bowey put an arm round her shoulders.

'Photographs,' Bowey said.

Sasha glared at his hand. Though she didn't panic the girl seemed to shrink. Her voice was smaller too. 'Please,' she said. 'They had nothing to do with me.'

'You're not even denying you know what I'm talking about?'

'No, but—'

'But what?'

Sasha said, 'I warned her. What was I supposed to do?'

Bowey's face was alive with the now familiar tremor of his rage. He gripped the girl tighter, a pink dot in the middle of each white knuckle. 'Warned? You forced her. Forced her! Admit it. You used her. Destroyed her with threats. And then . . .' He sniffed, licked his lips. 'She fought me off and I gave up. I *ran*. Because of *you*. It was your fucking fault! But no, not happy with that, you had to suck the blood from this man. *You murdering thief!*'

The boy's loss of control seemed to strengthen Sasha's resolve. Her jaw muscles – clearly visible in her little face – tightened, and the metal returned to her voice. 'What the fuck are you on about?'

A figure passing on the other side of the culinary sculpture came to an abrupt halt on hearing this and turned to look at us. A woman's outline, dressed in a navy blue jacket and skirt. She was six feet away from us, no more. Her blazer had gold buttons. They flashed in the chandelier light as the woman turned and walked quickly away.

'I'm who you've been blackmailing,' I told Sasha.

'*Me?* I'm the one that tried to stop her! She told you it was *me*?'

'She's said nothing. Not yet.'

'Well, it's not my fault if you can't make the silly bitch talk, is it?'

Bowey yanked the girl closer. She flinched, but quickly recovered, staring straight at him with a face that dared him to do worse. 'If you don't tell me who's sending that filth I'll kill you,' he said.

'Filth?' the girl said, and rolled her eyes.

I leaned forward then and eased Bowey's hand from the girl's shoulder. More people were passing through the lounge. We were in full view. If he kept on manhandling her some-one would surely intervene. 'This makes no sense!' I said to him. 'None at all!'

At which point Jo Hoffman walked through the archway. She was wearing a floor-length evening dress. It was black with a petrol sheen, the same colour as her hair, and she was talking to a man in a dinner-jacket with a name badge stuck to his lapel. In two steps they were past us. The dress was cut low on her back. The doctor's shoulder-blades were shockingly visible, the ridge of her spine, too. I only caught a glimpse of her, but in that second, before I turned back to Sasha and Bowey, the water closed over my head again.

Bowey was quivering beside Sasha, straining against an invisible leash, while she sat staring at him with her thin upper lip drawn high enough to reveal her teeth. I sensed Jo Hoffman stop half-way across the lounge. Bowey demanded Sasha tell us the truth. The doctor and her friend had turned to wait for a third delegate to catch them up. Her eyes must have swept right across our table.

'Truth about *what*?' Sasha hissed at Bowey. 'I don't know what she has against you, do I? I haven't seen her in weeks!'

Fighting to control his voice, Bowey started pleading with the girl. He explained, convolutedly, how the photographs must have forced Anna to fight him off in the sea. His broken flow lacked certainty: he sounded unconvinced by himself. I couldn't look after the doctor, couldn't tear myself from watching for Sasha's response. Yet even as the girl's smirking incredulity pricked my anger, drunken pleasure washed over me. The doctor was here. She hadn't fabricated the conference: Sasha was almost sneering now. I wanted to tear her mouth from her face. Yet when the black shape disappeared entirely from the end of the lounge I had to stop myself following it. Only the girl's raised voice nailed me in place.

'Drown herself? Because of *those* photographs? No, mate.' She shook her head. 'You've got that wrong. She couldn't have cared less.'

'She fought me.' Bowey repeated. 'Something made her – it stands to reason. Otherwise she'd have let me help. These pictures. You know who took them. You know who's to blame. I'm giving you one last chance to tell us.'

The girl blinked at him and said, 'Or what?'

She was hiding something, I saw that. The blinking was a hair-line crack in an otherwise flawless front. I could have said something then to prise open the gap and draw her through it, but Bowey, who was fiddling with one of his many pocket flaps, muttering, 'Or what? Or what?' shook his head and pulled out a knife. It had a wooden handle wrapped in twine. Making no attempt to conceal what he was doing he bared the knife's dirty blade and laid it flat on the girl's thigh.

Sasha said, 'You're going to use that here, are you?' and managed a brittle, hopeless smile. I felt a surge of affection for her: what face! Looking down I saw the cotton of her skirt bulging up either side of the flat blade. He was pressing down hard. My voice sounded distant telling him to put the knife away. He ignored me.

'Who took those photographs?' Bowey asked.

'I can't tell you that.'

In full view of the suits still milling into the lounge Bowey angled the knife so that its tip pressed into the girl's stomach. His cheeks were mottled with rage. The girl, by contrast, sat monumentally still. Her cotton top served to emphasize the softness of her belly and the knife's sharp tip.

I'm ashamed of what I thought then. It was: I must shield this from the room. What if the doctor were to reappear? I slid off my chair and knelt before the pair. I looked hard into Bowey's face. He allowed me to draw his hand back but would not release his grip on the knife-handle. He held the knife out at stiff-arm's length. I found myself scrabbling for the sheath, stabbing it down on to the blade.

The girl's expression hadn't altered. 'You *can* tell me who took the pictures,' I reassured her. 'I'll find out eventually anyway, because I'm the one they're blackmailing. There are ways behind a bank account. You're her friend and I'm her father. I won't let anyone hurt you, you have my word.'

I regretted this speech as soon as I'd come out with it; promising what you can't deliver always sounds pathetic in the end. The fact was that unless this girl explained what had gone on, I wouldn't know. Sasha gave a mechanical little laugh, but something I'd said made her think.

'Blackmailing you. How?'

'Threatening to publish the pictures.'

'But they'll have done that already,' she said. 'Unless . . .'

'Unless what?'

She laughed again. 'They must be shocking.'

'Well, of course they—'

'No, mate, as in, real duds.'

A shadow fell across us. I looked up and saw one of the uniformed doormen looming above me. 'Is everything all right?' he asked. He had some sort of accent – Greek perhaps – and he'd recently cut himself shaving. A tiny scrap of bloodied tissue still stuck to his throat. I could not look away from it, or reply.

'Fine, thanks,' said Sasha, brightly.

At the same time Bowey hissed, 'Fuck off.'

Bowey's face was still trembling; the doorman eyed him uncertainly, then looked back to Sasha, who smiled flirtatiously. 'We're waiting for my sister. She's a guest here. We won't be long.'

Her performance was based on sound thinking, which I suddenly understood. Bowey was under control now, but the doorman's interference could change all that. Who knew then what the boy might do? Sasha had waved away help because she thought she could cope herself, which meant that she had something to barter with. If I could just persuade her to tell me what she knew, then, then, then? The next step felt like it should have been obvious, but when I reached to take it I stumbled, as if I had struck out on a phantom limb. A dark shape flitted through my mind; more featherless wings beating, the doctor *here* in her petrol sheen dress. When I brought

271

the hotel lounge back into focus the doorman had retreated a few yards and Sasha was regarding me steadily.

'Sounds like a bad accident. I'm sorry.'

'There is no such thing as an accident,' I mumbled. 'Only shades of blame.'

Sasha's voice softened. 'The pictures were some sort of joke to Anna. She didn't care, she wasn't ashamed. About the only person she might not want to see them is you. If that lanky bastard has sent you some already, there's nothing worse she can do.'

I asked, 'Who is *she*?' at the same time as Bowey growled, 'Just give us a name.'

Sasha thought for a moment. 'I didn't believe her at first, so I can't say I blame you for not believing me. But I'm telling you the truth. Anna wanted the photos for some sort of art show. No blackmailer can harm you. The fool isn't worth your effort. Anna's the best person to convince you of that.'

There was grit in the sheath holding Bowey's knife; when he bared the blade a second time it sounded like a short, metallic intake of breath. 'A fucking *name*,' he hissed.

'Okay, okay. Suit yourselves,' she said. She pulled a pen from her bag and wrote on a coaster, fast and with the sneer still on her lips, like a debtor cornered with her chequebook. 'All I ask is you keep me out of whatever you have to say.'

Bowey snatched the address from her hand and strode towards the lobby, only pausing when I called out for him to wait.

I found myself apologizing to the girl. Her expression softened again, to something like sympathy, which I could not afford to entertain. Anna has a similar look. This Sasha, sitting hunched over her tattooed arm, was my daughter's friend; they shared something, I sensed that then. I told her I wouldn't reveal her name to anyone, that Anna would be grateful she'd helped. The look I gave the girl felt almost fatherly. It faded as soon as I turned away.

33

27 February

It's ten thirty in the morning but I haven't been to sleep – which makes it more of last night really – so I order a beer. The waitress brings a bottle beaded with cold droplets to one of the many vacant PC terminals where I sit to write this.

I once asked my dad if he ever thought he'd fall in love again.

– Again? he said.

I was in the middle of my first speed-drawing phase then – must've been about fifteen. From the look on my face he guessed he'd upset me with that answer – but what he went on with was every bit as wrong.

He said – I don't think your mum and I were old enough to be properly in love.

Then he stepped to the table where I was filling waste paper with sixty-second sketches. I remember him looking down to see I'd drawn the back half of a horse – I was never much good at their heads. He nodded appreciatively – but couldn't resist turning the page over to check I was working on a truly scrap bit of disaster report. Brushed the hair from my face and went on to make things worse.

– I've got you to love now he said.

– Not that kind of love.

He laughed. – I'm too old for any other sort.

He was a week short of thirty-six.

I take the first sip from my beer and see a new nonsense at the heart of this exchange. To have used himself up so early in his life he must have loved her completely. It seems to me you can live without caring much about anything before or after you've been in love – but not when you're in its grip. Then there's just too much to lose.

We came here in Bowey's pick-up. I sat next to him in a sort of awe – mesmerized by the way he drove one-handed – his steering elbow resting on the window ledge and his other hand cupping the gear-stick. Unmoving there for twenty – thirty – forty miles at a stretch! He was just driving. The dog lay between us on the bench seat with its squat black head pressing warmly against my thigh and its tongue lolling out but instead of pulling away I found myself not wanting that sensation to stop either. Though the radio played unrelenting pap I couldn't have been happier.

I told Bowey to stop the truck. There was nothingness to our left – a million flat beautiful grey-green miles of it – and the ocean lay to our right. I peered forward through the windscreen – up at the sky. Bowey laughed when I told him what I wanted but didn't object. I climbed down from the cab and up into the tray and I lay on my back there with a coil of rope for a pillow – staring straight up as we went on. Nothingness rushing above me. An empty canvas. I'd have stretched the ride further but wasn't wearing sunscreen and didn't want to burn.

Bowey has never been up this coast before. Before we set out he spent an evening trawling my guidebook – planning where to break the journey. I let him take control – it was sweet. First place we stopped was beside a house-sized banana – set back a few yards from the road. I'd overheard tourists talking about these big roadside things in the bar. They're dotted round the country – huge fibre-glass lobsters and shells and apples – for no good reason at all. People make pilgrimages to see them. Don't ask me why. Yet even this plastic monument seemed important as we stood before it. Like a Jeff Koons sculpture – kitsch and significant at the same time. Bowey took photographs. I'm in some – pointing at the banana like it's some top prize.

Later we stopped in a coastal town famous for its painted rock art. The folk there are happy for tourists to add to the graffiti. They sell little paint kits in all the shops and guest-houses. Even that sappiness touched me now. We went swimming and then spent an hour working on our own slabs of stone. I painted a passable monster truck for Bowey – he decorated his rock with the words *I want all of you*. I had to turn away when I saw what he'd done – muttering about whether his stone was small enough to carry away. It wasn't. I made him take photographs of that too.

Hurt once – Dad's petrified the same thing might happen again. I can appreciate now why a part of his heart has turned to stone. If I were to return to the hostel and find Bowey gone it would floor me too – and I've only known him a few weeks. Once you give yourself up to someone the important merging happens all at once – it seems – there's no control – no holding back.

The moon was so bright last night it made a negative of the sea. Silver foam seemed to rear up while the unbroken water tumbled forwards. The longer I watched the more convincing the illusion became – white-water looming and blackness crumbling – all out of sync with the crash-boom soundtrack. We sat on the beach up towards the rocks next to our unlit foil barbecue drinking a bottle of wine wrapped in a paper bag and eating potato salad with our fingers. Didn't light the barbecue because Bowey hadn't caught any fish. He looked like he knew what he was doing when he bought the rod and tackle in town – but I soon saw he hadn't a clue. We scrambled down the rocks beneath the lighthouse at dusk – with the sea all street-light pink. Evidently Brent – Bowey's brother – baited the hooks on their holiday expeditions. I'm thinking now he must have put them into the water too. Bowey's first cast caught his float in a crevice just in front of us. He was wet to the chest by the time he'd freed it. I sat there grinning – thinking how his cackhandedness reminded me of Dad except that Bowey didn't care about looking an idiot in front of the proper fishermen. Once he did finally manage to fling his hook he snagged it on the bottom reeling in. Cut his hand ripping the line loose. Then knocked the bait – sprats – nice if we'd cooked them – into a deep rock pool and after that we called it a day.

Yesterday I found myself jealous for the first time in as long as I can remember. We tied Vic to the back of the pick-up when we went to paint those rocks and before Bowey had had a proper chance to appreciate my truck he noticed the time and shot off to fetch the dog some water. I left our drying swimsuits behind in the rush to keep up with him. Ridiculous – competing for attention with a dog.

But it makes sense of Bowey's reaction late last night – in the bar. I was fetching us refills when a huge surfer wearing just his board-shorts reversed into me – knocking rum and Coke down my front. He was unsteady on his feet and slow to realize what he'd done and then insistent on buying another whole round. When I told him he didn't need to do that he put a plank of forearm across my shoulders. Said he wanted to marry me. Then tried to give me a kiss. I could see from the warmth in his blurry eyes that he was harmless enough and had already ducked out of his hug when Bowey somehow got between us. He just stood there – a snake before a buffalo – fixing the guy with his stare. If I hadn't pulled him away I swear there'd have been a fight.

Afterwards he was embarrassed. He spoke into the space over my shoulder – said now he could help out he couldn't just sit back and watch. I thought of his crisscrossed camera strap but didn't remind him of the cringing academic. The whole thing was as thrilling as it was daft to me. I took his hand and led him back to the beach and didn't let go until I could no longer tell where he ended and I began.

I've never felt this way before – sensitive to the point of numbness – everything mattering so much I've lost track of its meaning – each moment indelible and yet horribly fleeting at the same time.

I was right thinking Bowey wouldn't be interested in Sasha's parting gift. If I hadn't already embarrassed myself justifying how I came by it – wrapped in a pointedly saccharine thank-you card she left at reception in my hostel – I probably wouldn't have bothered myself. Most of the line blew off across the beach – but what didn't was enough to make me address the elephant riding with us.

– What happens after this then? I asked.

Bowey was inspecting his fishing injury – his hands moonlit grey. – We'll need to get some sleep eventually he said.

– No. I mean when I have to go home. After the end of this trip.

– You're forgetting I'm a farm boy. The only other times I've seen four a.m. I'd already been to bed.

– Please! I said.

He considered a moment. – You should see where I'm from before then.

– That doesn't answer the question either.

– Yes it does. Once you've seen all that emptiness you'll have pity. You'll take me back to London with you.

– Really?

He looked steadily at me.

– You could study.

– I don't know about that. But I could help you out on your course or something. He patted his camera. – At least see what comes of all those pictures I took.

I must've been more scrambled than I knew because his saying that left me staring at his camera full of anxious thoughts to do with how Aborigines used to fear a camera capturing their soul. They were right I saw. In trying to freeze time a photo just makes it more obvious that the moment is gone for ever. It shows its subjects a dead version of themselves – gives them less future to look forward to – puts them to sleep a second at a time. I tried to explain this to Bowey.

He laughed and agreed he was dog tired.

Then he led me back to the hotel. I lay on the bed next to him – but couldn't sleep. I didn't expect that gambling would land me with something so . . . uninsurable – that a project about acting a part would lead somewhere this real.

The stillness of him. I tried to calm myself by breathing in time with him – but love's invincible vulnerability hung in the fearful pause between each breath.

I started wondering how Dad will react to the news. He'll be welcoming – he'll offer for Bowey to stay at the flat as long as we want – he'll give us acres of space. And I'm sure he'll also give me whatever money we need. He'll see me happy and he'll do what he can to help that and he'll be genuinely pleased.

All that said he now doubts the love he felt for Marian at my age – so will he truly believe?

By ten this morning Bowey hadn't so much as rolled over – so I came here. And now my eyes feel scratchy looking at the screen. My beer bottle is blood-warm to touch – the plastic chair is sticking to my legs – I'm cooking in the prickly heat downdraught of this overhead fan. Time enough later to buy a new bikini. I need to cool down now. I'm going to dig Bowey out of bed and drag him into the sea for a swim.

34

I followed Bowey down the hotel's grand front steps, which still pulsed with the day's heat. Even now, at night, the cavernous black sky belittled the city in a way it does not back home. Bowey was walking quickly. When I took hold of his arm to slow him down I felt – or imagined I felt at least – a jolt, as if he were charged with static.

'What in hell were you thinking?' I asked.

He stopped, turned to me and waved the coaster in my face. 'It worked, didn't it? We've got what we came for.'

'Yes, but—'

He leaned towards me, so that for a second I felt threatened. Then he put his ragged hands on my shoulders and gave them a friendly shake. 'Relax. I knew what I was doing. I *know* what I'm doing now.'

Plainly he did not. Drawing myself tall in front of him I smiled and said, 'Just now we're going to do nothing at all.'

Frown-lines deepened on his street-lit brow.

'We're going to wait until morning,' I told him.

'We're going to do what?'

'We'll turn up first thing,' I said. 'That's the best time to confront this person. Not late at night. We're going to cool off this evening, collect ourselves. Tomorrow morning, before the day starts, we'll knock on the door in a rational state of mind.'

His nostrils flared and he gave the slightest shake of his head, but my suggestion seemed to slow him down and he allowed me to steer him round the side of the building towards a taxi rank. We returned to our hostel in silence. The air-conditioning in the taxi had broken. Bowey dropped his window, put his elbow on the lip of lowered glass, and sat staring at the coaster as he turned it between his fingers in the warm airflow. I could not stop myself saying, 'Careful with that.'

He handed it over. 'You keep it safe,' he said.

The taxi driver drove us a roundabout route home. Slick shop-fronts and gleaming apartment blocks slid evenly by. Our own area looked like a wall full of skewed pictures by comparison. An ambulance was parked opposite the hostel; as we climbed out of the taxi I watched two paramedics struggling to hold an old man still on a stretcher. They looked bored with the task, but his hands flapped like tethered birds.

'Your leg is broken, sir,' the female medic said. 'You'll have to let us lift you.'

'It's my coffin! I'll get into it how I bloody well choose!'

I followed Bowey inside. His head hung low; he walked with a slouch. I sympathized: confronting Anna's friend had drained me too. I felt like I was in one of those dreams – everyone has them – where you have to fight but cannot land a punch. The closer we got to the culprit, the more exhausting these swipes at thin air had become. I felt weak with the effort of chasing shadows, less and less able to stem the fear that they were cast by a phantom sun. *Connect soon*, the hostel's staircase creaked at me, *or collapse.*

Still, in the corridor outside our adjacent rooms, I took a deep breath – the air tasted of mothballs – and told Bowey again that I'd see him in the morning. It was only nine. He folded his arms and looked at his feet. I patted his wiry shoulder and repeated that we'd both cope better after a night's sleep. Then I turned into my room and sat on the bed waiting for the click of his door. I listened while he kicked off his shoes, tore back the bedclothes, and collapsed on to complaining springs. The wait was agonizing, yet I made myself lie back and echo Bowey's breathing as it chopped and slowed and finally softened. Once he was asleep I eased off my own shoes. Then I sat up, tucked them under my arm and stole from the room, careful to turn my key slowly in the lock, holding the mechanism's momentum back silent within itself until metal met metal and the lock had fully shut. Key stowed, I walked sock-footed to the lobby.

I hailed another cab and headed back to Martin Place. It felt like I was dashing for a door that was closing ahead of me. The wedge of light the doctor had shone through the gap was now no more than a sliver, and yet I could still see by it, just. If Jo Hoffman hadn't invented the conference she might still have used it as an excuse, she might yet be here in Sydney for my and Anna's sake. I bolstered myself in the taxi by thinking of the glimpse I'd caught of the doctor's face as she strode past me in the lobby, distracted, *pretending* to listen to the man with the name badge. I'd find her again and make her admit her true purpose here, which was – dream logic, irresistible as the tide – to reassure me with hope.

But before I reached her I ran into a problem. The cab driver, an Asian woman who spent the journey stifling a wet cough, pulled up outside the Westin and told the rear-view mirror I owed her fourteen dollars. When I reached for my wallet I found it empty. She blinked bug eyes at me as I turned out my pockets, then pointed across the street at a cash machine. Though I knew it was pointless, I stood in line and keyed in my number. The sense of futility that welled up within me rolled beyond the straightforward refusal onscreen. She was parked across a busy road. It occurred to me that I could run away. But I picked my way back through the traffic. Bending beside the driver's window I found I had undone my watch. Before I knew it I was brandishing the thing in front of her and muttering an apology.

The little woman glared at me, then looked through her windscreen and coughed a wad of phlegm into her mouth. I thought she might spit it at me. But she didn't. She dug in her pocket for a rag and used that instead. She seemed embarrassed. Waving my watch away she put the car into gear and drove off.

I stood on the kerb feeling cheated. The air smelt of hot static, hard to breathe. I managed to walk across to the hotel steps, but it felt like I'd floated there, and when I arrived I had to sit for a moment with my head between my knees. A memory came to me, clear as yesterday, of my father writing a cheque in the department store where we stocked up on Anna's first clothes, pram and cot. I could see the this-is-no-big-deal look on his face, and felt the hot dilemma again: it would dilute the promise if I mentioned more than once my intention to pay him back. I stared at the Pitt Street traffic. He would have had to pay for his own air fare out to Brisbane. Once I'd dealt with the fallout from Guatemala I'd reimburse him for that, too.

Happily the doorman Bowey had offended was no longer

on duty. His replacement did not look twice at me, but the very fact he might made me aware again of my shabby clothes. I strolled through to the gents' and did my best to collect myself there. With my shirtsleeves rolled to the elbow the crumpled cuffs were hidden from view; I appeared more purposeful to myself. I patted colour into my cheeks until I felt closer to the surface of my own skin. Then I set off in search of the doctor's conference dinner.

The concierge directed me towards the hotel's basement. Emerging from the lift, I saw a free-standing sign composed of little letters slotted on to a board. The first line spelled 'Critical Care Symposium'. Each truth – the fact that she hadn't lied about the topic, for example – was another brick added to the wall. I concentrated on the noticeboard itself, ignoring what it said. Something about the corporate ubiquity of the object helped, as did the rest of my surroundings. The basement was full of meeting rooms. Sumptuous red carpet pulsed underfoot; the walls felt like they had their backs turned on the corridor; each heavy door bore a brass plaque with the conference room's name – native Australian trees – in a solid font.

I'd navigated countless such plush interiors before and emerged with what I'd come for.

I followed an arrow on the sign to a door marked 'Boab' and pushed it open, realizing as I did so that there wasn't enough noise coming from inside for a conference dinner. I was right and wrong. It was quiet because the delegates were listening to an after-dinner speech. I heard the phrase 'like tapping blood from a funnelweb' and then the speaker – the only person in the room facing directly my way – stumbled. Had he just carried on with his anecdote I might have been able to slip away again unnoticed – I seemed to want that overwhelmingly now – but he looked up and lost his thread and heads began to swivel in search of what had distracted him. There were too many faces to take in at once; I stood there searching blindly, willing the doctor's not to be among them, as if her having skipped the speeches might somehow have helped Anna's fate.

But she was there. In fact, she was sitting at a table near to the door, and she was looking over her shoulder at me. I saw shadows move across the plane of her back as she twisted further round. Her mouth was open and her hand rose to cover it. She was so utterly separate, and radiant, and rattled by my presence. The other faces and the speaker coughing and pausing and trying to restart were blurred by comparison, and yet, as with the sun, I couldn't look at her for more than a second. I ducked back through the open door, blinking down at the red carpet, which now swam blue, purple and pink. It seemed to lead in all directions at once. I made it back to the signpost but had to steady myself against it when I got there, and then I was clinging to the thing for support.

'What are you doing here?'

I pushed myself upright. The signpost's raised lettering was Braille beneath my fingers, but it gave away no clues.

'Did your talk go okay?' was all I could say.

'Fine, thanks. But—'

'That's good, because—'

'Forget the talk, Wilson.'

I pressed on: 'Because you looked nervous this morning, and I know how that is. I give a lot of presentations. I sympathize.'

She considered this. 'Well, thanks. I *was* nervous, as it

happens, but I finished that hours ago and I can't say I've relaxed. I haven't stopped worrying since you left the hospital. That's the fact.'

I opened my mouth to apologize but she went on.

'After you left Byron I saw I'd failed – Anna, you and myself. Because there are routes around next of kin who refuse to give appropriate consent, and I've never had to take one before. I didn't want to have to start the wheels turning, but without you there . . .' She ran a hand through her hair, the workings of her forearm moving too visibly beneath her brown skin. 'When your father heard I was coming to Sydney and gave me that letter to bring, I was happy, because it meant I'd have another chance to convince you.' She looked up from under her hand. 'But I gave in so damn easily again! I let a stupid poxy drug dinner get in the way. So I'm glad you came down here tonight, because I need to make you see. I have to. I can't carry on with the thought of you disputing what has to be done.'

Despite the hotel's default evening light – and Jo's tan – there was colour in her cheeks. The scar on her neck showed white again. She stood braced with her feet apart and slightly turned out, an assertive pose, which accentuated the delicacy of her black dress and the gentleness of her words – which were still coming. She was also half a pace closer to me than people normally stand – probably because I'd been clinging to the sign when she approached. Her closeness made me look at the ground. Her toes were long and thin in open high heels.

'Christ,' she was telling the top of my head. 'Nobody wanted this to happen. Least of all you, but not me either—'

I let go of the signpost, reached an arm round her and pulled myself towards her. She stood stiffly while I pressed my face into the warmth of her shoulder and neck. My hands were on her back, the lattice of bone and muscle brittle beneath her skin.

'I know, I know,' I said. 'But it did.'

I thought I felt her relax – or breathe out at least – when I admitted that, but the moment my face came away from her neck she eased herself from me and smoothed her dress across her hips.

'I must get back.'

I nodded.

'But tomorrow. The conference ends at lunch. We could return to the hospital together.'

'Wheels,' I said.

She looked at me uncertainly. 'I flew—'

'No. For Anna. You said there were wheels turning.'

Jo nodded quickly, relieved to be back on solid, professional ground. 'Nothing will happen for now if I have your consent.'

'You have it.' The words came out of my mouth, but it felt like somebody else was saying them. Giving my consent, it seemed, was now a *brake*. How could that have happened? Now my 'yes' was Anna's last line of defence.

She began to walk away. 'Tomorrow, then,' she said.

After she'd gone I sank on to one of the bullet-hard leather benches lining the corridor walls. Would they ask me to switch the machine off myself? I shut my eyes and shifted on the seat. At what point would Anna stop being the doctor's patient? I leaned forward. Had the thought of that moment coloured my thinking? No. I gripped the bench-front with both hands. Now that I'd made the decision, it seemed as if I'd always been deciding, and would go on deciding for ever. This scared me, yet it was good: I didn't have to deal with everything now. Smooth leather, cold, hard upholstery studs. Repercussions would flow naturally, truthfully. I leaned back against the wall, trying to feel the relief that comes with having owned up to a lie, but something was jabbing at me. I dug in my back pocket to rearrange my wallet, and my hand surfaced with Sasha's cardboard coaster.

One side was decorated with the hotel's pompous crest, which showed an eagle gripping rumpled cloth. It looked like the bird was changing a bed. I turned the coaster over to decipher Sasha's cardiogram handwriting. I made out an address in a suburb called Edgecliff and saw she'd underlined a word immediately below that.

The word was *annals*, buried in a web address.

I stood up and ran a hand across my forehead and held it over my face. My fingers smelt of anticipation: storm dust. My feet began walking me back to the lifts and out through the lobby and into the street. I recalled what Sasha had tried to tell us about how Anna had convinced her of the truth of those photographs, and how Bowey had cut short her explanation with his idiotic knife. The fact that people seemed to be giving me a wide berth outside made me aware that I was looking at them oddly, *hungrily*. I slowed my pace. The first Internet café I came to I ducked inside. I sat down at the terminal nearest the door, trying to look like I knew what I was doing, but soon worked out I had to pay up front. I was shaking my head at myself when a teenage intellectual – tiny goatee, black turtleneck – asked if he could help. While I struggled to come up with a way of threatening him my hands dug mechanically for my credit card. Mercifully, he put it in his pocketbook by way of deposit. I wanted to stroke the soft bristles on his chin. But he'd gone, leaving me alone and online.

I started reading.

35

Halfway through the first entry it occurred to me that I had crossed a boundary, was now on private ground. I knew I should stop. I *wanted* to stop. But I could not. If I'd been forced to justify myself I'd have said that my hunt for a culprit licensed me to step across such lines. But I was beyond excuses: Anna was talking, I could hear her, and I would go on listening until the last full stop. I didn't slow down when it became obvious there was neither a culprit nor a crime, nobody to blame at all.

It was as if the outback sun had risen behind me. I'd known it would come up all along, had seen by its light for some time, and was now suffering its heat. Denying its presence by refusing to turn round was no longer possible. By the time I'd read Anna's last words I understood exactly what had happened in the run-up to the accident. That word, *accident*. Admitting its provenance was like grasping a burning coal, an unfathomable sensation at first, coldly factual in the instant before pain.

Banal bad luck, loss without liability: my worst fear.

In vain I reread the journal entries, fixing upon Anna's mother as a possible scapegoat, but Anna's preoccupation with Marian was not the cause of her drowning. I'd known about the letter, of course; Dad told me. Marian's fearful blitheness may have pricked Anna to experiment as she did, but that experimenting – the project, the photographs, the coke – altered nothing. In retracing Anna's steps and trespassing across the landscape of her journal I had done nothing but intensify my pain. Nobody drowned her, she didn't drown herself, and yet she drowned – by mistake.

I sat back from the computer, imagined Anna doing the same up in Byron Bay. She'd not intended these to be her last words. Her head fizzing with excitement, drink, tiredness – the coke must have long worn off – she tripped back to the hostel, roused Bowey, dragged him blinking through the molten morning to the sea. There she ignored the lifeguard's flags and took the shortest course into the waves.

Love's invincible vulnerability, she wrote.

She managed – as I did – to swim through the white-water and beyond the break. Bowey struck out after her. By the time he'd caught up she was already in trouble. Fatigue, cramp, the undertow: I can't know what caused her panic, but the panic made her fight Bowey off and the panic dragged her down.

I'd read to a soundtrack of two-fingered typing coming from the desk next to mine. I looked across now and saw a woman of about fifty wearing a cheap business suit with shiny elbows, shoulders and cuffs. Maybe it was the strip-lighting, but I could only perceive that woman in shades of grey. When she bent forward I saw pale roots in her charcoal hair. I'd finished reading, but I did not feel pain and I did not feel cheated and I did not feel relief. No, about Anna, those feelings all cancelled one another out, leaving me beyond numb. But watching the woman type filled me with dark sorrow. The peck-peck-peck of her anaemic fingers was too much to cope with just then. I had to get away from it. Paying my way no longer applied. I waited for the boy to turn his back, then left the café.

I trudged back to the hostel. I climbed the stairs and lay down in the dark, listening through the thin walls to what passes in a city for quiet: traffic groan, building hum, subway clatter, the hiss of air brakes, a siren's stab and train-track drums.

Something was missing.

I jumped up, put an ear to Bowey's wall and tried to pull the sound of his breathing from the background noise, but it wouldn't come. I tapped the partition, softly at first, and said his name, and then I slapped it with the flat of my hand and called out to him. He didn't respond. The tiredness had fallen from my limbs. I kicked the connecting door hard. It slammed open. Bowey wasn't there. I bounced on the balls of my feet and swore out loud and shook my head and set off.

In the hostel foyer I checked the map. Edgecliff didn't look that far from Kings Cross. I stripped Sydney from the wall and folded it into my waistband. Not long after I'd set off I rounded a corner and strode headlong into a crowd outside a bar. Football shirts wove before me. One ducked into a pretend tackle and I surprised myself by shoving it aside. Someone leaped after me and I ran away, drunken cheers trailing in my wake.

I kept running. Exertion made the night air unbearably thick and wet and hot. In no time my face was streaming, my feet were burning and my shirt was plastered to my back, but apart from pausing to check the map I jogged on, not just because I wanted to get there fast but because the effort of running blotted out the possibility of thought. I was soon among quieter residential roads overarched with lamp-lit palm fronds. At two in the morning most of the terraces had a blank, shut-eyed look. But the house I was making for glared at me from down the street. I stood on the pavement opposite, hands on my knees, aghast and out of breath. The lights could still be a coincidence. I had to squeeze between two wedged cars to reach the front path. The bigger of the vehicles, rammed boss-eyed up on to the kerb, was Bowey's pick-up. I stared at the house. Insects throbbed at me from the bushes; moths dog-fought against their sky of bright windowpane. I jogged to the front door. Through a gap in the curtains I saw a segment of stencilled wallpaper border. I rang the doorbell. Its chime sounded homely, domestic and wrong.

A lizard the size of my little finger raised its head from the porch ceiling but, that aside, nothing stirred.

There was a cat-flap in the bottom of the door. I bent down, intending to call out for Bowey through the hole. When I pushed the plastic panel open, though, the whole front door gave. I straightened on the threshold and swayed there a moment, unsure of what to do. When I finally said, 'Hello,' my voice served only to underline the resonant quiet.

I recognized the house as the place Anna had described in her journal. It smelt faintly of cat pee. I turned through the door immediately on my left, expecting to see the velvet wall hanging, studio lights and couch, and I did, but all of it was heaped in a jumbled mess with the television and coffee-table and armchairs at the near end of the room. There was another smell in here too, wine. Shards of green glass lay where they'd fallen on the carpet beneath the far wall, the middle of which was stained red with a shape like an inverted flame. I crossed the room and touched the wall and my finger came away wet. The streak of wine ran down to an electric socket at my feet, which hung half out of the skirting-board on exposed wires. Somebody had yanked a power cable straight out of the wall. The plug it belonged to clung tail-less to the ruined socket. I stared down, my heart beating fast, and felt the pressure of trying to breathe quietly as an ache deep in my shoulders. Those wires looked dangerous, a hazard, a *liability*. I wanted nothing to do with them. I turned to leave.

Bowey was watching me from the door to the hallway. His shirt was torn and open to the waist, revealing the ridge of his chest and his flat stomach, hairless and pale and adolescent in the yellow light. He pulled the shirt closed but there was only one button to do it up with. Eventually Bowey looked back up at me.

'You didn't need to come,' he said.

'What happened here?'

'You don't want to be any part of it.'

I glanced around me at the wreckage. 'What have you done?'

Bowey walked towards the pile of furniture in the centre of the room and stood before it, hands on his hips, thought-ful. He righted an armchair, pulled it clear of the mess and turned it towards me. With deliberate calm, he sat down.

'I know you're not right about Anna making it. She'll die, it's my fault, the least I can do is sort this for you.' His voice was tight with the effort of his trying to keep it steady, but wavered as he went on. 'You should leave. I've got it covered. Go now – I won't be long.'

'Anna kept a journal. I'll show you. There's nothing *to* sort out.'

He gave a tight little laugh and nodded at the door. 'Sure, you're right. Leave me to do nothing, then.'

I'd assumed, when Bowey appeared before me alone, that there was nobody else in the house. The alternative was unthinkable and therefore I hadn't thought of it when, in the middle of my saying, 'There's nothing to be gained trashing this woman's house, she didn't—' there was a loud thump on the ceiling, directly above us.

As soon as I heard the noise I sprang past Bowey and ran up the stairs. A cat erupted from nowhere, clawed up the carpet face ahead of me and dived into the bathroom. Bowey had to rise out of his chair, but he moved fast and was only a pace or two behind me when I reached the landing. I barged through the one closed door with Bowey trying to hold me back.

This room was in pieces too. I could not take it all in at once. I shrugged off Bowey's hand and saw a bed upended against the window, its mattress fallen forwards and draped with sheets. In front of it a wardrobe was on its side, door open, spilling shredded books and photographs. I saw a shattered computer keyboard and a piece of circuit board and a laptop bent back on itself and a mound of shiny black film, like seaweed on a rock, its tendrils poised to spread everywhere. I moved forwards. A plastic CD case crunched underfoot. The light moved with me across broken pieces of mirror and scattered compact disks. The room seemed to blink.

Beyond the wardrobe something moved.

Bowey said, 'There's really no point in you seeing this.'

She was on her side, on the floor, tied with electrical cable to a small chair. I crossed the floor to her and knelt down. One of her hands was white and the other was purple and they were big, mannish hands, bound together behind her with flex. I reached to untie them. She flinched from my touch and squealed, squirming sideways, her eyes rolling white in her long face. I touched her neck and whispered, 'What have you done to her?'

'I had to gag her. I used a strip of pillowcase.'

I turned to look up at Bowey. He was standing with his arms crossed, fingers twitching.

'This woman isn't to blame.'

He laughed and said, 'She's already admitted it. Named the bloke in the picture, contact number, everything.'

I tried to lift the woman up but she was heavy and lay awkwardly, her legs entangled with the chair. 'Help me,' I said.

Bowey leaned across me, took hold of a handful of the woman's hair and made as if to pull her up by it. I spun round and pushed him in the chest. He staggered backwards, nearly lost his footing, but managed to steady himself against the bed. When he came forward again he was holding his knife.

'With a cornered snake you clear the room,' he said. 'But someone has to kill it.'

Laughter spilled out of me. I didn't have time to stifle it. I was so frightened, and so relieved I'd got there in time, and so anxious to make him see. But my laughter tipped something in Bowey. His eyes began to blink and he started panting and he waved his knife in my face. I stepped back instinctively. He shoved past me, yanked the chair and the woman upright and hauled the woman's chin to one side. She began to choke against the cloth. I thought of water filling a throat, pressing down.

'It wasn't anyone's fault,' I whispered.

'We're way past that,' he said. 'This woman took the photographs. I made her show me. She's the one who's been stealing your money.'

'None of that matters.'

'Course it bloody matters!'

The woman's long neck was cabled with veins and arteries, sinew and muscle. It looked like marble, she sat so absolutely still. I thought of Anna, inert in bed. Bowey gripped the woman's chin with a hand that showed dark against her skin. Yet the knife was still at his side. I understood then. He'd been here hours. He'd bound this poor woman to the chair and driven her into an animal terror. But he couldn't find it within himself to take the next step because the panic had hold of him too. I knew in my heart that if I'd been in his position I'd have frozen here as well, and that fact made him real again, real and close. I began to tell Bowey about Anna's diary again but he cut me off.

'What else did we come for?' he was shouting. 'If you're not up to it, you should just . . . go. Go!'

'Bowey,' I said.

His voice dropped. 'I didn't want to involve you in this.'

I went towards the two of them slowly and I knelt before the woman again and began to untie her hands, only noticing then that I was shaking all over. Bowey let her chin drop.

Her face fell forward towards me, slick with tears. My fingers struggled with the knot of cloth at the back of her head but I didn't stop working at it until the knot loosened and the gag came away. My breath was burning in my chest and I was willing Bowey to step further away. He did eventually. He moved backwards and sat down and put his face in his hands.

'She saw your advert.'

'I don't care.'

'Reckoned you must be rich.'

'Fine.'

'I made her call her bank.'

'Go fetch some water.'

Bowey stood up. 'They're wiring the money to my account. I'll have them send—'

'Water!' I shouted.

He left the room. I managed to undo the knots. The woman's wrists were as thick as ankles; each of her hands was a dead rock in mine. I tried to rub the circulation back into them and it seemed I could feel the pores in her cement-grained skin. Her face, turned to one side and staring down, was granite. Everything about her seemed stony and inert, except when she spoke. When I gave her the glass Bowey brought back into the room she had a surprisingly soft voice.

'Thank you,' was all she said.

EPILOGUE

The walls are freshly painted, a blinding, flashgun white.

Brightness pours down on them through skylights in the ceiling and bounces around the space, defying shadows, exploding among the wine bottles and jewellery and lip-gloss, the wristwatches, the foreheads, the shiny teeth.

I lift my eyes above the crowd. I blink at a streak of contrail fading in one of the blue squares high above me. I run a finger round my collar and shoot my cuffs and I head off a sense of anticipation, a lightness in my stomach, by looking back down at Bowey and saying firmly, 'Thank you for this.'

Beside the boy Jeanette shakes her bleached head. 'He's the grateful one,' she says.

I did not fly north with the doctor, because I had no means of buying an air ticket, but I told her I would meet her at the hospital and I drove there with Bowey beside me in the pick-up's passenger seat. Just outside a place called Coffs Harbour we passed the ridiculous banana sculpture Anna wrote about in her journal and I realized this was the route she and Bowey had taken just weeks beforehand. Aside from stopping to refuel, we drove without a pause. We made Byron Bay on the evening of the same day I'd found Bowey at the woman's house. Already the events of the small hours seemed distant. I suspected that was a result of the numbing effect of the road, but as soon as I saw Anna again I understood that the enormity of what lay ahead of us had simply cancelled out what lay behind.

She seemed much smaller than before. Her exposed forearm was the same bluish white as the sheet it lay across. The machine breathing for her was louder than I remembered. Either that, or the silence around her had deepened. I was half-way through introducing Bowey to my father before I realized I was speaking in a whisper.

Dad flew home a month ago now. I did not tell him about the exhibition. Though I'm sure he'd understand, I've decided not to trouble him with realities I should never myself have uncovered. Perhaps I am using that as an excuse, to save myself the embarrassment of explaining what I found out. But this way both truths about Anna persist.

I knew, as soon as I finished reading her journal, that I would have to deal with the consequences of invading Anna's privacy. I began that first night, by apologizing to her. After my father had taken Bowey, drunk with tiredness, back to his hotel, I sat with her and I told her what I had done. My confession was no less heartfelt for my knowing she could not hear me, yet it left me owing her something more. I sat there listening to the ventilator, trying to think what Anna would want me to do next.

It turned out my father knew all about Guatemala. More

than me, in fact. Penny had tracked him down and, because he was willing to listen, she burdened him with that disaster too. The syndicates won a preliminary ruling saying we had misrepresented the G-Com risk. Although Dad didn't admit it, I think he suspected my trip into the outback had something to do with fleeing that fact. I made sure he was in the room when I telephoned Taylor Blake's lawyers with instructions for them to meet what liabilities we could. 'Yes,' I confirmed aloud, 'I understand that means winding the company up.'

Brent's big shoulders sit well inside the sheath of his new suit, but I can't help noticing, when he shakes my hand, a crack in his thumbnail etched grease-gun black. Bowey tells me his brother spent the last fortnight framing every picture in this room, and he hung the lot last night, working by eye, in under an hour. Their father has insisted on self-catering the private view. Town food, he calls it: miniature spring rolls, bacon-wrapped cocktail sausages, tiny slices of quiche. Every time I go anywhere near the trestle table he's had Brent set up near the gallery entrance he says, 'Bloody marvellous!' and tries to give me something else to eat. I stay put in the middle of the room and confine myself to occasional glances at the door.

The doctor arrived for work in the morning, dressed normally again, in a vest top, pedal-pushers and trainers, her hair wet and black. She brought a smell of cut cress into

Anna's room with her, and a hospital administrator – a little man in a brightly coloured waistcoat – with paperwork for me to sign. I felt sorry for the clerk; he could not look any of us in the eye. Jo and my father moved around one another with an ease that helped assuage the guilt I felt, now that he was before me, at having forced Dad to cope alone for so long. The administrator left. We gave Bowey time to say goodbye to Anna first, and then my father kissed her pale forehead. Neither of them wanted to be there at the very end.

Mounting this exhibition seemed an obvious thing to do, but I had to convince Bowey it was right. He feared his pictures weren't good enough, that we'd have trouble finding a proper space to show them, that nobody would come. I almost let him talk me out of it, but a week after she died, when Dad returned to England and I decided to stay on here – I've nothing pressing to go back for and there's another month until my visa expires – I came across the exhibition flyer that the blind hitchhiker gave me in Bourke, and before I knew it I had picked up the phone. The gallery was resistant to the idea of an unknown exhibitor at first, but some rules don't change: the blackmail money Bowey retrieved proved persuasive. I suspect it might have been my conversation with Jeanette – Bowey was slow in coming to the phone – as much as my appeal to him that this was what Anna would have wanted, that changed the boy's mind.

Not all the pictures are of Anna. I asked the boy to

choose his best work, knowing that that was what she would have wanted us to show. I'm not sure I get the distorted shots of machinery and tourists and open space. But those photographs Anna is in are luminous in their stillness, as she was that last morning, stretched out and framed on her hospital bed.

Jo Hoffman asked if I was ready.

I replied that I was.

I kissed Anna's cheek and let my forehead rest on her chest. My eyes closed. I felt the misleading warmth of her body against my face through the thin hospital gown. My head lifted and fell with breathing that belonged to a machine, and then the noise of the machine stopped and we were both still.

I lay listening to her silence for a long time, empty and complete.

When I stood up I saw the doctor's back was turned, that she was staring through the blind at a blood-red bird perched upon the window-ledge. It was a strange thing to find myself whispering reassurances to Jo, but that was what I did. The bird pecked at nothing visible. I put a hand on the doctor's arm and struggled to help her in her fight to keep all expression from her face.

'You never lied,' was all I could come up with.

There was a pause; her shoulder grew warm beneath my palm. Eventually she shook her head and said, 'That's not quite the case.'

'Course it is,' I reassured myself.

'No. The conference in Sydney.' She turned to me, her eyes glinting black. 'I didn't have to be there. You thought I was in Sydney for you and I denied it, but you were right.'

Jeanette is congratulating Bowey on the good turnout. I have to agree, but the room is still empty for me. Jo said she would come; I believe what she says and so have every reason to be hopeful. If I look long enough through the crowd at the gallery entrance and glare beyond it I am sure, eventually, to blink.

Acknowledgements

Thanks to the following for their help with this novel:
Christopher Booth, Kate Eshelby, Hannah Griffiths, Carol Jackson,
Jason Lawrence, Stephen May, Ian Mitchell, Hazel Orme,
Betsy Robbins, David Sheasby, Sid Smith, Anna Valdinger
and Gita Wakling.

I am particularly grateful for the editorial judgement
and guidance of Jonny Geller and Maria Rejt.